MAY 2010
DONALD, ANN, DARYL & JULIANS'
TRIP TO KUCHING.

Children of the Monkey God

THE STORY OF A CHINESE HAKKA FAMILY
IN SARAWAK, BORNEO
1850-1965

By

F. S. Choo

Third Millennium Publishing
A Cooperative of Writers and Resources
On the INTERNET at 3mpub.com
http://3mpub.com

ISBN 1-934805-22-X
978-1-934805-22-0
278 pages

© 2009 by F. S. Choo

All rights reserved under International and Pan-American Copyright Conventions. Published in the United States of America by Third Millennium Publishing, located on the INTERNET at http://3mpub.com. No part of this publication may be reproduced, stored in a retrieval system, or transmitted in any form or by any means, electronic, mechanical, photocopying, recording or otherwise, without the prior permission of the copyright owner.

Front Cover

The photograph is a family portrait of the author's paternal grandparents together with six of their children. It was. taken in either 1923 or 1924.

Third Millennium Publishing
PO Box 14026
Tempe, AZ 85284-0068
mccollum@3mpub.com

CONTENTS

MAP 1: CHINA AND SOUTHEAST ASIA IV

MAP 2: NORTHWEST SARAWAK AND WEST KALIMANTAN V

THE GREAT GRANDFATHER 1

CHILDREN OF THE MONKEY GOD 27

THE GRANDPARENTS 45

COUNTRY VISITS 85

TOWN LIFE 113

STREET FRIENDS & CLASSMATES 135

RELATIVES 183

GHOSTS, DEMONS & MONSTERS 205

WITCHCRAFT AND WITCH DOCTORS 235

EPILOGUE 260

AUTHOR BIOGRAPHY 264

BIBLIOGRAPHY 266

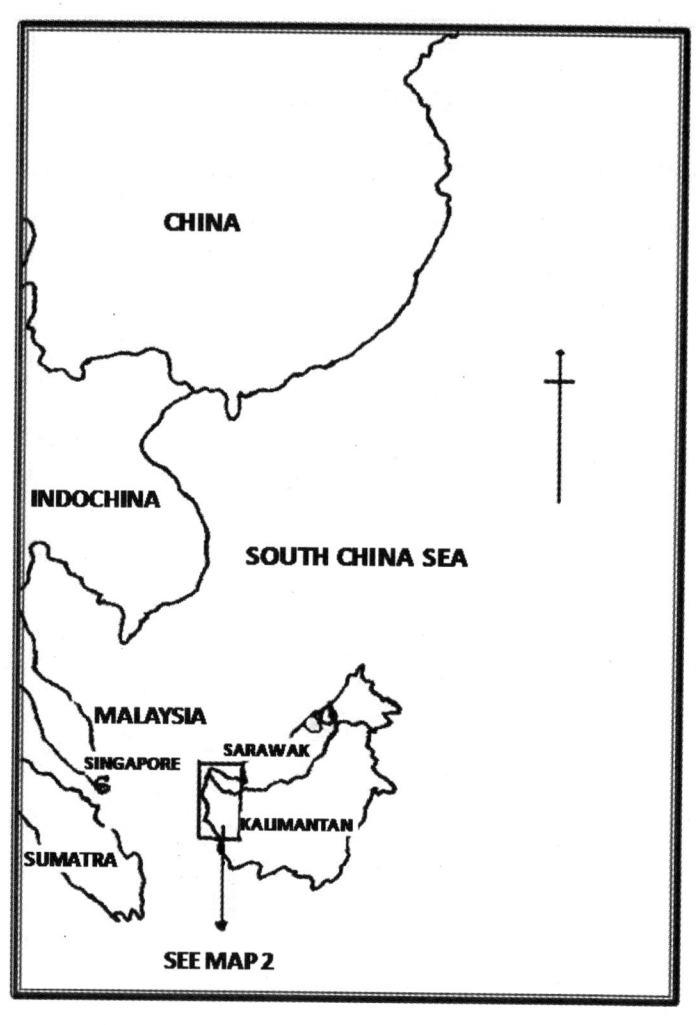

MAP 1: China and Southeast Asia

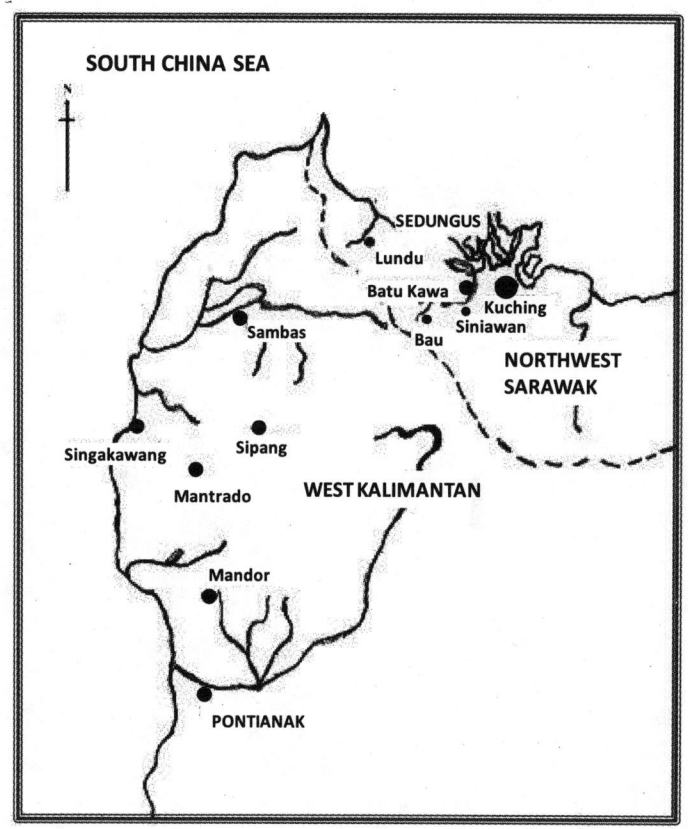

Map 2: Northwest Sarawak and West Kalimantan
Showing Points of Interest in the Story

Legend

● Cities and Towns   - - - - National Boundaries

THE GREAT GRANDFATHER

"An attack by the Rajah is imminent. He will do so with numerous Iban troops. Stay alert at all time. Stay sober. Post guards everywhere."

"Tragically they didn't. Most of them were too drunk with rice wine to heed the words of the Monkey God and they were mercilessly slaughtered as they lay in a stupor following a wild night of celebration." Ah Kung said.

These words of the past came to me as I sat next to the mound of impoverished clay soil housing the remains of Ah Tai[1]. It was the annual festival of Ching Ming, the day when the deaths were remembered and honoured with prayers, food and drinks.

It was a small and simple grave, a far cry from some of the bigger and more ornate graves seen in the Chinese cemeteries of suburbia Kuching. Covered by partially trimmed *lallang,* a local weed with long, narrow razor-sharp blades, and with its ebony-hued ironwood burial tablet already rotted to a small splintered stump, the only other indication that it was a grave was the tortoise-shaped mound protruding from the ground.

The food consisted of a bowl of steamed rice, a

---

[1] *Ah Kung and Ah Tai are terms for 'grandfather' and 'great grandfather' in the Hakka dialect. The Hakka are a diverse dialect group of people found mainly in the Guangdong and Fujian provinces of southern China.*

poached chicken, a braised duck, a thick slice of plain-boiled belly pork and a bowl of mixed fresh fruits. The drinks were held in two porcelain cups - one containing rice wine and the other thick brown tea. Once the food and drinks had been properly laid out and the customary invitation to our venerable ancestor to eat had been carried out, I sat next to these ancestral offerings for the duration of twenty to thirty minutes.

This was the normal length of time considered to be adequate for the offerings to be consumed by the spirit guest, although confirmation of this still needed to be sought. This was done by the simple expedient of tossing two twenty-cent coins into the air and the question respectfully posed as to whether the said venerable ancestor had finished his meal. A resultant two heads or tails would be an answer in the negative while a head or tail combination would be an answer in the affirmative.

As I sat waiting amidst the heavily–scented smoke of the burning joss sticks which, mercifully, kept at bay the numerous mosquitoes hovering in mid-air, I reflected on my grandfather's words, telling of an event that took place in 1857, more than one and a half centuries ago. (Keeping the mosquitoes at bay was, of course, a side-effect of the joss sticks, its main purpose being to alert the gods and friendly spirits to the devotions carried out by the devotees.)

It was, after all Ching Ming, a time of remembrance.

Close to four thousand Chinese gold miners were killed on that fateful day in 1857. My great grandfather and his youngest brother were among the few lucky ones who managed to survive the massacre of Sir James Brooke, the first White Rajah of Sarawak, Borneo.

He and his brother managed to slip unnoticed behind

the enemy's line and escaped by swimming downstream with the currents of the Sarawak River. Perhaps instinct and an uncanny sense for survival guided them in taking off north into the very area from whence the enemy had originally mounted their attack. Perhaps it was pure luck in merely running through the first available opening in the enemy's dragnet.

But above all, it was, according to my grandfather, because they heeded the warning of Sun Wukung and, staying sober and alert, they were able to make good their escape.

The remnants of the rebel force made a desperate bid to retreat south to their headquarters in Bau, still a good seven kilometres away. Tragically, they were either finished off by the pursuing Rajah and his men in Bau or by the Dutch troops waiting on the other side of the watershed border that Dutch Borneo shared with Sarawak.

"He killed a Manchu officer, you know, and that's why he had to flee China," my grandmother whispered to my eldest aunt.

My grandmother must have thought that all the children were already asleep when she spoke these words. My brothers and cousins were definitely somewhere far away in a dreamland of their own. I could even hear some of their snores as the eight of us lay on our lumpy kapok-stuffed mattresses in the small living room of my grandfather's shop-house in Padungan Road.

I was never a light sleeper. Sleep never came to me easily. Perhaps it was the street noise that continued until quite late into the night. Perhaps it was the soft street lights that intruded into the living room through our open windows, making certain that the room was never enveloped in complete darkness. This low visibility of the room made it possible for me to play my nightly games with the denizens who had made the wooden ceiling of the shop-house their habitat. Nightly, a black, jagged palm-sized knot imbedded into the ceiling and situated right on top of my sleeping space, would turn into a terrifying fire-breathing dragon, a giant lizard or a soaring eagle. Eventually I would drift into sleep. For years that dark knot kept me awake but it also helped me to drift into sleep.

The words of my grandmother, Ah Por (Hakka for grandmother), however, had fired my curiosity on a rebellious great grandfather who had to flee China for his life. Years later I questioned myself on whether I had really heard those words clandestinely whispered in the dark. My elders never talked to me about this flight of my great grandfather from China and I never asked them about it. To do so would have revealed to them that I had been eavesdropping on them, on words not meant for the ears of young children. Yet questions remained.

Ah Tai was certainly no different from the hundreds of thousands of Chinese migrants who left the shores of Southern China in the mid-19th century to seek fortune and work overseas. China was at that time ruled by a repressive Manchu dynasty that had already lost its claim to govern because of the withdrawal of its 'mandate of heaven' to rule by the gods. It was a regime that had come to the end of its dynastic tenure and, like all the other preceding dynasties in their death-throes, it was coming apart at the seams with devastating effects. Widespread civil wars, social unrests, chaos, poverty and hunger were the order of the day, and to escape these horrors, hordes of poor and displaced Chinese migrants left the country, leaving behind wives, parents, children and other family members to seek a better life overseas.

The gold fields of Dutch Kalimantan on the southern hub of the Borneo Island were one of these destinations, and that was where Ah Tai and his brother were headed. Was it work and fortune he sought or was it a desperate flight from the Manchu authority? Or was it perhaps a combination of all these factors?

Whatever the reason for their decision to leave China, the gold fields of Kalimantan beckoned, and Ah Tai and his younger brother arrived in Dutch Kalimantan sometime in the late 1840s to 1850, barely twenty years of age.

Like most Chinese migrants intending to go back to China in "silken robes" and with money in their pockets after the necessary stint of work or business undertaking overseas, they, like millions of others, in fact, stayed on in the adoptive country, never to return to China again.

The anguish my great grandfather must have felt at having to leave his family and country behind was never conveyed to us. Although the Hakka are known to be a down-to-earth people, and therefore not easily given over to sentiment, there could have been no doubt that he and his youngest brother must have felt great remorse at having to leave behind their parents, brothers, sisters and other relatives. Some migrants left even their wives and children behind, perhaps never to see them again.

Thus, Ah Tai and his younger brother never went back to China and never saw their family members again. I have, over the years, come to the conclusion that the reason they never went back was not because they didn't want to, but because they were unable to. The soft words I thought I had heard being whispered by my grandmother to one of her daughters might not have been my imagination after all. My great grandfather and his brother might well have been involved in some act of rebellion against the Manchu regime, and that being the case, might have really gone to Borneo to escape their clutches. They would have been wanted men in China, a strong enough deterrent against them ever wanting to return to their homeland.

Ah Tai died in his mid eighties in 1918, two years after the birth of my father. According to my grandfather he died a debilitated old man. Bed-ridden for the last few years of his life, his body was a mere shell of the robust man he once was. It was a body ravaged by the opium he was addicted to for almost his entire life. The hard, lonely life of a gold miner in the gold fields of Kalimantan was enough to turn him and thousands of other migrants into life-long addicts of that pernicious substance. And who could blame them? For opium was a soothing balm that took away all the aches and pains caused by the performance of hard uncompromising menial work, the day-to-day bane of millions of 19th century Chinese migrant coolies all over the world. It was no different with the migrant miners of Dutch Kalimantan, as they tried to eke out a living in the gold fields of a hostile country far away from their homeland.

Ah Tai died without leaving behind a photograph or even a hand-drawn portrait. Perhaps there was a portrait or two that were either lost or damaged with the passage of time. They might even have been destroyed. Ah Kung might not have been too happy to have a portrait of his father's emaciated image in the house. Perhaps it was too depressing to be constantly reminded of the ravaging effects that opium addiction had had on his father. All that remains of Ah Tai and his brother are two barely marked graves on a piece of land bought by Ah Kung in Sarawak, on the island of Borneo at Sungai Tiram, near Mt Santubong.

In actual fact, Ah Tai's grave faces directly into the southern face of Mt Santubong – assuming an unmoving, confronting and uncompromising stance that some family

Children of the Monkey God

members would claim to have an adverse and everlasting influence on the future generations of his line. According to my grandmother, Ah Por, it was bad 'feng shui'[2] to have his grave situated thus. She never stopped chastising Ah Kung for the strong-willed, stubborn, and difficult children she bore as a result of an ancient grave incorrectly sited. The spirit or soul of a dead person should not be permitted to assume such a stubborn stance against a mountain, especially not a mountain like the legendary Mt Santubong, she said. It was a stance too presumptuous and arrogant to take, even for a venerable ancestor. This trait would surely flow through the family line and be passed on to future generations, as had already been indicated on numerous occasions, she added.

Ah Kung however, with his strong bias for strong-willed and proud offsprings, was not overly concerned with Ah Por's claim of adverse feng-shui, however. He took her chastisement in good spirit whenever she decided to let off steam at him for our misbehaviours, merely smiling his all-knowing smile without uttering a word. After all, he was the one who chose the site of the grave and what my grandmother claimed was a negative thing might not have been so to Ah Kung.

Although Ah Tai worked and lived for most of his life in Sarawak, he and his brother did not start off as gold-miners there. A few months after they left their village in the province of Guangdong, China on board a Chinese junk, they arrived in Sinkawang, Kalimantan, the southern half of Borneo Island belonging to Indonesia. They would have

---

[2] *Feng shui (pronounced "fung shui") is the ancient Chinese art of geomancy involving the placements of objects and articles together with the use of space in order to achieve harmony with the environment.*

boarded the Chinese vessel most probably between the months of October to February, when the north-easterly winds of the monsoon would be at their strongest and, therefore, most favourable for the merchant vessels of Guangdong and Fujian, the two neighbouring provinces of South-eastern China.

In the port-town of Singkawang, they would have found a huge, well established community of Chinese gold miners made up of Hakka folks from the towns, villages and hamlets of Huichui, Haifeng, Lufeng, Kityang, Taipu, to name a few. They would have come across many of their own Hakka clansmen of the Huichui speech group as well as other Hakka members of various mining organizations called the "Kongsi" in Hokkien[3]. Also known as "Kongtse" in Hakka, the Kongsi were self-funding, independent organizations that had been largely responsible for the Chinese gold-mining activities in Kalimantan since the mid-18th century.

They would have already heard tales of these organizations back in their village in China from clansmen and relatives who, after a stint with the Kongsi, would have not have held back in their boasting about the fabled riches of West Kalimantan. In all probability, these returned adventurers would not have related to the hot-headed and impressionable youths of their villages the hardships, pains and tribulations they had gone through as Kongsi members, or very little of these, at the very most. Instead, they would

---

[3] *People of the Fujian province, on the south-eastern coast of China. Calling themselves "Hokkien" in their own native dialect, they are also known as "Fujianese" in mandarin and are the dominant Chinese dialect group in Taiwan and Singapore.*

have filled their heads with stories of the fabulous riches of the West Kalimantan gold fields and the adventures to be had there, very much in the same vein as the returned old-timers of the gold rushes in USA, South Africa and Australia. The desire to boast, the need to put on an appearance of success and, above all, the supreme importance of not losing face in public meant that deeds of romance, adventure and success would mainly be the ones told. Not that these youngsters needed much encouragement, anyway. The dire financial situation that my great grandfather and many other Chinese like him, young and old, found themselves in, would see hundreds of thousands of them departing in droves from the shores of China in the decades to come.

Singkawang, where Ah Tai and his brother landed, was one of the ports of West Kalimantan traditionally called upon by Chinese junks trading with the Nanyang, the Chinese name for the Malay Archipelago. Situated by the western coast, it was a port of call of these junks as they followed the north-east winds of the monsoon in the later or the early part of the year, and returning to China in the middle of the year with the south-west monsoon winds at their backs. Like many pioneer towns established in the Nanyang over the years, Singkawang's two rows of wooden shop-houses filled with all sorts of Chinese goods and paraphernalia would have oozed a familiarity that would have reminded them of the provincial towns of their homeland.

Moving among their own clansmen in this outpost far away from China would have, somewhat, soothed their longing for family and home. A further reminder of home was the immediate area surrounding Singkawang. For, as far as the eye could see, numerous Chinese farmers and vegetable gardeners worked tirelessly to supply the towns, the mines, the villages and their inhabitants with native and Chinese vegetables, rice, chicken, ducks, geese, pigs and pond fish.

However, not far beyond that tamed and cultivated landscape rose the wall of the tropical rainforest; a constant reminder that they were still far away from their native village of Guangdong. They had now before them the fabled tropical rainforest of Borneo – that seemingly endless mass of ancient vegetation. It was a landscape extremely dense and highly inaccessible, consisting of myriad inter-twining creepers, heavy musty-smelling undergrowth and strange-shaped buttresses with formidable giant trunks that seemed to stretch forever into the sky. Every plant, every shoot, every vine and every tree seemed to carry on its branches thick green leaves and foliage of all shapes and sizes. A thick, green canopy enveloped everything. Although it acted as some sort of filter and, therefore, respite against the harsh tropical sun, the high humidity was still quite unbearable. To these two "sinkheks" or new 'guest people' from China this vast and old tropical jungle was an alien world all of its own – seemingly hostile, unworkable and uncultivable.

From Singkawang, my great grandfather and his younger brother would have been taken to another Hakka town called Sipang, some twenty kilometres directly east of the port-town, to be formally initiated into the mining Kongsi of Shum Tio Kau (The Three Creeks) before they could be formally accepted as members.

Sipang was, and had been for quite a number of decades now, the headquarters of the Shum Tio Kau. In Sipang they would not have felt out of place, as some of the members of this organization would have been clansmen and kinsmen hailing from the same district in Guangdong, if not the same village – the result of decades of recruitment carried out by that organization among their own kind in that part of southern China. Ah Tai and his youngest brother would have been their latest recruits and they would have been encouraged to join, their trust and confidence perhaps bolstered by the knowledge that members of the Chu clan were one of the dominant clans, if not the dominant clan, involved in the running of the Kongsi.

As "sinkkehs" they would have been initially boarded in the quarters of the Kongsi. Their initiation as members of the Kongsi would have involved them in the taking of an oath of loyalty before the shrine of the deity of the Chinese immigrants, namely, Tai Pak Kung, centrally located in the main hall of the Kongsi building. This hall not only served as a meeting place of the members but also a function area where guests were welcomed and entertained, as well as a place for other social activities such as gambling and the holding of religious festivals, of which there were many. These were keenly looked forward to – especially by the bachelor members of the Kongsi – as the fares served would be better and more bountiful and the rice wine would flow more freely.

They were the "sinkheks" because, ironically, they were the latecomers. Other Hakka miners had already come before them. In actual fact, they were preceded by the first group of miners by more than a hundred years. Mining activities in West Borneo started in 1740 when a group of 20 Chinese miners were recruited from Brunei by the sultan of Montrado to work in his gold mines. So successful were they that more miners were recruited, this time from the Guangdong province of China.

Word soon spread around the hamlets, villages and towns of that part of the province that gold was to be found in Borneo, and what started off as a trickle of human traffic became a deluge. Other mines were opened in competition to that of Montrado. The local chiefs of Pontianak, Sambas,

Singkawang and Moro joined in the mining activities by ceding mining areas to other groups or clans of Chinese. Consisting mainly of male members, these groups of Chinese mining workers started to organize themselves not only into cogent work-forces but, more importantly, into self-governing associations or societies – bodies that had their roots and origins in the kinship and clanship organizations of rural China.

These societies had always been of vital importance in the vast countryside of China, where little or no reliance could be placed on a rapacious central authority consisting of an emperor and his rather large retinue. Among these were the eunuchs, mandarins, minor court officers, functionaries and other hangers-on, too often more concerned with their own pleasures and survival than with the welfare of a hamlet or a village located thousands of miles from the seat of the central government.

To prevent their own hamlets or villages from descending into a spiralling cycle of chaos, anarchy and self-destruction, the people of these communities, whether large or small, had little option but to come together to organize themselves into self-helping, self-supporting and sometimes into self-governing bodies. Often headed by a committee of elders, these organizations would be responsible in the overseeing and organizing of tasks relating to areas of self-defence, as well as that of other cultural, social and economic activities; in particular in the irrigation and distribution of water.

The functions, objectives and nature of these organizations made it imperative that mutual loyalty and trust became the mainstay of their survival and, more often than not, this would mean heavy reliance being placed on their own kinsmen and clansmen. This was easier to achieve in those communities where the majority of the residents carried the same surname than in those where the people merely spoke the same dialect or sub-dialect. The latter categorization into dialect and sub-dialect is important in drawing attention to the fact that the Hakka people are not mono-lingual or even mono-cultural by nature, and that within this big group of people there are sub-groups of Hopo, Taipu, Fuichui, Kiaying, Sin-On to name a few. However difficult it was to achieve, the ensuing galvanization and assimilation of kinsmen and clansmen into pockets of self-governing communities of peasants or miners for a long stretch of time would eventually result in the development of extremely strong bonds between people carrying the same surname or even speaking the same dialect.

All migrating people, especially when travelling in groups, take along with them to the adoptive country the social, cultural, religious and economic practices of their mother country, despite the effect this has in making them objects of racial prejudice and ridicule. The Hakka were no different from other migrants in continuing with the practices of their forefathers when they first arrived on the shores of West Kalimantan. Here in the jungles and gold fields of Borneo they would have encountered almost the same situation that they and their forefathers before them had experienced for centuries in China – the necessity to fend for themselves in the face of an unhelpful, uncaring and self-absorbed central government.

And while the Malay overlord who had granted them the mining concession would have to be acceded to, he was not, however, the emperor or even his appointed or official representative. Moreover, he did not command from them the same sort of loyalty as that of the Chinese emperor and while most migrating Chinese of that era would still consider themselves loyal subjects of the emperor, or at least until he had lost the 'mandate of heaven' to rule, there were in West Kalimantan no officers or representatives of the imperial court who could exact any form of loyalty from them. That is not to say that they would discard their allegiance to the throne the moment they landed on the soils of West Kalimantan. Far from it, they still considered themselves subjects of the Ching Dynasty and, as a token of that loyalty they and their children would continue to wear the pigtail or queue until the overthrow of that regime in 1911 by the republican movement of Dr. Sun Yat Sen, himself a Hakka and the "Father of Modern China".

Thus in West Kalimantan in the period between the mid-18th to early 19th century, there were mainly the local Malay chiefs to deal with in the negotiating of mining concessions and licenses. They were also mainly the people responsible in the granting of trade agreements for the sale and purchase of grains and other produce and most importantly, opium, although this hold that the local overlords had over them would wane in the passage of time as the Hakka miners prospered and grew in the years to come. Other than that, they were left pretty much to their own devices and, as we will see, this would eventually result in the formation of their own self-supporting and self-governing organizations – the Kongsi. The formation of these organizations would also mark the beginning of a new era in which they would eventually become masters of their own destiny.

In retrospect, it is doubtful that the formation of the Kongsi by the Hakka could have occurred in China, or perhaps anywhere else in the world, during that particular period of the mid-18th century. The socio-political and economic conditions for their birth in West Kalimantan could not have been more conducive, and it is arguable whether these conditions were ever fully present in China or other parts of the world where Hakka migrants might have happened to settle. And we are not talking about the presence of just one Kongsi, we are talking about dozens of them – a unique development multiplied numerous times over. There are several reasons why this could only have happened in West Kalimantan.

In the first place, the de-humanizing, constrictive and repressive feudal land-tenure system of China, with its hierarchical pyramid stretching all the way from the local government officers and landlords to the emperor, was not a factor here for the Hakka migrants starting a new life in West Kalimantan. And it is safe to say that its comparative local and native counterparts did not exact from them the same debilitating taxes demanded by a huge centrally-based and despotic bureaucracy which, among other things, had been the cause of the downfall of many a family back home in China.

It is safe to say that here in West Kalimantan they were practically given an almost clean slate on which to write their own script. Furthermore, operating in a foreign land, they didn't feel that they were in any way carrying out acts of rebellion or disloyalty against either the Ching emperor or even the local Malay Overlord in the formation of their own government – the self-sufficient and self-governing Kongsi. Even if these acts could be construed as rebellious or treasonous acts, the imperial court of China was too far away to cause them any concern. It was also more likely the case that their Malay Overlord would have encouraged them to form into groups to take care of their own welfare, rather than hindering them, as would have been the case back in China. The first few groups of Hakka miners, small in size as they were, were undoubtedly hired as coolies to work in the mines of the local Malay chiefs. However, as they grew in size and complexity, the Malay chiefs undoubtedly took the view that it was better for all concerned that these immigrants took charge of their own affairs. Indeed, not only did the Malay chiefs have no desire to implement such programs of self-rule, they would not have possessed the necessary knowledge and resources to successfully implement them anyway. Thus it was more by default than by design that the Hakka miners were given the opportunity to be masters of their own destiny, and given that opportunity, they lost little time in making full use of it.

In the second place, a subtle change was beginning to take place in the way that latter groups of miners were starting to organise themselves; different from that of the original pioneers of 1750 who had come to this part of Borneo with very little capital to their name. While early smaller groups would have started off as coolies under the employment of the local Malay rulers, subsequent bigger groups would have been treated with better equity. The resultant concessions to mine the land for gold would consequently and subsequently be treated as joint ventures between the Malay rulers and the miners, as they, the miners, began pooling together what little resources they had between them. The mines and the surrounding farmlands would be properties ceded to them as a collective group by the local rulers. This in turn would be treated as communally owned properties by the miners as equal shareholders. This, then, became the foundation on which equal partnership between the miners would be based. It, therefore, became an easy matter to extend their native clan practices into the gold fields of West Kalimantan, if it had not already happened.

In the third place, the constant political manoeuvres of the local sultan and his court officials plus the occasional raids carried out by marauding bands of native tribes on outlying mines meant that they had to work as a strong cohesive group in order to survive. The harsh conditions of the jungle in which they had to work also made it imperative that they pooled their meagre resources. With mainly their muscles and their own ingenuity to contribute to the success of the Kongsi house, they had to work as a group or perish for want of trying.

Egalitarian in both concept and practice, the Kongsi house thus became an extension of the clan system that had already existed for quite a long time in rural China. It is also possible that they might have been influenced by the system of grass-root governments prevailing among the Dayak tribes of Borneo. These were the indigenous people who lived in communal longhouses, farming and hunting with a democratically elected headman in charge. This was not inconceivable in view of the high incidence of inter-racial marriages between the miners and the native tribeswomen, which could easily have resulted in the borrowing of some of these ideas by the Hakka.

Unique in terms of their scale of operation, their efficiency and their ability to embrace grass-root democracy, the members of the Kongsi were more or less equal contributors in ability and means. They were also equal shareholders with the right to elect and sack office-bearers of the Kongsi house and the right to stand for election as office bearers themselves. Important decisions of the Kongsi house had to be referred to open general meetings of the members for review and discussion. Often boisterous and noisy and occasionally breaking out into fisticuffs, these meetings were, nevertheless, the burgeoning signs of grass-root democracy.

These fraternal practices were not restricted to the formal activities of the Kongsi alone, and, in true egalitarian fashion, meals were eaten communally in the meeting hall with leaders and followers partaking of the same simple fares of rice, vegetables and dried or salted fish. As bachelors, and new arrivals, my great grandfather and his brother did not have a place of their own. The Kongsi house was their home and they lived and slept in it, sharing its facilities with other sinkkhek members. With no family, and lacking female companions, the social activities of the Kongsi' members consisted mainly of drinking, gambling and – most sinister of all – opium smoking.

Opium was a balm to soothe the loneliness and anguish many of these sinkkeks must have felt in having to leave their family behind in China, not knowing when or, indeed, if they would ever see their loved ones again. It helped to alleviate the hardships, both emotional and physical, that the miners went through everyday. It was inevitable that many miners became addicted.

There was little doubt that life for the Hakka miners of West Kalimantan in the mid-19th century was a hard one. They had to wake up before the crack of dawn and, except for a noon break of a couple of hours, would then have to work right through the day until early evening. On top of that, they had to keep themselves trained in the art of kung fu and warfare in readiness for any attack from their enemies. These were numerous, being from the various Dayak tribes, rival Kongsi houses and Dutch colonialists. The harsh life, hard work and longing for home, plus the stress of not knowing whether they might soon be a casualty of the frequent warfare waged against them, were factors that conspired to turn even the most reluctant non-user into an addict. Above all, opium-smoking was a way of life, socially and culturally acceptable, and the dark odious substance was readily available, sold to the workers either by the Kongsi or at least under their sanctions.

My great grandfather was never able to rid himself of his addiction to opium – an addiction which he would take to his grave many years later. My grandfather told us of his father's devastating dependence on opium and how he had to scrape enough money to feed his father's craving for the obnoxious substance and the debilitated state such addiction had inflicted on his father. Having seen these devastating effects, Ah Kung never failed to remind us, his grandchildren, of its evil nature.

To digress for a moment, I should say that I had seen opium smokers in operation myself as a mere seven year-old. It happened one afternoon after my father picked me up from school. On the way home he veered off to Carpenter Street, Kuching, proffering no explanation as to why he had not taken the usual route home.

He proceeded to park his second-hand Austin Seven in front of a shop-house in the extremely narrow road of Carpenter Street. Still, without any explanation as to what we were doing here, he let me tag along as we walked from the car and up the steep narrow staircase into the first floor of the building. He opened the door that faced us at the top of the staircase. He walked in; I followed.

It took my eyes quite a while to adjust to the darkness that confronted me. Although it was just past mid-afternoon and bright and sunny on the street outside, the room where I found myself was enveloped in almost complete darkness. Although there were no curtains, the timber shutters of the louvers facing the street were more than effective in blocking out the bright sunshine. A simple light bulb hung from the ceiling; unlit.

And then I saw them.

Seven to eight old men – bare to their waist and wearing only loincloths in either drab grey or khaki. With their ribs sticking out through their dark tanned skin, browned from too much exposure to the tropical sun, they looked emaciated and severely malnourished. They were all reclining on long, hard wooden benches with the ball of their elbow as a means of support and making loud gurgling noises with the long water opium pipes on which they sucked. The air was thick with the pungent smoke spewing from their pipes. I could not help myself, but stood there and stared. My father had a short conversation with one of the men. He finished talking and we left. Later on in the car he told me he was trying to recover some money owed to him by the man he was talking to. He was a rickshaw puller, as were most of them.

Opium-smoking was not the only "recreational" activity Ah Tai and his younger brother took part in. There were, of course, the occasional gambling and drinking sessions with the other miners, but these never induced the dreamlike effects of opium. Like social drinking in pubs and bars so prevalent in western culture, there was no lack of companions with whom to share a pipe or two of this odious stuff. Devoid of female companions – for most of the migrant miners were bachelors – the opium also took the place of sexual pleasure.

At the height of their power at the turn of the 19th century, there was something like fifteen major Kongsi organizations in West Kalimantan with a total membership of approximately two hundred thousand. All had their own administrative headquarters and military strongholds in places like Singkawang, Sipang, Pontianak, Semanis, Montrado, Mondor, Larah, Sambas and Bangka. Among the bigger and more powerful of the Kongsi houses were Lan-fang (The Orchid Fragrance), Ta-kang (The Great Port), Shum Tio Kau (The Three Creeks), Hsin Wuk (The New House), Man-ho (The Perfect Peace), Tai-ho (The Peace and Harmony), Chieh-lien (The Link), Lao-pa-fen (The Old Eight Shares) and Hsin-pa-fen (The New Eight Shares), among others.

The Hakka had a near complete hold on these Kongsi, to the exclusion of all other Chinese dialect groups, with the Hakka sub-dialect groups of the Hopo, Fuichui, Sin-on and Chia-ying, to name a few, also being involved and forming part of their membership.

Of all the founders and leaders of the Kongsi, perhaps the greatest and most venerated was Lo Fang-po of the Lan-fang Kongsi. A Chia-ying Hakka, Lo was highly respected as a great visionary leader, a poet and a highly-skilled military strategist of tremendous courage – a general who would not shrink from personally joining the front line in the thick of battle. Extremely charismatic and deeply loved by his members – numbering thirty to forty thousand at the height of their power – he refused to be crowned king, even when the Lan-fang dominated other Kongsi. He preferred, instead, to accept their votes to grant him the title of 'the great president' (Ta-tsung-Ch'ang) and the description of their Kongsi as a 'presidential system' or republic (Ta-tsung-chih).

While there have been some debates among interested contemporary historians and academics as to whether Lo was the president of a true republic, there is no doubting that he, his followers and the other Kongsi Hakka had in their own ways made significant contributions in their relentless search for a better and more democratic government. And, it is thus that with the supporters who claim the Kongsi was a true republic that another claim would also be made on its historical significance in its formation at about the same time as that of the Republic of the United States of America. On my part, I feel that it is of more historical and political significance that the formation of the Kongsi preceded that of the Chinese Republic of mainland China by nearly 150 years. The fact that Lo Fang-po of the Lang-fang Kongsi refused to be crowned king by his followers, tempting as it must have been for him, choosing instead to be the elected head of a representative organization is a further indication of its democratic nature. This step taken by the Hakka people was a step towards greater political maturity, which, if it had been allowed to continue, would have had more far-reaching consequences on the Chinese people as a whole. It was not to be, however. The powerful forces in existence at that time, and the subsequent changes in the social, political and, above all, economic conditions would conspire to make certain that this move towards more representative government would be snuffed out before it could be fully developed. And there is little doubt that debates as to the true nature of the Kongsi will continue to take place in the future among historians, anthropologists and academics.

Suffice it to say here that even if the self-governing Kongsi with their own army, law-enforcement agency, judiciary, mint, sovereign flag and other instruments of self-rule had not quite fully achieved the qualities of what many 'experts' would consider necessary to constitute the equivalent of a modern republic, there was every indication that they were on their way to becoming one. Above all else, the Kongsi was a government of their own creation – brought into fruition by their own ingenuity to serve their own needs and to help them achieve the objectives they had set for themselves.

Unfortunately for Ah Tai and his brother, the Kongsi houses were already in decline as an economic and political force by the mid-19th century, their fortunes going the same way as their mines, with the earlier rich deposits of gold ore having been exhausted and new mines barely able to support their existing members. Intermittent, and sometimes protracted, energy-sapping inter-rivalry wars carried out between the Kongsi houses had all but robbed them of the powers exerted during the halcyon days of the mid-18th to early 19th century.

There were also the marauding natives, their greedy local chiefs and the Dutch authority to contend with. The Dutch were of particular concern, at this time paying more attention to the activities of the Kongsi houses and initiating policies that would curtail, and eventually wipe out, the sovereignty of the Kongsi houses.

Furthermore, the rise of a merchant class, namely the towkay, literally meaning the heads of a family in Hokkien, in the early to mid-1800s had already reduced the numbers of democratic practices previously enjoyed by the members. A few of these practices were still in force but the increasing control exerted by the towkay as large and powerful shareholders also meant a corresponding reduction in the freedom of the ordinary members' ability to elect office bearers of their choice or in obtaining a genuine consensus in general meetings.

Both my great grandfather and his brother were members of the Shum Tio Kau Kongsi or the Three Creeks Kongsi with its strongholds in Sipang. Although they were not members of the biggest or most successful Kongsi, there was a sense of fulfilment in belonging to a brotherhood where they had near equal rights with other members. Furthermore, many clansmen with the surname of Chu from the same area of Haifeng and Lufeng in Guangdong and who spoke the same dialect as them were there to make them feel at home. Everyone was a brother to everyone else. And in spite of some humorous and light-hearted banter traditionally reserved for the 'Sinkheks', they felt accepted.

Ah Tai and his brother's stay in West Kalimantan were short-lived, however.

He and his brother were on the move shortly after their

arrival there – the result of an inter-rivalry war with the Ta-Kang Kongsi house fuelled by the Dutch authority. The Dutch had always viewed the Kongsi houses as a scourge on their rule and a threat to their authority in West Kalimantan. The existence of the Kongsi houses with their own governments and, therefore, independence, was an anathema to their control over the Indonesian people as a whole and a challenge to their monopoly on all economic and trading activities. For the hundred years or so of the Kongsi existence, punitive expeditions carried out by the Dutch had not been very successful in eroding the power nor the influence that the Kongsi houses had exerted over their members. Numbering at least twelve big houses with a collective membership of two hundred thousand during their halcyon days, they were the bane of Dutch rule in Kalimantan.

However, with the rise of the towkay (i.e., the merchant class) in the 1840s within the Kongsi houses, and the corresponding decline in their own power and influence due in no small part to the dwindling gold deposits, Dutch inroads into the sovereignty of the Kongsi houses became more successful. Collaborative by nature, the towkay were more than willing to help the Dutch in curtailing the power of the Kongsi houses, seeing in the Kongsi's decline a means of further advancing their own position and control over the miners. This was not an insurmountable task, for the Kongsi houses had seen the best of their glory days and the few remaining ones were a mere shadow of their former selves.

Of the three big Kongsi houses still in active operation in the mid-19th century, the Lan Fang (Orchid Fragrance) – the most powerful house until the early 19th century – had already accepted Dutch suzerainty together with the Shum Tio Kau, the smallest of the three houses. For the Dutch,

Children of the Monkey God

there only remained the Takang (the Great Port) to be dealt with. This was the Kongsi in which Hakka with the surname of Chang were one of the dominant clans. With the help of the towkay in the Shum Tio Kau, the Dutch decided in 1850 to mount a series of punitive military expeditions against them.

In their retreat from the Dutch attacks on their headquarters in Montrado, large numbers of Takang began to make incursions into Shum Tio Kao territory in Singkawang, Seminis and Sambas. Killing and wreaking destruction as they fled from the Dutch, members of the Takang were not sparing in exacting vengeance on members of the Shum Tio Kau for the assistance their Kongsi house had given to the Dutch. Decades of inter-house rivalry and hostilities boiled over. The smaller and weaker house of the Shum Tio Kau was no match for the larger and stronger Takang. Some of their members decided to take flight across the watershed into North West Borneo; three thousand of them, in actual fact.

Ah Tai and his younger brother were two of these three thousand refugees.

And so began our family history in Sarawak.

Sarawak – often referred to as the Hakka's 'home away from home'.

CHILDREN OF THE MONKEY GOD

"They ignored the warning of the Monkey God and were slaughtered in their sleep after a wild night of drinking. Luckily for your great grandfather and his younger brother, they heeded the warning of Sun Wukung. They stayed sober and awake, thus making good their escape."

This tale of our great grandfather's escape from the clutches of the White Rajah of Sarawak and his troops of local Malays and Iban warriors was recounted to us, his grandchildren, many times over by our grandfather. A keen student of world and family history, I was always a willing listener.

It was to me an engrossing tale, liberally interwoven with myths, legends and history to give it a touch of colour and mystique. And the warning of the Monkey God gave it that extra touch of exoticism, for was it not him who took up arms and rebelled against Heaven for its perceived injustices, single-handedly inflicting more than a few defeats upon the warriors of the Jade Emperor before he was finally subdued by Buddha? He would be seen as the guardian of all freedom fighters and the Hakka miners - his children.

The event was the so-called Bau or Chinese Rebellion of 1857 and it occurred seven years after the exodus of the three thousand or so members of the Shum Tio Kau out of West Kalimantan into Bau, Sarawak.

Crossing the watershed, a trek of nearly 75 kilometres through mostly hilly virgin rainforest that formed a political and natural border between Dutch West Borneo (Kalimantan) and the territory now known as Sarawak, the refugee members of the Shum Tio Kau were soon absorbed into the Hakka mining community of Bau. In actual fact, they more or less overwhelmed it.

There were less than a thousand miners and farmers working in the Bau area of Sarawak at that time, and the arrival of these three thousand Shum Tio Kau members swelled the Hakka community there to nearly four thousand. Some of these miners and farmers working in the Bau area were an offshoot of the West Kalimantan Shum Tio Kau Kongsi, having moved there in previous years in their search for new mining areas. Several other smaller mining Kongsi were also there; eleven of them, in actual fact, and these had already merged with the Shum Tio Kau to become the Twelve Companies (the "Ship Ngee Kungtse"). With this latest arrival of desperate refugee members from across the border, it was not hard for the Shum Tio Kau Kongsi to establish itself as the dominant partner in this merger by virtue of its numerical strength.

The exodus, however, precipitated a political crisis that had been brewing for quite some time between the then white Rajah of Sarawak, Sir James Brooke, and the Hakka community of Bau. Situated about 25 kilometres from Kuching (the capital of Sarawak and Brooke's administrative centre), Bau (meaning "foul smell" in Malay, although it was more exotically called "Shak Lu Mun" or "Gate of the Rock Caves" by the Hakka) was one of many Hakka pioneer settlements of West Borneo that had sprung into being largely because of the gold deposits found there in the early 19th century. Although never quite on the same scale nor in the same league as that of its Kalimantan counterparts in terms of its social, cultural, economic and political developments, Bau and its Hakka community would achieve historical renown in the days to come. This would come about in the shape of a bloody conflict to determine who should govern Bau – the Kongsi or Sir James Brooke.

Through his gunboat policy and by clever political manoeuvrings, Sir James Brooke, an English adventurer from Somerset, England, had obtained from the Sultan of Brunei an area of land encompassing the Sarawak River from Tanjung Datuk to Samarahan.

Appointed the Sultan's governor of Sarawak in 1841, he lost little time in embarking on a policy of progressive territorial expansion. Wearing down local resistance from the local Malays and Dayaks as he merrily continued on his road of expansionism, he soon encountered resistance from the Hakka in Bau.

Having obtained from the Pengiran Muda Hashim, Brunei's representative in Sarawak, the right to mine gold in Bau since 1830, the Hakka saw no reason why they should submit to the rule of the rajah, whom they considered to be a latecomer to the scene. Considering him to be a downriver upstart who had no business meddling in their affairs, the Hakka felt that they had every right to guard their independence from the encroachment of the Brooke regime.

The Kongsi government was, after all, an efficient self-governing body with its own currency, laws and judiciary system. It took care of all their daily needs -including the dubious supply of opium resin. It provided them with food and work. With the exception of female companions, for which there was an acute shortage - as the vast majority of the migrants were male - the Kongsi was the overall provider of all their needs. They were freemen in a socio-economic-political system created and run by themselves and their elected representatives to serve them in the conditions that confronted them.

Although they were not yet a nation, they were very close to becoming one. The fact that they flew their own flag - the flagpole still stands to this day - was a testimony to the pride they had in themselves and their own independence. Basking in the security of the Kongsi aegis, they thus saw no reason why they should submit themselves to the rule of the rajah. In actual fact, they resented it and sought to resist the rajah at every turn.

The Hakka are a proud people with a long history of resistance against authoritarian rulers and it was perhaps significant that the event popularly known as the Bau Rebellion took place at a time of great social and political uprisings in China, for it was around this time that the Taiping Rebellion (1851-64) was also gathering momentum in China. Hakka-led and Hakka-inspired, with the bulk of its followers drawn from the province of Guangdong, it sought to overthrow the Ching dynasty of Manchu rulers in the mid-1850s to 1860s. Some of the Kongsi members in Sarawak and West Kalimantan would have relatives of mostly poor peasants in the massive ranks of Hung Xiuquan, the rebellion leader, himself a Hakka. Britain, in its aggressive military campaigns in the Opium Wars (1839-42) and in the assistance that it gave to the Manchu rulers in putting down the Taiping Rebellion, would have been looked upon as an arch-imperialist. Sir James Brooke, the white rajah, with his policy of colonial domination and expansionism would have been viewed in the same light.

Although it is not suggested that there was any link between the Taiping Rebellion and the so-called Bau Rebellion in Sarawak, it is noteworthy that both movements took place against a background of widespread anti-Manchu and anti-British feeling among the Chinese both inside and outside China. This was particularly the case with the southern Chinese, with the Hakka at the forefront of such

Children of the Monkey God

movements.

Thus it was of no surprise that the decision of the rajah to impose an opium tax on the Chinese community of Bau was seen as a means to place the town and the Kongsi house under his suzerainty. To add fuel to the fire the recent formation of a British trading and mining company with the help of the rajah, the Borneo Company, was to them a further indication that he intended to take over their mining activities as well. Not willing to give up either their independence or their gold-mining activities without a fight, the Kongsi decided to strike first.

A force of six hundred Bau Hakka miners decided to attack the capital, Kuching, situated on the south bank of the Sarawak River, including the home of the rajah, on the north bank, in the early hours of 19th February 1857. Ah Tai and his younger brother were among this force of miners.

It was, by all accounts, an ill-conceived and ill-prepared campaign.

Kuching was a good twenty-five kilometres from the miners' headquarters in Bau and the ragged band who assembled in front of the Kongsi' temple on 18th February, 1857 marched part of the way to Tundong, five kilometres in fact, where they then boarded a fleet of boats that would take them downriver to their target. Led by their headman, Liu Shang Pang, a two-pronged attack was made on the enemies on their arrival in Kuching. One party attacked the house of the rajah, while another headed towards his stockade with the intention of capturing it.

The rajah was asleep in his house at the time of the attack and only managed to avoid death by jumping into the Sarawak River and subsequently taking refuge with one of the local Malay chiefs. Two of his officers were killed in the ensuing attack together with two young children. Mistaking one of the officers killed to be the rajah, the miners thought that they had achieved their objective. They had also learned that the rajah's nephew and heir-apparent, the then Charles Brooke, was on his way back to Kuching from River Skrang with a large contingent of Iban warriors. They had no desire to wait for their arrival in Kuching, feeling, no doubt, that they would be better off retreating to the security of their own headquarters in Bau.

In a meeting hastily called by the leaders after the end of the initial fighting, some form of proposal was put before a few of Brooke's more influential men and the local Malay chiefs. The miners made it clear that they wished their sovereignty to be respected. Each side should only enforce their jurisdiction within their own borders. The Kongsi would have control over the upriver area of the Sarawak River, while the Europeans and the Malays, the downriver area.

The meeting over, the miners decided to march back to their headquarters in Bau. As they retreated, however, one of the Malay chiefs reneged on the "agreement", mounting an attack on their rear, to which the miners retaliated by attacking Kuching. Sporadic fighting again broke out in various parts of the town and the surrounding villages between the miners on the one side and the townsfolk and villagers loyal to the rajah on the other.

Reprisals by the rajah followed fast on the heels of the miners the next day as they continued on their way back to Bau. Coming out of his hiding place, the rajah was able to assemble a small group of loyal Malay and Dayak supporters with the purpose of harassing the miners in their retreat to Bau. These earlier sorties of the rajah's smaller force were, however, successfully repelled and it was not until the following day, when the rajah was joined by his nephew, accompanied by troops of Skrang Iban warriors that retreat by the miners to their strongholds in Bau turned into a desperate run for safety. A humiliating defeat at the hands of the rajah was almost a certainty should they fail to make it back in time.

"The rajah was a tricky devil. After having arrived at a peace settlement with the miners, he sent them rice wine to celebrate." Thus my grandfather related the tragic events that were to take place, as recounted to him by his father.

Pursued by the rajah and his troops, the heavily outnumbered Hakka rebels soon found themselves holed up by the bank of Sungai ("River" in Malay) Sarawak Kanan, not far from Siniawan - a tiny Chinese hamlet about eighteen kilometres by road from Kuching and less than seven kilometres from their headquarters in Bau. With their backs literally to the wall, they were determined to make a last stand.

They made one final, desperate bid for peace, however. The rajah responded by offering the Hakka envoys arak or tuak, a strong locally brewed sweet rice wine, perhaps bought or commandeered from the nearby longhouse residents in nearby Siniawan or surroundidng areas. Rice wine, next to opium, was a substance much favoured by the Hakka miners in their constant search for a gateway to pleasure and solace. And it is almost certain that an experienced campaigner like the rajah would have known this.

The Hakka, who viewed this gesture as a genuine peace offering, received these jars of wine with great joy. This optimism was not only misplaced - as events were to show later – but also one matched by cultural naivety. Perhaps it was an optimism falsely created by the desperate situation they found themselves in, blinding them to the possibility of enemy subterfuge. In any event, it was a false hope that was to have dire consequences.

For, unbeknown to the miners, the rajah had no intention of negotiating a peace settlement or of allowing them to reach Bau to recoup and fight another day. He saw before him a golden opportunity to rid the country of the rebellious and troublesome Shum Tio Kau Kongsi and the Twelve Company. The ringleaders of the Hakka miners - many of whom he suspected to be triad members - and their main contingent of fighters were here, cornered and right in the palm of his hands. Furthermore, the rebels had provided him with the justification to exact reprisals for their unprovoked attack and he would make sure they suffered the consequences.

The rajah was a seasoned military campaigner and not one to shirk his duty. As far as he was concerned, this was a battle no different from those he had already conducted against the Dayak and other native tribes of Sarawak. This was only the start of a whole series of military campaigns that he and his nephew would conduct over the coming years.

This was, after all, warfare.

Meanwhile, much merriment began in the Hakka camp as the wine flowed freely. Drinking had barely begun when one of their members went into a deep trance. Assuming the persona of Sun Wukung, the Monkey God, with the necessary body language to match, he warned the miners against letting down their guard and partaking of the drink.

> "An attack by the rajah is imminent. He will do so with his Iban troops. Stay alert at all times. Stay sober. Post guards everywhere."

Ah Kung said: "Nearly all of them ignored this warning.

Children of the Monkey God

Only a few didn't. Your Ah Tai and Mon Tai (Hakka for youngest great granduncle) were among these few. They pleaded with the others to heed the warning of Sun Wukung. But did they listen? No, they didn't. As far as they were concerned, your great grandfather and his brother were youngsters. Who were they to tell their elders what to do? Fortunately for them, they did not join in the merriment or the drinking. They stayed sober and they stayed alert."

"And they survived?" I asked.

"Of course they survived; otherwise you wouldn't be here today, silly."

It makes sense that Ah Tai and his brother's plea was ignored by the rest of the party. They were still young men barely in their mid-twenties. Except for their participation in the flight from West Kalimantan when they were attacked by members of the Takang seven years earlier, they had no other military campaign to their name. Quite a few of the other miners were veterans who had fought in various inter-rival Kongsi wars in West Kalimantan. So, who were these youngsters to tell the veterans what to do?

The attack of the rajah, when it finally came, was ferocious. The rebels, whether drunk or half-drunk, put up as much resistance as they could muster. Mayhem reigned as the rajah's Iban and Malay horde descended upon them. Liu Shan Pang, the leader of the miners was himself cut down and killed.

"It was fortunate for your Ah Tai and Mon Tai they managed to escape in the confusion." Ah Kung said.

Fortunate, indeed. Perhaps the fact that the attack was carried out in darkness made it possible for them to slip through the cordon of the rajah, unnoticed. More than twenty-five days had elapsed since the Chinese New Year and there would have been no or very little moon in the sky. The dense foliage of the rainforest trees would also have blanketed them in near, if not total darkness.

In the confusion, they also lost contact with the rest of the miners, now almost certainly leaderless and in complete disarray. It proved to be a stroke of luck, however, as events would show later on. Ah Kung never told us why his father and youngest uncle broke away from the main party of surviving miners or why, indeed, they took off in the opposite direction.

"They headed north towards the river, in the very direction from whence the attack of the rajah and his troops was originally mounted," he said.

In effect, they went behind the enemy's line. As it turned out, it was a fortuitous act, for in their pursuit of the main body of the enemy the rajah and his men were too busy to notice those miners who had managed to slip behind them. They were too preoccupied with their main objective of finishing off whatever was left of the band of miners fleeing south towards Bau. As for Ah Tai and his brother, they were confronted by the Sarawak Kanan, a tributary of the main river and there was nothing they could do but to slip into it. Swimming quietly and with the aid of a fairly strong current - for the waters in the upper reaches of the river always seemed to flow downstream - they drifted away from the scene of the slaughter that was still taking place behind them.

They eventually arrived at Batu Kawa, about 15 kilometres downstream, a small riverbank hamlet of Hakka shopkeepers and farmers sympathetic to the cause of the miners. It was there that they took refuge for a number of years.

In my younger days when this story was told many

Children of the Monkey God 37

times over, I would imagine my great grandfather as a man with the superhuman ability to foresee the impending doom awaiting them had he and his brother joined the others in their retreat to Bau. Now tempered by age, I have come to the realization that it was perhaps no more than a case of their decision to stay sober, as well as having luck on their side.

A number of breaks must have occurred in the cordon set by the enemy. The jungle terrain made certain of that, thickly populated as it was by rainforest trees with trunks of mammoth proportion and myriad creepers of all descriptions. To maintain a tight and disciplined cordon in these conditions would have been a near impossibility for the rajah and his nephew. It was also likely that in their zeal to collect the heads of the miners as trophies to hang in their longhouses, the Skrang Ibans - the main contingent of the rajah's troops - most probably broke ranks, creating openings here and there for those miners still sober enough to make use of them as escape routes. It was more likely than not that Ah Tai and his brother, realizing the hopelessness of their situation, made a break for it at the first available opening. As fate would have it, that opening happened to lead north. Desperation, an instinct for survival and common sense would have guided them, rather than foresight.

Ah Kung said, "The remnants of the Hakka fled to Bau, where they were slaughtered by the rajah and his men. The rivers of Bau and Siniawan ran red with their blood for days. Do you know how much blood would spew from a human body that has its head chopped off? Plenty."

Pursued by the enemy troops, the surviving members of the rebel force fled to their stronghold in Bau to join the other miners, believing that there was greater safety in numbers. There was also no other way to go. Leaderless, confused and hotly pursued by the enemy, they and the rest of the Hakka populace in Bau could do nothing but scatter and flee.

A number of them, mostly women and children sought refuge in a nearby cave. They were not to be spared. The enemy troops simply set fire to both entrances of the cave. Not a single person survived.

Later generations of Bau Chinese settlers named it the "Ghost Cave" – for it was claimed that the anguished cries of their spirits could still be heard in the dead of night after all these years despite the construction of a small temple at the entrance of the cave to appease the souls of the fallen. Perhaps it was merely the howling echoes of the wind as it ripped through the channels of the cave. Who could tell for certain?

Those who were still able to tried crossing the watershed into Dutch Kalimantan, only to be confronted by Dutch troops waiting on the other side. Very little evidence exists as to what actually happened to them. As for those who were spared or who managed to escape, it is doubtful whether they ever crossed back over the border to return to Sarawak again.

From all historical accounts of this sad episode in the history of Sarawak, no prisoner was taken by the rajah and his troops and no trial ever took place. Out of the four thousand or so Hakka population residing in Bau prior to the uprising, only a handful survived. My great grandfather and his younger brother were two such survivors.

The uprising of 1857, if one could call it that, was, by all accounts, ill-conceived and ill-prepared. The abortive campaign of the miners had come at a great cost for the Hakka in Bau. Other than the loss of lives, the Shum Tio

Children of the Monkey God

Kau Kongsi and the Twelve Company were totally wiped out; never to be revived, their mining activities taken over by the Borneo Company.

Historians, especially Brooke historians, have described the event of 1857 as a rebellion or an uprising[4]. That is only true if one takes the perspective that James Brooke had sovereignty over Bau and, therefore, over the Hakka who took up arms against him. As far as the Hakka were concerned, he had no such rights.

There was no doubting James Brooke intended to impose his rule on as big an area as he could gain in the course of warfare and which, as it turned out, would eventually be much larger than the territory originally ceded to him by the Sultan of Brunei.

The Chinese Hakka in Bau was not the only group of people he fought against during his reign in Sarawak; there were also the Malays, the Melanaus and above all, the Dayaks, and, in particular the Ibans, who at various stages of his rule resisted his propensity to expand.

Brooke was, after all, only acting in character with other European colonialists of that period such as Rhodes and Raffles, who saw in the European colonization of Asia,

---

[4] *I must mention here that almost no official literature exists recording the Hakka perspective on the Bau Rebellion. Likewise there is scant mention of the battle near Siniawan or the incident at the "Ghost Cave". The official British perspective is that these events never took place. The Hakka of Bau, Batu Kawa and Siniawan have a different tale to tell, however, and, even in the 1950s and 60s, continued to relate these events in quite graphic detail to interested listeners. I should also mention here that Liu Shang Pang, the leader of the ill-fated rebellion was himself buried here, his marked grave situated not very far from the shop-houses of Siniwan, perhaps further evidence that the battle of Siniawan really took place as claimed by the Hakka of that general area.*

Africa, the Americas and Australasia a god-given right. They were the strong and able representatives of a growing capitalist system that had already prevailed in large areas of the world. As the latest champions of this new socio-economic and political force, they were merely bringing to fruition the energy, dynamics and spirit of this new colonial system. Translated into concrete terms, this meant the formation of commercial enterprises, big and small, that would span the entire globe; the creation of huge plantations in the far reaches of the world; and the extension of the slave and indentured labour system into new areas that would affect millions of families in the colonies. In addition, it was responsible for the migration; both forced and 'unforced', of millions of people, whose displacement would have a huge impact on the social, cultural, political and economic make-up of hundreds of countries in the years to come.

They were also the geo-politicians of their time, equipped with a world-view second to none, commanding a wide vista of world events, past and present, that would stand them in good stead against all foes – a political acumen that would grant them victories in almost every conflict, whether big or small, military or non-military.

Compared to them, their opposing counterparts like Liu Shan Pang, the leader of the Bau Hakka, were mere novices who had very little understanding of the socio-economic forces at large and of the political dynamics at work. For how else could one explain the defeat that the Hakka miners, with their superior numbers, suffered at the hands of Brooke who in reality had only a handful of European administrators in whom to put his trust?

Perhaps the answer lies in the local alliances that Brooke had forged with the indigenous chiefs, which could only have come about through his understanding of local politics. The Hakka, on the other hand, had no such alliances, perhaps feeling that there was no necessity for them.

Unlike the Brookes and the Raffles, they were not colonialists, and they had no ambitions other than to work the goldfields. It is true that they might not have completely isolated themselves from the indigenous people - for some forms of trade were conducted from time to time with the Malays and Dayaks and inter-marriages between some of the Hakka men and indigenous women were not uncommon. But very little was done to forge a deeper alliance with the native people, however, while at the same time displaying little awareness that such a union could act as a means of protection from hostile third parties.

They were, by and large, an alien community living in a sea of Malay villages and Dayak longhouses. Brooke, by contrast, was very much involved in local politics from the moment he set foot on Sarawak soil. Using the alliances he had formed with the local chiefs, he was able to harness warriors to quell the Hakka (as well as other indigenous tribes during his rule). The Hakka, by contrast, had no local support to call on when the counter-offensive was mounted against them and evidently had never even considered such an alternative course of action.

The Hakka miners saw in their fight against the rajah a war between two sovereign states, while Brooke and his supporters saw in it the quelling of a Chinese triad uprising, an unjustified and disloyal attempt to usurp his powers. Hence, its labelling by Brooke's historians as a rebellion. From the Hakka perspective, it was a war, and, as such, it is suggested that consideration should be given to rename the conflict "The Bau-Kuching (or Sarawak) War of 1857," rather than "The Bau or Chinese Rebellion of 1857".

And what of the Kongsi? What started off as a great

socio-economic-political initiative by the Hakka people of West Kalimantan more than two hundred and fifty years ago became, through the passage of time, a thing of distant memory. It was a great initiative, resulting in the formation of an autonomous, democratic system of government. Yet, sadly, except for some interest from various historical and anthropological quarters, it scarcely forms part of the social awareness of later generations of Hakka.

The word "Kongsi" is now more widely used than ever - for almost every Chinese enterprise, whether private or public calls itself a Kongsi – the contemporary English translation being "company", which in the modern context is a correct description of Chinese businesses around the globe. These organizations, however, are a far cry from the original Kongsi in every respect. Patriarchal and pyramidal in nature, including their method of distributing profits, the word "Kongsi", or "Kung-tse" in Hakka, has literally and ideologically been "shanghaied"; its original colloquial meaning of "sharing and sharing alike" renders meaningless. This term, used by the Hakka to describe the organizations they established in the goldfields of West Kalimantan and Sarawak, was a faithful reflection of the passions and objectives they had at that time.

A final ironic twist was delivered in the way the heads of a modern Kongsi were, and still are, reverently called in the Nanyang – "the towkay". They were the real and final victors.

Whereas the towkay might have played a major role in the final demise of the original Kongsi of West Kalimantan and Sarawak, the real culprit, ironically, was gold. Although it was gold that initially help them to create and sustain their members, it was also gold that was responsible for their death, turning the once flourishing goldfields on both sides of the Borneo border into their graveyards. And while it was gold that provided them with the rationale for the trials and tribulations they went through as Kongsi members as well the reason for the many battles they fought against each other, the natives and western colonialists - thus turning them into a potent social, political and military force - it was also gold, or the lack of it, that undid them in the end, for there is little doubt that the gradual depletion of the once rich goldfields also led to a corresponding decline in their strength, power and influence.

The effects would not have been so devastating had there been an alternative support system that the Kongsi could have relied on, similar to the European trading organizations of the same period. Thus, while companies such as the East India Company, Guthrie and the Chartered Bank, for example, enjoyed the support of their mother country, and were, in fact, an extension of their colonial policies, the Kongsi stood alone, being quite independent of the Chinese imperial court. Indeed, not only did they operate against the wishes of the emperor they were, in fact, illegal. This was because of an imperial edict going back to the Ming Dynasty that forbade unapproved emigration by its subjects.

Unlike Britain, France, the Netherlands, Spain and other Western powers, Imperial China was not only a non-colonial power, it showed scant interest in such ambition. Thus, the millions of Chinese who migrated overseas during the reign of the Ching Dynasty did so at their peril, even though the Chinese Government was too inept to take action against this exodus.

Thus, while Western European companies and other organizations flourished as a result of firm backing from the mother country, their Chinese counterparts, in particular the Kongsi, floundered and ultimately perished. Some Chinese entrepreneurs were allowed to continue, provided they posed no challenge, albeit as either junior partners or adjuncts of the bigger European trading houses.

In conclusion, it could be said that as long as gold deposits were in plentiful supply, however, the Kongsi remained strong and influential, their strength only waning with their inevitable depletion. In practical terms, an abundant supply of gold meant an active and vibrant Kongsi membership and this was the real strength of the Kongsi. It mattered not that there was no colonial China they could rely upon for aid. Truly self-supporting and self-governing, their members were all they needed in carving a new world for themselves. They might have been successful in doing that for only a century or so, but in that short period of time they showed both to themselves and the world the true meaning of democratic self-government.

THE GRANDPARENTS

(Also known as "The Sea Turtle, the Monkey & the Crocodile")

After their escape from the rajah, my great grandfather and his younger brother became itinerant farmhands in Batu Kawa. Not quite yet the Hakka stronghold it would become in later years, Batu Kawa was nevertheless a Hakka area, where a number of Chinese farming settlements had already been established - mainly by former miners of the various Kongsi houses. It is possible that they saw the supply of food to the mines as a more viable means of subsistence than working in the mines itself. Some of these farmers would have known that these two young Hakka were escapees from the rajah, as word of the rebellion would have already reached them. As Hakka themselves with many of them also former miners, they would have been sympathetic toward their plight and it is most likely that these two young refugees would have received food and shelter from the residents of Batu Kawa.

Although Ah Kung never talked about the relationship between the two brothers, I suspect it must have been a very close one. In actual fact, I rather doubt that they would have survived the rebellion if they had not looked out for each other all the time; not only during the time of the rebellion, but in all the trials and tribulations that they went through together.

Perhaps an indication of their closeness was the fact that Mon Tai never left the side of his older brother until his own death many years later. He died a bachelor; marriage to a Hakka clanswoman being something of a near impossibility in the early days of pioneering migration when male miners formed the bulk of the migrant population with the women heavily outnumbered. Although a more balanced demography of the genders existed in other Chinese dialect groups, particularly among the Hokkien and Teochew,[5] taking a wife from these dialect groups would mean having to overcome the social and language barriers then in place which, in most cases, would have proved quite to be insurmountable. It was a situation not too dissimilar to that of inter-caste marriages in Indian society where it was considered an act of sacrilege for a person to marry another of lower caste. Similarly, the Hakka farmers and miners in Sarawak were looked upon as people of a lower social group from that of other Chinese dialect groups.

Many of them ended their life of bachelorhood and loneliness by taking as wives women of the native tribes of Borneo. In Sarawak, these would mainly be women of the Bidayuh tribe, the predominant indigenous tribe in the Bau, Lundu and Siniawan area, coincidentally also areas where Hakka population tended to concentrate. Some miners however, chose to remain single. My great granduncle was one of these miners.

My own great grandfather did not marry my great grandmother until he was nearly of middle age. And I am certain it was not by choice that he married so late in life. The near non-availability of Hakka women, the near impossibility of marrying outside their clan and the brothers' own financial circumstances were factors that conspired to

---

[5] *Teochew, also known as "Chaozhou" in Mandarin, is a dialect of the people of the Chaoshan region of eastern Guangdong. A dialect of southern Min it is also spoken in Hong Kong, Singapore, Malaysia, Thailand, Indonesia, Vietnam and Cambodia.*

Children of the Monkey God

make certain that one brother would stay single for life, with the other unable to marry until he was a middle-aged man. The strict traditional requirement of a suitable dowry payment demanded by the intended bride's family would have made it extremely difficult for a couple of itinerant farmhands to convince them of their marriageable worth; for that was how a man's worth was still measured in those days. Landless and drifting from one job to another, they were considered unsuitable candidates for marriage and nothing much could be done even by professional matchmakers, who would only be paid their agreed commission after the celebration of a successful union.

They were landless because they were unable to take advantage of the liberal policy of the rajah in freely granting lands to Chinese migrants willing to take up rice, pepper, rubber and coconut farming in those early pioneering days. Their participation in the rebellion of 1857 made certain of that. They would, for the rest of their lives, avoid having any contact with officialdom; fearful of making any application for free land and just as fearful of buying any with their own money; fearful even to board a boat to leave the country to return to China. To put their name down on any official application or document might invite official investigation into their past, something which had to be avoided at all costs.

They were hired hands to farmers and shopkeepers for a considerable period after the rebellion of 1857 in the Siniawan and Batu Kawa area. Both of them still bachelors and with no other family members yet to support, their earnings – Ah Tai now supplemented his income as an herbal practitioner - were spent mainly on foods, drinks, gambling and opium. My grandfather would recall in later days the spendthrift ways of his father with some disdain and bitterness, admonishing us never to take up these harmful activities.

Yet in spite of his poverty and his lack of assets my great grandfather still managed to secure for himself a young bride in his middle age. The exact circumstances of how this came about were never talked about in the family except that it was quite widely known that my great grandparents' arranged marriage was not a happy one. Perhaps the difference in their respective ages of twenty years or so was too huge a gap to close; a chasm that would continue to fester like an open wound throughout their married life and perhaps even thereafter. While Ah Tai's name was often mentioned with great respect in the family, my great grandmother's name was seldom mentioned, if at all. While Ah Tai's exploits in the war of 1857 were elevated to the stature of a legend, my great grandmother's standing in the family was all but non-existent. She was a persona non-grata as far as her son, my grandfather, was concerned; a shadowy figure consigned into the ever-expanding shadow of an ever-expanding extended family.

A stern and oft-times harsh man, my grandfather never got over the anger he felt against my great grandmother, nor forgave her for taking up with another man a few years after the death of my great grandfather; an act flying in the face of a Confucian taboo. He was the only son of their marriage and, while he had six sisters, our family remained in contact with only the youngest one. The other five sisters, like my great grandmother and her grave - for no one in the family seems to know or care where she was buried - drifted out of the family's collective consciousness and into eventual oblivion.

One or two years after his twentieth birthday, Ah Kung decided to have a wife. To attempt to obtain one from Kuching or from any of the other towns populated by the people of Hokkien and Teochew dialect groups was out of

Children of the Monkey God

the question. The social and class barriers then in place were far too forbidding. Any matchmaker worth her commission would not waste her time trying to match a poor landless Hakka - only seasonally employed as a hired hand to farmers and shopkeepers - with any of the daughters of the Hokkien or Teochew merchants and shopkeepers.

Not that Ah Kung had any intention of marrying a woman from outside the Hakka clan, in any case. For him it all boiled down to a question of practicality. Maidens of the Hokkien and Teochew were, according to him, too soft and "genteel"- and therefore unsuitable - for a farm life. The Teochew women with their bound feet were particularly so. "A cruel practice; painful and foul-smelling," Ah Kung would say of the practice of foot-binding. In his stints as a hired hand to the Teochew shopkeepers he had seen how their young daughters of a few years' old would start with their first binding. The long cotton bandage, wet and stained with blood and pus - and heavy with the stench of putrid flesh- was changed every morning and every night. This daily practice of binding and changing bandages would continue into their teenage years when by that stage their toes would have been forced to bend and fold under their feet, forcing them to assume a small and stumpy appearance. "Neat and petite" was how some old-timers used to describe them. Although a young woman's marriageable value would be increased by the binding - for it was considered to be a sign of beauty and gentility by Teochew men with a foot-fetish, the poor girl would have to hobble about for the rest of her life. Shod in tiny soft cloth shoes, tailor-made for that purpose, she could only move about with the aid of a walking stick, a servant or a helpful family member, her freedom of movement substantially curtailed as a result.

"A woman like that would need to have servants all her life; how could she be of any help as a housewife, let alone a farmer's wife," Ah Kung concluded.

For Ah Kung, only a Hakka wife would do - with her big feet strong, free, unbound and unrestrained.

Looking for a suitable Hakka woman did not prove to be an easy task for Ah Kung, however. Although recent waves of Chinese migrants had tended to redress the imbalance in the Hakka population somewhat, the male population was still in inordinate disproportion to the female population.

Ah Kung's quest for a Hakka wife naturally began in the area heavily populated by Hakka; in the very area where he was born and where his family lived. The small towns of Siniawan, Batu Kitang, Batu Kawa and Bau and their nearby hamlets and villages were the places he began making enquiries of eligible young maidens.

Certain decorum must be observed however, for it would not do for a young stranger to simply ask a family for the hand of one of their daughters unannounced. The traditional ways in which these things were done must still be strictly followed. A local matchmaker must first be engaged as his agent and go-between in every town, village, hamlet and Hakka settlement that he decided to visit. His commissioned agent for the moment, the matchmaker, invariably a woman, would then present his credentials to the family of the bride-to-be. They could not have been too impressive. Poor, landless and still getting by as an itinerant farmhand or shop assistant he would not have been able to offer much by way of a dowry, let alone a bright future for the bride-to-be.

Although Ah Kung tried to explain later on in life that his difficulties in finding a wife among the Hakka community in these areas was the result of his own choosiness, I rather suspect that his less-than-impressive marriage credentials had more to do with it than he would care to admit. Those families with daughters of marriageable age would have other suitors with better prospects to pick from and the imbalance in the population would have afforded them the luxury of turning down poorer suitors like Ah Kung. It was a seller's market as far as the bride-selling trade was concerned. It was therefore not a surprise that his earlier attempts at finding a wife were met with failure.

Having failed to find a bride in Sarawak, Ah Kung decided to look farther afield. He decided to go to West Kalimantan to continue his quest.

It was going to be a perilous journey, he realized. He had to take the same route that his father and uncle took with three other thousand members of the Shum Tio Kau Kongsi when they took flight from the attacking members of the Takang Kongsi in West Kalimantan more than forty years ago. Except that, unlike his father, he was going into it and not away from it. Not quite the same thing as going into the enemy's lair but quite close to it.

It was also perilous because no paved roads had yet been constructed to link the towns of Sarawak and West Kalimantan, and what accessible tracks could be found were smugglers' and traders' trails, roughly hewed through the thick virgin jungle. Whereas smugglers and traders had the sense to travel in groups, Ah Kung was going to make the journey alone. His destination was Sambas - directly west of Bau and a good hundred kilometres from it. It would be a journey of at least one week by foot because of the trek he had to make through virgin rainforest for nearly half the trip.

"I had only with me some money, a change of clothes, a thin blanket, some dried provisions, a pot, a parang (a Malay machete), a musket and a piece of plank," he said.

I could understand the other items he took along with him – the money to help him pay his expenses along the journey and for use as a dowry payment, the musket and the machete for use in the jungle, but what, I wondered, was he going to do with a piece of timber plank in the middle of the jungle? Surely it was not going to be part of the dowry offered to the family of the bride-to-be or a required item in some sort of quaint Hakka's betrothal or marriage ceremony?

"For use for sleeping in the jungle," he added, with a twinkle in his eyes, smiling his trademark all-knowing smile.

It was his mattress, he explained. The moist and sometimes damp ground of the jungle made it necessary to have something dry to lie on. A strong and rustic man in his young days, he would not have found the plank too uncomfortable to lie on.

The Borneo jungle, however, was another matter. Although the roughly hewn and much trodden tracks marked the route he had to take, they would have been partially overgrown by creepers, vines, branches and saplings. His parang - a thick and broad single blade machete much favoured by the Ibans for headhunting- had to be put to constant use to cut and slash his way through the jungle paths; for it only takes days for a clearing or a path to be quickly covered by the undergrowth of the tropical rainforest. His dried provisions, consisting of rice and salt fish had to be supplemented by jungle ferns - mainly the young shoots of the pakis and beeding - other wild vegetables and fruits. Fresh water was not a problem however, as the mountain range forming the watershed had numerous streams and brooks running through it.

The jungle was largely uninhabited and what settlements there were – whether native or Chinese - were few and far in between. It was a lonely trip, punctuated only

Children of the Monkey God

by the occasional panicky scurrying into the thick undergrowth of perhaps a mouse deer or a wild boar alerted by the sound of his footsteps. Tribes of the grey-haired macaque monkeys and families of orange-haired orang-utans swung from branches high and low as they made their aerial journey from bough to bough and from tree to tree in search of wild durians, rambutans, mangoes, mangosteens and other wild jungle fruits, relentlessly foraging as they moved along. Sometimes he could hear the rustling and scratching sounds made by various species of reptiles and snakes - mainly monitor lizards, and pythons - as they slid and slithered their way through the undergrowth.

It was in the night when the jungle would come to life, he said. A crescendo of shrill sound greeted him as the sun set every evening, made by the courtesy of myriad unseen tiny crickets and cicadas. Other nocturnal creatures chipped in with their mating calls, perhaps also demarcating their territory or merely making their presence felt. The "tiong", a species of hornbill, with its loud piecing mono-syllable toot could also be heard; the night owls with their softer hoots; the "wok-woks" of the small but agile gibbons; and worst of all, the irritating buzzing sound of scores of mosquitoes. Despite their size, they were an irritation that hampered his attempt to sleep at night. He had to create a smoke screen around his makeshift 'bed' at the start of every evening before he lay down to sleep. He did this by gathering plenty of twigs and dry leaves to start a fire, which he would use for cooking his rice in a small metal pot. With that out of the way, he would put a lot of damp leaves and twigs on the flame, enough to create a thick column of smoke but not too much to completely smother it.

The ground he was going to lie on was borrowed ground and a prayer must be said to Tu Ti Kung, the god of earth for permission for its use; to Datuk Kung, the local

Malay god of Chinese migrant-creation, custodian-protector and lord of the forest and jungle for his generosity for letting him travel safely through his realm. Finally a prayer would be made to Tai Pak Kung, the guardian-protector of the Chinese migrants in the Nanyang for his guidance and protection. That done, he covered himself with his thin blanket from neck to toe for protection against the mosquitoes - for they would come again as soon as the flames died out, taking with it the smoke - and with his unsheathed parang and musket beside him he would lay down on his "mattress."

It was not too difficulty to sleep, he said. Exhausted from his day's trek through the jungle, sleep was not a problem. The jungle held no fear for him, he said. This was not the first time he had spent the night alone in the jungle. A keen hunter of wild boars and mouse deers with his musket he had on other occasions spent the night alone in the jungle in the Siniawan area. He was used to it. What you have to bear in mind, he said, was that you should always respect the gods and the spirits of the woods and no disaster would befall you. Never utter either a foul word or any curses and always seek permission from Tu Ti Kung and Datuk Kung when you have to clear your bowels or urinate on their ground. Thanks must also be offered to them for any fruits, vegetables, fish and animals obtained in the jungle and for the use of their land.

He finally came out of the watershed after a few days' journey over the mountain range. He was now in West Kalimantan and, although it was a different country ruled by a different government, the landscape and the inhabitants were, in many ways similar to that of Sarawak. The Hakka in this part of the world spoke the same dialect as his and, like him the younger ones were descendents of gold-miners. Those of the same age as his father were mainly ex-miners and ex-members of the powerful Kongsi houses of forty or fifty years ago.

With the demise of these Kongsi houses, these former members had turned to subsistence and cash-crop farming and other occupations for a living. They were the families he sought out in his quest for a wife. Although he was still as eager as when he first started, he was careful to continue to observe the same protocol that he had practised in Sarawak. He might have been in a different country now, but he was still among his own Hakka clansmen, and certain customs remained the same as in Sarawak. The local matchmaker of each town, village and hamlet, including even very small Hakka settlements, must still be engaged as his go-between.

However, unlike Sarawak, looking for a wife seemed to be a lot easier here; the Hakka population on this side of the border was more established and hence bigger, the proportion of female to male better balanced. One thing had not changed though. He was still very particular about the woman he wanted as a wife, he said.

"I can't recall how many Hakka settlements I went to and how many girls I met. Some were too weak and thin; not having the required strength for farm work nor the child-bearing qualities I wanted. Some were too fat, good for farm work and child-bearing but not much to look at," he related.

It was in a village near the town of Sambas that he finally met my grandmother, Ah Por (meaning grandmother in Hakka). She was in his eyes, the right woman for him. Not too thin and not too fat; strong yet not flabby. There was an alertness in her eyes that he had not seen in the other women. They were bright and showed a keenness of mind that he would appreciate throughout his life. She was pretty without the softness that normally accompanied prettiness. His quest was now over.

The wedding ceremony was a small and short affair. The groom's family was back in Sarawak and across the watershed. Only Ah Por's family members were present, consisting mainly of relatives and clansmen with the surname of Chang. Ah Por was a Chang and her father and his father before him were members of the Takang Kongsi. It was the very same Kongsi that was responsible for chasing her recently acquired father-in-law and other members of the Sham Tio Kau out of West Kalimantan and across the watershed into Sarawak more than forty years ago. The very watershed she must now cross with her husband.

They didn't cross it until a few days after the wedding and when she finally had to leave with her newly-wedded husband for Sarawak, she cried. She wept a lot, she told us grandchildren, especially when the finality of her home-leaving hit her. It might have been out of filial piety that she wept, for all Chinese brides were expected to weep out of a sense of duty; to show to the gods and the world their sadness at having to part from their parents who had hitherto nurtured and supported them. It was more likely that she cried because she knew she would probably never see them and her siblings again and also because she was barely twenty years' old and this man who had taken her for a bride was still a stranger to her. There are very few women in the world who could lay claim to being happy as the bride of an arranged marriage; Ah Por was not one of these women.

For his return trip across the watershed border with Ah Por, Ah Kung was careful to allay her fears of travelling on their own. His impatience at finding a wife now sated, he took time to ask around the town of Sambas as to whether there were any traders who might be planning on making a trip across the border soon. He knew it shouldn't be too difficult a task as there was quite a brisk trade between the Chinese merchants of Bau and that of the traders of West

Children of the Monkey God

Kalimantan, whose wares of mainly crocodile and snake skins, especially that of python's, and dried tobacco leaves had a ready market across the border. It didn't take him long to come across a few traders who were, in actual fact, planning on such a trip. It was a tearful farewell for Ah Por and her family when they finally had to leave. She couldn't remember much of the trip except that she wept for much of the time.

It didn't take Ah Por too long to be accepted as the latest member of the extended family system of her newly-wedded husband or to get used to life in Sarawak. The Hakka farming way of life in Siniawan, Bau and Batu Kawa was not that much different from that of West Kalimantan. As for Ah Kung, he returned to his job as a shop assistant and an itinerant farmhand and it was not until he was in his mid-twenties that he managed to buy his first piece of land.

The family was still landless up until then and, although Ah Tai had by now become quite an accomplished herbalist - his age and his near opium-ravaged body making it nigh impossible for him to work as a farmhand now - the larger family that he and Ah Kung had to support meant that it had become extremely difficult to gather enough money to realize their ambition of owning their own piece of land, an ambition that they had been harbouring for quite sometime. There was also his addiction to opium, which continued to be a drain on the family's earnings. It was at the very best a hand-to-mouth existence for all of them, with hardly any savings to their name.

However, an opportunity to buy a piece of land came by one day when Ah Tai was paid three hundred dollars for the treatment of the daughter of a rich Kuching towkay suffering from menses. In the traditional fashion in which fees were paid to the practitioners of Chinese medicine, the grateful father's small red paper wrap containing the payment for Ah Tai's last visit was more than the few dollars he was normally paid. In true Chinese traditional fashion, the packet was not opened by Ah Tai until he reached home - for it was considered extremely rude to unwrap any gift or payment in the presence of the benefactor. The discovery at home of the $300 sum contained in the packet prompted him to go back to the towkay, who in turn assured him that the payment was not a mistake and that he meant it as a bonus to Ah Tai for a job well done.

It was a fair bit of money in those days; enough to buy a small plot of land to start their own farm. Ah Tai didn't want to buy the land himself - his fear of officialdom again a factor in his decision - and the money was given to Ah Kung for that purpose. Ah Kung was also his only son who, in the absence of a will, would, by Chinese tradition, inherit everything he owned. The three hundred dollars was all he had to give to Ah Kung.

Ah Kung had by now a small family of his own to support and it had been his ambition for quite some time to start his own farm. He had felt that something must be done to break the cycle of poverty and landlessness that the whole extended family had found themselves in. His father and uncle were getting old and his own family would only grow bigger. He was by now the most able-bodied breadwinner out of the three of them and it fell on his shoulders to do something about their situation. It had never been easy to put aside enough money to buy a farm of their own, working as they had as hired hands to farmers and shopkeepers. This $300 bonus payment changed the situation somewhat. He had now the funds to buy a piece of land and a decision had to be made as to what type of land to buy and where.

He began his search for his own farm by making enquiries of available lands in the surrounding area of Bau, Siniawan and Batu Kawa. Nothing suitable was found and

Children of the Monkey God

he had to extend his search further afield. What eventually turned up after a lot of enquiries was a piece of land of roughly ten acres in size in Sedungus - situated on the northern coastline and forming the other part of the river delta of the Sarawak River from Santubong. It was suitable only for planting coconut trees, however, something in which he had neither experience nor much knowledge.

The experience he had hitherto acquired as a hired farmhand had been that of a rubber-taper, pepper grower and picker, and although he would have liked to remain in these areas of farming, any land that could be purchased with the money available to him for these types of farming would be too small in area. Coconut planting and the production of copra was not a bad thing to go into, he thought. It was a cash crop that was starting to have an increasing demand. He might have no experience as a coconut planter but he was young, strong-bodied and he was prepared to work hard. He would also learn as he went along. On top of it all, the family would have a piece of land and a home of their own; something that been denied them for so many years because of their poverty and his father's past. His mind made up, he took the plunge and sealed the deal that would be the turning point of his and his family's life.

Ah Kung 's entire extended family of about ten members consisting of four of his own children, wife, father, mother, uncle, and a couple of unmarried sisters didn't wait long to set up home by the coast after the purchase of this small piece of land. Although he never talked about it, most, if not all of his sisters would have been married by that time with husbands and children of their own. The gender imbalance of the Hakka community in Sarawak where males outnumbered females would make certain of their marriages at a very young age. This would most certainly have happened before the family made their move to Sedungus and possibly before Ah Kung's own marriage. The family's poor financial circumstances would also have been a strong factor in their decisions as marriages of these young maidens would not only have meant fewer mouths to feed but the grooms' dowry payments would have been of tremendous financial help.

Although Ah Kung never said it, and I rather doubt he would ever have admitted it, their arrival at the farm would have been only the second time he had seen the sea. The first time would have been when he had gone to view the land before its purchase.

I came to this view, with a fair degree of justification, from Ah Kung's own account of his first encounter with a sea turtle soon after the family's move to the coast.

He related, with some abashment, the following account of that first encounter:

"One day, towards evening, I was standing on the beach when, out of the water, I saw this lumbering sea monster coming towards me. It was fearsome and ugly in looks and it seemed like it was going to attack me. Fearing for my life, I scrambled up the nearest tree for safety. I was up there for a short while and I only came down when a passing Malay man from a nearby village combing the beach for clams and other shellfish, assured me that there was nothing to fear from this sea creature." Standing next to the turtle, the Malay man seemed to have no fear of it at all.

Reassured, Ah Kung got down from the tree, albeit gingerly and still with some apprehension. The fisherman explained to Ah Kung that the turtle was a pregnant female, quite harmless by nature and who had merely come up to the beach to lay her eggs in the night and that she would return to the sea as soon as she had finished her task in the morning.

The eggs, he said, were a delicacy and could be eaten like chicken eggs. They would only be buried under a few feet of sand and, if Ah Kung were to come back to more or less the same spot the next morning he would find them waiting for him.

Ever curious and always eager to learn new things, Ah Kung went back to the same spot early the following morning and found, to his delight, the nest of eggs as was promised by the Malay man. Helping himself to some of these fresh-laid eggs, for they were still warm to the touch, he took them home and the family had boiled turtle eggs for the first time in their life.

Ah Kung and his family soon learned how to run a coconut farm. It was not difficult, he said. However, what was required was a lot of hard work to ensure that the coconut trees, especially the young shoots and saplings, were not choked by weeds. The land had to be constantly cleared with the sickle, the scythe and the parang to keep at bay this creeping army of undesirable undergrowth.

Drainage canals had to be strategically dug, and regularly maintained, to ensure that the roots of the coconut did not stay water-logged, as well as having the desired effect of depriving other unwanted plants of their water supply.

Coconut trees that had grown too old and too tall bore fewer fruits and were too hard to harvest, their tall height making it difficult even for the long sickle-attached harvest pole to reach the fruits at the very top of the tree. New saplings had to be regularly planted to help with the regeneration of the coconut crop.

The soil of the farm was poor, consisting mainly of beach sand but the coconut trees thrived in it and no fertilizers were required to ensure their growth. Only the brown old coconut fruits were harvested, the unripe young ones with their delicate, but delicious flesh not suitable for turning into copra. The brown furry fibres of the husks of old fruits were either turned into brooms or mosquito-smokers or for use as mulch. The tough, hard shells took the place of firewood and together with the husks, were used as fuel in the copra smoke-house, as well as in the kitchen.

Ah Kung's small plot of land was part of a bigger area of two hundred acres situated on the western side of the Sarawak River estuary as it joins the South China Sea. A rivulet on the southern side, flowing from east to west, and scarcely twenty feet wide in its widest part, separated it from the mainland and had all but turned the two hundred acres of land into a partial islet. The northern beachfront faced the South China Sea while its eastern side formed part of the Sarawak River estuary and faced Mount Santubong. And while the near-islet was composed mainly of poor beach sand, the other and southern side of the rivulet was made up of acres and acres of mangrove swamps, forming part of the Salak mangrove wetlands.

The area teemed with marine and wild life. While it provided Ah Kung and his family with food and sustenance it also caused him a few problems. This was especially so with the squirrels and monkeys, he said. And while he had little tolerance for the destruction caused by the squirrels, it was the monkeys, he said, who were the most ruinous of the tree creatures. There were two main species of them - the proboscis and the macaque. The proboscises were not a problem, he added. The larger proboscises, with their long orange-coloured fur and inordinately long, soft flabby noses — cheekily and rather unkindly dubbed the Dutch monkeys ("holung hel" in Hakka) by the local farmers - tended to keep to the southern end of the farm where mangrove trees abounded. Shy and reclusive by nature, their diet consisted mainly of fruits and leaves and they showed scant interest in either the green or brown coconuts. Their tribes were also considerably smaller than that of the macaques.

The smaller fruit-eating grey-haired macaque monkeys, however, were a different matter. Vivacious, gregarious and mischievous by nature, they were a menace to coconut planters in particular, and fruit farmers in general. Travelling in tribes of twenty to thirty members, they would wreak havoc as they foraged for fruits far and wide, whether it was in the jungle, plantations or farms.

"I wouldn't have minded if they had not been so destructive. They would just strip a whole tree of its young fruits, using their hands and feet to pull, kick and yank until they fell onto the ground. They would do this from one tree to another. Do you think they were satisfied with just one or even a few trees? No. They were only happy after they had wrecked lots of trees. By the time they had finished and had left, the whole place would be strewn with young coconuts - nearly all of them spoilt and split open from their fall from the top of the tree. What was worse was that only a few of these were actually eaten by the monkeys. The rest were simply left to rot under the sun. What a waste! What a waste!" Ah Kung said with a shake of his head.

Ah Kung's strict adherence to the Confucian ethics of frugality was considered something of a legend in the family, but surely he couldn't really have thought to apply it to the antics of a bunch of monkeys - or could he?

Initially, Ah Kung turned to his hunting gun to rid his land of these marauding monkeys. It worked for a while. He was a good shot in his young days, and although the monkeys were very agile and mobile, Ah Kung was still able to bring down quite a few of them. Frightened by the sound of the gunshots and worried for their own safety, the monkeys stayed away, foraging elsewhere and avoiding Ah Kung's land.

They did not stay away for too long, however. They came back soon after and in larger numbers. Whether it was a case of hunger or running out of areas to forage or simply a case of bravado was hard to tell. But, either way, back they came to Ah Kung's land.

They had also become more cunning and cautious. They learned to keep their distance from Ah Kung. They stayed out of range of his gun and Ah Kung found it hard to get close enough to shoot at them. Sometimes, they would bare their sharp teeth at him as they gave out aggressive screeches. At other times, they would tease him with their hoots while bouncing up and down on the branches they were standing on. Any slight approach made by Ah Kung would be reciprocated by a retreat of a similar distant by these unwelcome and mischievous visitors, presenting their bare and pinkish bums to him as they did so. Ah Kung swore that they were teasing him and, what had started off as a simple matter of merely pointing his gun at the monkeys and shooting, had turned into a battle of will and wits. Ah Kung had the will, I knew that, but had he the wits to deal with these monkeys I wondered.

"I had a plan," Ah Kung said, with a twinkle in his eyes and smiling his usual all-knowing smile.

Ah Kung's plan began with the trapping of one of the monkeys. Using a bamboo cage with a trap door and a few tempting juicy fruits as bait - mangoes, star-fruit and banana, etc., - he managed to capture a rather young, imprudent male member of the tribe.

The poor creature was then neatly trussed and tied up

by Ah Kung with the help of a couple of other members of the family, for although it was trapped, it was still a cornered animal and must be treated with extreme caution. Having done that, Ah Kung proceeded to shave off its fur with a sharp cut-throat razor blade. The monkey was now bare-skinned and pink. Its body was then dabbed with all sorts of bright-coloured paints - yellow, red, blue and green. It was put back into the bamboo cage after the paints had dried.

Ah Kung waited for a few days for the tribe to return before he decided to release the now very colourful monkey. But not before he finally strapped the juvenile simian in an old pair of shorts and a colourful shirt.

Once released, the poor but extremely relieved creature lost no time in rushing towards his mates with the intention of re-uniting with them, but not before presenting his bum to Ah Kung as a final act of defiance.

It was not going to be a happy re-union for him, however.

He had no inkling of the sight he presented to his mates when he approached them; for any resemblance he had to a monkey had been disguised by a thick layer of bright multi-coloured paint and the human garb forced upon him. To the other monkeys, the creature that was coming towards them was not a monkey, let alone a member of their tribe. In their eyes he was just some monstrous creature chasing after them. He neither looked nor smelled anything like one of them.

Screeching in fear and alarm they backed away from him, scrambling out of his way and fleeing. The poor painted monkey couldn't understand why his mates were running away and, doing the only thing he could do under the circumstances, he kept up his pursuit. They continued to run from him, their destructive foraging of the coconuts now forgotten. The more he pursued, the farther they ran.

This "game" of chase and run continued for quite some time until their disappearance into the mangrove wetlands towards the southern end of the farm. They didn't come back to bother Ah Kung again for quite a long time and when they did, he would simply scare them off the farm by using the same ploy again.

There were other coconut farms other than that of Ah Kung's in Sedungus but most of them were uncultivated, which left the family with very few neighbours. It also made them quite isolated from the outside world.

The house they lived in was small and simple; built of wooden stilts with bound bamboo stems for the floor and thatched attap leaves for the roof and the walls. No public services of any type – including roads, sewerage, piped water or electricity - served the area. Their main link with the outside world was via the sea and rivers. Obtaining a regular supply of water was not a problem, however. The land was a mere two feet above sea level and the wells that Ah Kung constructed had only to be sunk eight feet deep to provide the family with an ample supply of fresh water.

The soil was not rich enough to support the planting of any type of rice - wet or dry - and this and other essential items such as sugar, tea, coffee, kerosene, matches, clothes, shoes, etc., were obtained mainly from Kuching, the capital, nearly thirty kilometres away. This would be carried out three or four times a year after the sale of a boatload of copra to the towkay in Kuching.

In the early days when he still had to get by on his timber boat fitted with a pair of oars, that journey would involve at least half a day of rowing. Coconuts, and the copra processed from them, were cash crops and the proceeds from the sale of each cargo would partly be used for the purchase of these essentials. Any funds left over would be put away by Ah Kung as savings, not in any bank but safely tucked away in some secret hiding place in the farm that only he and Ah Por knew about. I had always suspected it to be under their mattress.

The family looked forward to Ah Kung's return after each outing, for other than the essential items, he would also bring back fresh meat such as pork and chicken. Although Ah Por had got a chicken coop going, plus a pigsty rearing pigs, as well as free-ranged ducks and geese, these farmyard animals still had to be supplemented by the occasional purchase from the town. Manure from the chicken coop and pig sty was used to fertilize her small vegetable garden of star beans and the long snake beans, pumpkins, bitter gourds, yams, tapioca, duckweed, bamboo and fruit trees of banana, papaya, star and jak fruit, mango, red-haired rambutan, lime, mangosteen, sugar cane, etc.

There was no lack of fish, crabs, prawns or shellfish. The waters surrounding Sedungus abounded with marine life. The family learned how to use the long dragnet, the casting net and crab traps. From the dragnet the whole family would be involved and basketfuls of whitings, anchovies, herrings, cobblers, cods, mullets, blue-mantra crabs and prawns, would be their normal catches.

The rivulet yielded scores of prawns when used with the casting net, and the crab traps would haul in numerous mud crabs. Another smaller variety of hairy-legged climber crabs had to be caught by hand in the mangrove swamp at night and would only be eaten after a period of pickling them in salt and rice wine.

The beach and the estuary mud of the mangrove

swamps were home to myriad species of clams, cockles and edible sea snails. Locating and harvesting them presented no difficulties to the family, especially when they were willing to learn these same skills from friendly nearby villagers and neighbours. The refrigerator was still a thing of the future and the humid tropical heat made it necessary that nearly every catch had to be consumed on the same day. There were still plenty that could not be eaten in a single day and these would then be dried, smoked, salted or pickled. Guts, heads and shells were turned into fertilisers. Leftovers were turned into animal feed. Nothing was wasted.

In time, Ah Kung's hard work and frugality started to pay off and the profit made from each consignment of copra began to grow. Copra was fetching a good price and his savings soon became quite substantial; enough for him to cast his eyes on neighbouring plots of land. Only a few of them were actually farmed, and with enough funds in his hands, it was not too difficult to buy these untended farms from owners who showed scant interest in coconut farming. Akin to the old Chinese saying that "a journey of a thousand miles begins with a single step" he began to make progressive purchases of these neighbouring plots.

They were straightforward transactions, except for one purchase where the vendor claimed that he had not been paid and refused to complete the transfer of the land. All of Ah Kung's purchases had been made in cash from his accumulated savings and there was no other evidence of the transaction. This fact did not deter Ah Kung from filing a complaint with the appropriate authority against the seller and taking him to court over the matter. It would be his word against that of the vendor.

"The case was fixed for hearing early in the morning. I had to be there by seven o'clock. Fortunately for me the tide was flowing the right way. I found that out from the Tung

Children of the Monkey God

Tsu"[6], Ah Kung recounted.

Throughout most of his adult life Ah Kung had with him a Chinese almanac, called "Tung Tsu" in Hakka, which he would buy every year. An annual publication in Chinese, it has sections containing the moon-phase, Chinese astrology and the traditional twelve animals of the zodiac. A self-taught man in Chinese written characters, Ah Kung would often go through the book for consultation on matters of auspicious days to conduct an affair, feng shui and the choice of names for his children and grandchildren. It was also invaluable to him as a guide on the ebb and flow of the tide. He never rowed against the tide, he said. Going to upriver Kuching, one must go with the rise of the tide and, coming back to the farm - a downriver trip - one must follow the ebbing tide, he further explained.

After due consultation with what I considered to be his bible, he decided that the best time to begin his journey was just after midnight. To take advantage of the tide he had to almost row non-stop with just a few short breaks in between. It was an exhausting effort in the standing position in which he had to row. Although the long oars made of tropical ironwood were sturdy, they were also heavy and, while the blades cut through the water with ease, the right rhythm had

---

[6] *Tung Tsu, meaning the 'Book of Myriad Things', is an ancient almanac reputed to be over 4200 years old and is more widely used than the 'I Ching' among Chinese communities in the world. A book of geomancy, fortune-telling, divination, physiognomy, palmistry, moon phases, tide predictions, moral codes, numerology, astrology, etc., the book is treated as a powerful spiritual instrument. When unused, Ah Kung's copy was always reverently hung next to the family's Kuan Yin shrine.*

to be maintained at all times. Each downward stroke had to be carried out by a forward bending of the body and, as the oars were pulled through the water by drawing the handles towards his chest, his back had to be straightened to continue with the momentum as well as letting him to lift the blades out of the water in readiness for the next stroke. Although there was neither the sun nor the oppressive tropical humid heat to deal with yet at that time of the morning, it was still a backbreaking job.

He arrived at Kuching just at the crack of dawn. Mooring his boat at the jetty at Pangkalan Batu, he made his way to the government courthouse, a mere stone's throw from the jetty.

As the plaintiff, Ah Kung started first, with the defendant following after him. Both parties stated their case and gave their version of the transaction. It was one man's word against another and no other witnesses were called. The court was presided by Sir Charles Brooke, the second rajah of Sarawak who, as a young man had helped his uncle Sir James Brooke and the first rajah of Sarawak, in putting down the "uprising" of the Hakka miners in 1857 with his troops of Iban warriors from Skrang. The rajah asked questions of both parties and decided in favour of Ah Kung at the end of the case.

"A good man and a wise ruler," Ah Kung said of the second white rajah. Acting as his own lawyer, he loved telling his grandchildren of the one and only courtroom appearance he had ever had in his life and of the proud moment of his victory achieved before a distinguished ruler. This was in spite of the fact that Sir Charles Brooke was, together with his uncle Sir James Brooke, one of the two main characters responsible for the quelling of the miners in the "Bau Rebellion of 1857." Perhaps the fact that the event had taken place more than 50 years' ago might have

Children of the Monkey God

something to do with it, for in all the times that Ah Kung related this story and that of the "Chinese uprising" he never sounded bitter toward the Brookes. To him and perhaps to his father, it was warfare and consequences such as deaths, injuries and other losses and sufferings were part of it. If anything, Ah Kung was more bitter towards the Kuching towkay for their perceived treachery in siding with the rajah than with anybody else.

I have often wondered whether Ah Kung's view of the rajah would have been the same had he lost his case. I also wonder sometimes if it was really the rajah who had sat at his case, taking into consideration that he had never met the man before or since the hearing. A further consideration would be that one Brooke officer would not be that much different from another in the eyes of Ah Kung.

The extended family of Ah Kung came to an end when he was in his late thirties. His uncle died in his seventies and his father in his eighties. His mother left the family home within two years of his father's death. With his sisters already married, he was now left with Ah Por and four young children, consisting of two sons and two daughters.

His four or five trips to Kuching every year to sell copra and purchase provisions would leave Ah Por alone to look after her young children and the farm. On those occasions, Ah Kung would leave with her his Winchester double barrel hunting gun. Not a hunting person herself, Ah Por seldom found it necessary to use the shotgun. There was one occasion, though, when she did have to use it. It was on a day when Ah Kung had just left for one of his trips to Kuching.

Ah Por related the incident to me later on in her life.

She said: "It was just about to get dark, when I saw our

lecherous neighbour walking towards our house. I knew him to be that way inclined because he had been rather suggestive in his behaviour as of late. He must have known your Ah Kung was away in Kuching. I had no intention of letting that demon near my house. How dare he think to come and molest me while your Ah Kung was away? I was carrying your toddler of a father at the time when I saw him walking towards the house. I gave your father to Tai Koo (eldest aunty) to hold. I went to get the gun and I loaded up both barrels. I aimed and I fired. **Pooon!** He fell to the ground. I thought I had killed him. Good. Good. Wah, he didn't die, he got up. I took aim again. I fired again. **Pooon!** He ran for his life and he was out of sight before I could reload. He never dared to come to the house again. He was lucky I was not as good a shot as your grandfather, otherwise he would have died an early death. Ha, ha, ha, ha."

As Ah Kung's farm expanded, he found it necessary to recruit hired help. There was no shortage of available young men, as there were quite a few Malay villages nearby with Sibu Laut to the west, Santubong to the east and Salak to the south. One Malay hired hand by the name of Bujang was particularly hard-working and stayed on the farm as a live-in helper. For the rest of his life, he became Ah Kung's companion until his death in his early seventies.

They were also joined by one of Ah Por's brothers who trekked all the way from Sambas with his only son, a young boy, after the death of his wife. He was our favourite granduncle who, like Bujang, was an invaluable help to Ah Kung on his farm. He remained a widower for the rest of his life and was the only sibling of Ah Por's to join her in Sarawak. A kind and gentle soul, he was extremely skilful with his hands, creating the most exquisite kites from bamboo splints and rice paper. Brightly coloured and

Children of the Monkey God

decorated butterflies and centipedes would result from his frail hands after hours of work spent patiently shaving the bamboo splints and pasting and painting the papers. They were wonderful presents to have and my brothers and I would be the street's only proud owners of these works of art, much to the envy of our friends. The only problem with them was try as hard as we could, my brothers and I could not make them fly, their bulky size and heavy weight a distinct disadvantage in a town that seldom experienced strong winds. Ah Kung, with his usual harsh, pragmatic thinking, considered them to be a waste of time and money.

The growth of Ah Kung's farm also made it necessary to have a bigger smoke-house and this was built near the small river at the southern end of the farm. The construction of a timber jetty next to it also made it easier for him to load and off-load his cargo. While the beach on the northern and eastern sides of the estate had the water flowing right to its edge, inclement conditions made it unsuitable for use as an access to the outside world. Strong wind and surf pounded it during the monsoon season and, without any form of windbreaker acting as a buffer, any jetty constructed would be smashed to bits or washed away. While the high tide would bring the waterline within a few yards of the farm, the low tide that followed a few hours later would leave bare acres of empty beach with the waterline more than a mile away from the farm.

The small river at the southern end of the farm was thus the artery used by Ah Kung to link his farm to the surrounding areas and to Kuching. Partially sheltered from the elements by the plantation's coconut, mangrove and other trees it was a waterway thickly covered with the putrid-smelling mud of the mangrove. While the water serving it would be reduced to a trickling shallow stream during the lowest point of the ebbing tide, it would become full flowing during periods of high tide.

Mangrove saplings sprouting on its banks, and some even in the middle of the river, had to be regularly removed or trimmed back to prevent them from choking the waterway. It was only usable during periods of high tide and Ah Kung's use of it had to be carried out with a good knowledge of the ebb and flow of the tide. The small river was therefore his lifeline.

A salt-water crocodile that had taken up residence there nearly spoilt it for him, however.

Its presence in the river came to the attention of Ah Kung one day while returning on his speedboat from a successful overnight hunting trip across the estuary at Teluk Bandung, his rowing boat now fitted with a small two-stroke Azani out-boat motor. Teluk Bandung was an area forming part of the north-western slope of Mount Santubong.

In the days when my grandfather was eking out a living as a coconut farmer on the other side of the estuary, Teluk Bandung, before it was developed in the 1970s, was part of the rainforest system; its virgin jungle largely uninhabited, unspoilt and undisturbed; its waters pristine and crystal clear. Renamed "Damai Beach", it has since become the site of at least two international-style resorts, as well as a golf course.

It was also a favourite hunting haunt of Ah Kung who found the numerous wild boars roaming its hill of tremendous value in supplementing his family's meagre supply of meat. The Malay - and therefore Islamic - residents of Santubong village, situated a few kilometres further south of this virgin area, had no great fondness for these wild animals, its consumption being forbidden by their religion.

Ah Kung was, therefore, only one of a handful of

Chinese cash-crop farmers of coconut and fruit trees from nearby areas who hunted these animals. The optimum time to hunt, according to Ah Kung, was in the dead of night when these, normally shy and cautious creatures, would come out of hiding and forage for food. One pig would normally last two weeks, with the family eating fresh meat within a day of the successful hunt, and smoked and salted wild pork for a further fortnight or so, depending on the size of the kill.

Ah Kung normally took as his hunting companion his eldest daughter, my most beloved of all aunts. She was a kind and gentle soul, yet possessed an inner strength second to none. She was to become the extended family's midwife. Although untrained, she managed to acquire the confidence and skills necessary to be the family member solely responsible for the successful delivery of at least a score of nephews and nieces in the plantation.

On those hunting trips with Ah Kung she would be responsible for looking after the boat, especially its small but valuable motor, while at the same time making certain that it would not be beached, especially during periods of ebbing tide. She would also help Ah Kung to carry the kill, especially if it was a big one. In the meantime, Ah Kung would enter on his own into the Teluk Bandung's thick undergrowth to hunt.

"Weren't you frightened looking after the boat all on your own in the night with nobody else around for miles?" I would ask my eldest aunt when I was a young boy.

"The first few times I went there with your grandfather, I was" she would reply, "but I got used to it and what bothered me in the end more than anything else were the bites of the mosquitoes and sand flies. Your grandfather was a lot bolder than me in going into the jungle on his own," she would continue, "especially into Teluk Bandung, which had an extremely bad reputation as a haunt of evil spirits and demons. None of the villagers from Santubong would dare to go in there, except in groups of twos or threes at the very least, let alone on their own," she would add.

On this particular trip when my grandfather had his first encounter with the crocodile after a successful hunt, there was no mention made of my eldest aunt being with him. Perhaps she was, but in the telling of this favourite family tale, her name and her minor role in it were most probably pushed into the background.

Thus it was that my grandfather noticed this half-submerged reptile approaching his boat. Perhaps it was attracted to the smell of blood coming from the dead wild boar that he had on board and which he had shot not long ago. But whatever it was that had attracted the crocodile, it was coming towards him as he slowly approached the wooden jetty on the bank of the small river. It was a monster of nearly ten feet long. Grabbing his gun, which was still loaded, he shot at it. It was a hurried shot made at the spur of the moment. The unexpectedness of the encounter and the necessity of also having to carefully negotiate his boat in the narrow channel had made his shot a poor one. He didn't entirely miss, for blood was pouring from the crocodile into the river, indicating that it was wounded. But, before he could take another shot, the wounded creature had disappeared into the murky water. Although he knew he had only wounded it, he was also hoping that the wound would eventually become fatal. Perhaps it had died, he thought, for there was no sight of it for the next few weeks.

It was not to be, however.

His next encounter with the creature nearly cost him his life. He was net-casting for prawns at the river mouth of the

Children of the Monkey God

rivulet - at its eastern end where it joined the estuary - when the crocodile surfaced and lunged at him. Fortunately, he was standing in less than one foot of water when it happened, and he moved swiftly enough to avoid its snapping jaws. It was fortunate that he was standing on the firmer ground of the beach at the time, albeit in one foot of water, and not in the soft sinking mud of the mangrove swamp, the riverside. Had he been standing there he would have found it nigh impossible to jump out of the crocodile's way, the soft and fluid grey mud of the mangrove acting like quicksilver in restricting his footwork. It was all he could do to make a quick retreat up the beach and on to dry ground.

There were a few more encounters with the creature after that incident. All he had to do was to go near that river and it would surface, making its presence known to him. Even a cough made by him as a means of testing whether it was safe to approach the river, would bring it to the surface. The creature was not only mean and nasty but it was treating the river as its domain, and Ah Kung its target for a personal vendetta, presumably for the wound he had inflicted.

"He seemed to have remembered the wound I had given it and was taking it very personally", Ah Kung said.

The river was vital to Ah Kung. It was not only a food source in respect of the clams, prawns, crabs and other shell fish he and the family were able to obtain from it, but a vital arterial link between the farm, Kuching and the surrounding villages.

Something had to be done about it, Ah Kung decided. He knew he couldn't get near it to make a shot that would count. The aggressive behaviour of the crocodile had seen to that, and its alertness at his very presence on or near the river seemed to make it a near impossibility for him to take a clean shot.

He next tried catching it by tying a rope to a big hook and using a chicken as bait. But it was to no avail. The chicken would be eaten. The hook would come out of the water clean and shiny. "No crocodile and no chicken", he said. In all probability the other residents of the river, such as fish and crabs, ate the bait even before the crocodile had a chance to get at it. Ah Por lost a few chickens that way and, though she was not happy about it, she could see the necessity of Ah Kung using them as bait to catch the cunning creature.

Quickly running out of options and now quite desperate, Ah Kung decided on the next best thing to do to get rid of the crocodile. He made up his mind to hire a crocodile charmer to do the job for him as he had heard they were adept at catching crocodiles.

He made inquiries of the nearby Malay villages for the services of a traditional practitioner of this age-old craft. He finally settled on an old Malay shaman who was reputed to have powerful skills in catching crocodiles. With his fees agreed upon, a day was fixed for him to be on the farm to perform his traditional skills.

He appeared at the farm a few days later carrying with him the paraphernalia of his trade; a small bag, a big barbed hook, a length of strong rope, a dead chicken with its feathers stripped off, and a small round ceremonial vessel with a stand. He explained to Ah Kung that he had already carried out the necessary cleansing ceremony on himself at home and he was now ready to catch the crocodile. He told Ah Kung that the jetty was the best place to carry out the ceremony and for Ah Kung to bring along his hunting gun.

"I had it in mind to take my gun along anyway, just in case things didn't go according to plan," said Ah Kung in his narration of this episode of his life on the farm.

Children of the Monkey God

"In any case, I wouldn't have gone near that river without my gun," he added.

With his gun slung over his shoulder, Ah Kung took the shaman or 'bomoh' to the jetty where the ceremony was to take place, whereupon the old man attached the chicken to the hook and tied it with the rope. Setting it down on the jetty, he sat down next to it and, with small pieces of frankincense taken from his bag he then placed these into the ceremonial vessel. Lighting the strong fragrant resins with a matchstick, he was able to get a small fire going in very little time. Satisfied that the fire was burning properly, he began to say his prayer. This was soon followed by a chant. His body swaying in rhythm to the chant, his hand would occasionally reach into the small bag and, producing tiny pieces of frankincense, he would sprinkle them into the ceremonial vessel. This went on for a few minutes, chanting and sprinkling, sprinkling and chanting, with columns of aromatic smoke rising into the mangrove trees. He then got up and, picking up the chicken by the hook ring, he made a few turns of it around the ceremonial vessel, all the while chanting away. With that accomplished, he then secured the loose end of the rope to the trunk of a big mangrove tree growing next to the jetty. He then threw the chicken into the middle of the river. Sitting in the middle of the jetty crossed-legged he continued with his chanting, still swaying as he did so.

He was calling to the crocodile, Ah Kung said. In no time at all, Ah Kung saw the half-submerged head of his old foe moving towards the partially submerged chicken. Its approach was slow, calm and deliberate and showed none of its usual aggressiveness, Ah Kung related. Then, just as calmly and slowly it opened its jaws and the chicken disappeared inside its mouth. Almost immediately it started to thrash and twist as the barbed hook set into one of its jaws.

The old shaman on the jetty called on Ah Kung to shoot at it immediately. He had by now stood up and had stopped his chanting. Ah Kung took aim but it wasn't easy with the creature still twisting and thrashing in the water. A clear shot seemed quite impossible under the circumstances but he managed it somehow. A slight pause by the creature to get back its breath was all it took for Ah Kung to aim at a spot just above its eyes and pull the trigger.

The mangrove swamp reverberated with the sound of the shotgun. Blood poured out of its body as it continued to thrash and twist, albeit more slowly. The thrashing and twisting came to a gradual halt as its life force finally drained away from its body. When it finally went limp, Ah Kung knew he had finally triumphed over the creature and that he had reclaimed the small river that was his lifeline. It was his, once more.

Life on the farm returned to normal with the death of the crocodile. Ah Kung continued with his copra production, earning more as his farm expanded with the acquisition of more neighbouring plots. With the purchase of a few cows and a few bullock carts he had also abandoned the traditional but backbreaking method of transporting his coconut and copra. Prior to the acquisition of this small herd of cattle, he had to carry them on two big rattan baskets hanging from a five-foot long ironwood pole slung over his shoulders. While this method of carrying made it easier to handle heavy loads, it was also tough work in such humid conditions. A bigger farm also meant more coconut and more copra to be handled and processed. The cows and the bullock carts were, therefore, his answer to deal with this heavier workload. The cows became his latest helpers.

In the meantime, Ah Por kept herself busy with her vegetable garden, fruit trees, chicken coops, pig sty, ducks and geese. Thieving otters and the occasional pythons and monitor lizards could result in the loss of quite a few fowls in a night of "bad luck". She was now in her mid-thirties and had already borne Ah Kung five children.

It was while she was working in her vegetable garden one day when she felt her left calf pricked by a sharp broken twig protruding from the branch of a small sapling. It bled a little bit and she gave it little thought, continuing with her gardening. When she got home she cleaned the wound and applied some herbal remedy to it.

It became quite swollen the next morning and got progressively worse during the next few days. The wound had now become sceptic and the swelling had become bigger and redder with plenty of pus oozing from it. She had also developed a high fever in the meantime. She was now in great pain, very weak and could hardly walk. The pains were worse in the night when the wound would throb with greater intensity. The herbal remedy she had been using had not worked and Ah Kung decided that help must now be sought in Kuching.

One of the farm's bullock carts was used to take her to the jetty and she was carried onto the boat by Ah Kung. One of the farm's small wooden boats was used for the trip and, with the aid of the rising morning tide they were very soon in Kuching.

There were only a few privately-owned western clinics in Kuching at that time and Ah Kung decided to seek these out in the treatment of Ah Por's leg. She was unable to walk by now and Ah Kung had to carry her piggyback style everywhere they went. Public transport was non-existent then and the few cars that were running around the town most probably belonged to government officers of the Brooke regime or to rich towkay; people he hardly knew - let alone people he could ask for help.

They attracted a lot of looks from passers-by wherever they went; looks of curiosity as well as disbelief - the Chinaman with a woman on his back – committing an act of deep violation against a male social taboo. Not a few of them had expressions of open contempt written all over their faces. To carry a woman on your back was to suffer the worst form of male indignity and humiliation. It was a shameful act for any man to voluntarily perform, to have a woman on his back. It invited ill-luck of the worst kind; better to let the poor sick woman die and take another one for a new wife. Although most of them would consider this an unthinkable loss of face, Ah Kung was hardly bothered by this or their contemptuous stares or even the odd snide remark. All he was concerned about was getting the best treatment for Ah Por to see her well and on her feet again.

My grandmother said of this episode of their life: "Your grandfather saved my life on that trip to Kuching. I couldn't walk at all and he had to carry me all the time. It was worse going up and down the narrow staircase of the lodging house we stayed in. We attracted a lot of looks from the townspeople. They felt he had lost face carrying his wife on his back. But your grandfather didn't care. We went to see quite a few doctors. Each of them would give me some medication. I would try that for a few days. When it failed to work we would renew our search for another one. We did that a few times. Nothing seemed to work and I was getting quite desperate, almost giving up hope. Then by chance one of the residents in the lodging house told us of a German doctor whom he said was very good. We took his advice and went to see this doctor. All he gave me was a jar of cream to apply to my wound. It was like a miracle and the wound got better after only a few days. It healed up eventually and we went back to the farm when I was able to walk again."

But Ah Por would always walk with a limp after that

Children of the Monkey God

infection. The wound might have gone but the scars would stay with her for the rest of her life. Ah Por was always proud to show off those scars to her grandchildren. Pulling up her sarong she would show us her left calf and, there it was; an indentation the size of a big hand would be revealed with dark hardened folds and creases taking the place of smooth skin, veins and muscles. Invariably she would again recount to us the care and devotion Ah Kung had shown towards her during that particular period of her life. Like a war veteran, she would carry the scars with pride for the rest of her life. More than just mere scars, they were special marks permanently imprinted into her leg - a reminder of the strong bond of love and affection she and Ah Kung had for each other.

COUNTRY VISITS

I took my first trip to my grandfather's farm when I was four or five years' old. I remember because I was seasick even before the motor launch had started its journey. It was also the earliest memory I have of my childhood. One of my older cousins was going to get married and our family, consisting of my parents, my two older brothers, my grandparents, plus other relatives and close family friends were going to form the entourage of well-wishers from the town.

Ah Kung and Ah Por had been in semi-retirement for nearly five years and were living with our family in the townhouse in Padungan Road which he had purchased in 1947 for that purpose.

The motor launch that was to take us there was called "Lizzie", named after the youngest daughter –Elizabeth - of the third and last white rajah of Sarawak, Sir Charles Vyner Brooke. It was a slim-built thirty-five foot timber cargo boat that Ah Kung had acquired a while ago to take care of the bigger loads of copra coming out of the coconut plantation. It was powered by a noisy diesel engine and, perhaps it was a combination of the pungent fume of the idling but running motor, grease, oil, diesel fuel and the fish I had had for lunch, which made me throw up. My mother had rather unwisely fed me pieces of Ikan Terubuk together with some of its eggs, a local delicacy, I may add. The rather strong, oily stuff proved to be too much for my young stomach to handle.

Mamah was sitting down on the hard timber panelled

bench lodging me in her sarong-clad legs with her hands on my shoulders to steady me against the swaying motion of the boat when it happened. I remember the incident as causing a fair bit of consternation followed by a lot of advice from relatives and friends on what should be done next.

I have very little memory of the journey itself; only of the boat pulling away from the jetty in Kuching and chugging along as it took off down the Sarawak River towards the farm. I also remember a pig being slaughtered, squealing and struggling as it was held down for the kill. And I remember lying on my mother's lap as I fell asleep and crying when I woke up hungry to find all the food gone. Nobody had remembered to leave any for me.

Five or six years were to pass before I made my next trip to the farm, although by that time it should properly be called a plantation. Ah Kung had, after the Second World War, expanded his original holding of about ten acres to nearly two hundred acres. He had bought up most of the surrounding plots of land and he and the family now owned nearly the whole of Sedungus. The post-war boom had helped him to make a handsome profit through the sale of the plantation's copra in the period following the end of the Second World War. The huge surge of demand of a world hungry for cash crops and other commodities helped push the price up many times over. As luck would have it, my grandfather was a beneficiary of this post-war surge in demand.

He was not only able to purchase neighbouring plots of the farm, but a shop-house in Padungan Road, a lodging house in India Street - "the tallest building in central Kuching when it was built," said Ah Kung of the three storey building - and a few other plots of land in the Santubong area, the most significant of which was a plot at

Children of the Monkey God

Sungai Tiram of twenty-one acres, containing the graves of his father and uncle. Sedungus, as the family land, would have been a logical choice as the burial site for these two elders, but it was too low-lying - the water-table a mere few feet from the ground surface. Ah Kung had chosen a burial site on a hill at Sungai Tiram with better feng shui, except that Ah Kung had sited Ah Tai's grave to face defiantly into the peak of Mount Santubong, a fact constantly pointed out, and lamented, by Ah Por. The land at Sungai Tiram, however, was privately owned and payment had to be made by Ah Kung to the previous owner for its use. There was, therefore, no certainty that the graves would not be desecrated at a later stage, and Ah Kung's purchase of the land was to ensure that this would not happen and, indeed, that they would be well cared for. It was an act of filial piety which he felt he had to carry out as a son.

My second trip to the plantation became the first of a yearly trip that I would make with my older second brother for the next five or six years. My mother had decided we had become too much of a handful for her and that she needed a break from us at least once a year. Taking advantage of the end of year school holiday break, we would be sent to the farm for a period of three to four weeks.

We went on the "Lizzie" again and I didn't throw up this time. My youngest uncle or Say Papah (meaning "youngest daddy" in Hakka) was the pilot/navigator in charge of the launch, while my cousin, Ah Hian Koh, (the only son of my eldest widowed aunt, Tai Koo) was the mechanic in charge of the diesel-propelled motor. There was no panel control or dials for the pilot of the boat – it was that simple and basic - and he had to indicate his requirement of a forward or reverse thrust to the "engine room" by way of a bell attached to a pulley system. A single ding meant "slow forward," two dings would put the boat in reverse and three dings would put the boat on cruising speed. Any extra dings would indicate going faster than cruising speed.

"Lizzie" was the pride and joy of my grandfather and perhaps justifiably so with very few motorised launches yet in operation on the Sarawak River in the 1950s. The family took pride on how fast she was able to cut through the water and how we were able to reach the farm in two to two and a half hours, depending on the flow of the tide. There was no other boat that could travel faster than "Lizzie" they claimed, except for the so-called "tiger boats."

These were boats of the Sarawak's Customs and Excise Department. Constructed of steel or aluminium hulls, they were used by the government to patrol the coast and rivers seeking out smugglers and dealers of illegal contrabands. Called "tiger boats" because of their loud roaring noise, they were an awesome sight with their high bow, churning up huge waves as they went about their business of bearing down on smaller, slower boats, as well as sweeping aside all river debris in their path.

We were boarded by two officious-looking members of the crew of such a "tiger boat" half-way through our journey on the meandering river. "An inevitable occurrence", said Ah Kung, as we weighed anchor waiting to be boarded in mid-river. With their stern faces amplified by their starched and stiff uniform of khaki pants and grey short-sleeved safari jackets displaying impressive ranking pips on their shoulders, they made a show of searching the boat, looking into every nook and corner. They didn't find any smuggled goods or illegal contrabands. Not that they expected to, for there was none, and they knew it. They simply had to go through the motions of conducting a search.

Their search and inspection over, they had a short conversation with my youngest uncle, the skipper. It was in

Children of the Monkey God

Malay and I couldn't understand much of it, except that I saw my uncle passing a few dollars to each of them at the end of their discussion. "Just something to see them off and to keep the peace", Ah Kung said later on of this delinquent toll-collection activity of Her Majesty's servants. It seemed that all boat owners were in one way or another coerced into "seeing them off and keeping the peace" with a few dollars as a parting gift.

Thankfully, we didn't meet any more "tiger boats" for the rest of the journey. I spent most of the time leaning over the bow watching small slim flying fish - aroused by the launch looming over the top of them - making daring leaps across its prow as the boat sliced through the water. I would occasionally look into the mangrove trees growing along the banks in the hope of catching my first sight of the shy proboscis or Dutch monkey. I was to be disappointed, for there was just the odd tribe of the more common macaque monkeys to see.

Our arrival at the jetty in late afternoon was greeted with a lot of barks and yelps from a pack of hyperactive mongrel dogs. A pungent smell of smoked coconuts wafted from the smokehouse situated less than ten yards from the jetty. Ripe brown coconuts were piled in one of the corners of its open deck, with brown husks and empty shells already split open and processed in another corner.

Ah Kung's main farmhouse, or "big house", was situated two hundred yards from the jetty. It was visible from where we were gathered and we made our way towards it walking on the bullock tracks, deeply carved into the ground by the heavy wheels of the carts. It didn't take us long to arrive at the house.

A close examination of it revealed that the main and front part of the house was built on a concrete foundation raised two feet from the ground. A rectangular area of roughly six by eight feet formed the covered front porch of the house and had low wooden steps on its left side. A crude ceramic jar filled with water was placed next to the steps and I was told to use the split half of a coconut shell resting on the edge of the jar to scoop up the water to wash the sand off my thong-clad feet before ascending the steps. This was a ritual everyone must perform before entering the house.

Walking through the front door, I entered the living room and was immediately confronted by the huge and fearsome portrait of Kuan Ti, the Chinese god of war, his big piercing eyes taking in everybody and everything in his sight. On a small table below his portrait, and centrally located, was placed a sand-filled ceremonial brass vessel containing the burnt-up stumps of joss sticks. A low brass candleholder on either side of the vessel had blood-red unlit candles sitting on them, ready to be used.

Next to the altar was a door leading to the main bedroom belonging to my grandparents. Two other bedrooms on each side of the living room were used by the family of my fourth and youngest uncles, respectively.

The floors of both bedrooms and living room were of bare unpolished concrete, while the walls of the bedrooms and, indeed, this part of the building were covered in light lime-green paint. The zinc roof covering this section of the building had the unfortunate consequence in making it quite intolerable to sleep in this part of the house on warm, humid nights.

A covered timber veranda on the left of the living room led to the back of the house. Unlike the concrete floor of the living area, this was raised on stilts and contained a timber floor and thatched attap roof. (Attap is a low, prolific-growing tropical palm tree found mainly in the mangrove swamps). This veranda led to the rear section of the house containing an area almost as big as the living area. It also housed both the kitchen and the dining area.

Here it was that my grandparents would tell family stories, Chinese history, myths and legends.

There were two water wells serving the house; one for drinking, the other for bathing and laundry. Big bamboo stems split in half were used as conduit pipes to convey drawn water to big ironwood tubs located in both the outside bathroom and the sunken area of the kitchen. I was told never to take my bath from the drinking well, as used and dirty water might seethe back into it. It was possibly for this reason that the drinking well was also situated about fifty feet at the back of the house and separated by about the same distance from the well used for laundry and bathing.

I was soon exploring the house and its surrounding area. It was then that I saw something very strange. Not more than ten feet from the drinking well was a small open outhouse constructed simply of a thatched roof of brown attap leaves raised on timber stilts, roughly seven feet in height.

The structure itself was roughly eight feet in length and six feet in width and was a shelter to a timber platform, again on stilts, of roughly three feet in height, seven feet in length and five feet in width. On top of this platform lay two huge ugly-looking coffins placed side by side. Made of belian - the tough and resilient dark tropical ironwood of the Sarawak jungles – they were the type of Chinese coffins displayed in the few shops of coffin-makers in Kuching, especially in Khoo Han Yeang and Carpenter Streets. Covered with a thick sheen of shiny black stain these two coffins looked ominous and to a ten-year old boy - frightening.

Coffins, I thought, contained dead people and should be buried underground in cemeteries. What were these two doing here - aboveground and at the back of Ah Kung's house, I wondered.

Fah Shoon, the eldest son of my youngest uncle, and a few years my junior, was with me at the time and I asked him whether there were dead people in the coffins.

"Oh no, they are empty," he said rather casually and with the air of someone who had a secret to share.

"If they are empty what are they doing here?" I asked.

"For use by Ah Kung and Ah Por when they die," he answered.

"Are they going to die soon?" I asked.

"Oh no, they are going to live a long life because of the coffins," he replied still rather casually and by now rather smug at the ignorance shown by the town boy standing next to him.

"How so?" I asked.

"They bring good luck," he said. "It's nothing to be scared of," he added, "It's a good place to hide when you play hide-and-seek, also when my mother comes after me with the rattan rod. The only trouble is you need two persons to lift up the lid to get into them."

I decided there and then that I was not going to play hide-and-seek with my many country cousins, the children of my third, fourth and youngest uncles.

I became quite focused on that pair of coffins for the rest of the time during that trip and on subsequent visits. I would look at them whenever I was within their proximity, whether I was going to the bathroom or merely looking out of the kitchen windows. It took a lot of effort not to look at them and, although they occupied my mind, I could not bring myself to ask my grandparents nor any of the adults why a pair of coffins was in readiness for them when they were still healthy and well. Although they were in their late sixties, they had not shown any sign of illness. They might have already gone past the prime of their life but they looked well and healthy to me.

I was plagued by these questions, yet I could not bring myself to seek answers other than the one that had already been given me by my cousin. Perhaps I was worried that I might be overstepping some boundaries or perhaps I was fearful of the answers that my inquiries might bring. Were they really there for "good luck" or was it their way of accepting death? A way of taking away the stresses of aging and dying and telling the world and the Chinese God of Hades that they were ready for him and did not fear the inevitable approach of death. That factor in itself might have prolonged their life somewhat and, in a sense, my cousin – who most probably was given that answer when he had himself asked one of the adults - might have been right when he said that the coffins were there to ensure that they lived a long life.

There was also, of course, the possibility that they were there by virtue of some practical calculation and consideration of my grandparents and had nothing to do with the claim made by my cousin. It might just be that it had something to do with the logistical difficulty of transporting an extremely heavy coffin to the farm from Kuching by boat within forty-eight hours after the death of either one of them, for any period longer than that would cause the body to decompose. The heat and humidity of the tropics would see to that. But I was not to know that at the tender age of ten.

Evening times on the farm - after the consumption of the somewhat bland but hearty Hakka fare - were times of tales and stories. The conditions leading up to their telling could not have been more conducive. The plantation was not powered by electricity and, isolated as it was from the rest of the world the only form of mechanical entertainment was an old hand-wound gramophone. It might or might not be put into use later on in the night, but not just yet - not immediately after dinner, for the evening belonged to the legendary heroes and historical figures of the past, to the gods of both major and minor statuses, to the ghosts, demons and monsters and, above all, to dead ancestors.

The setting was simple and spartan. Lighting was provided by the few kerosene lamps casting dim flickering lights and occasionally supplemented by the few wayward fireflies drifting into the house from the nearby mangrove swamp. With smoke still drifting into the house from the few strategically placed hanging baskets of smoking coconut husks and pungent mosquito coils placed under the long dinner table, armies of mosquitoes and sand-flies were thus mercifully kept at bay.

Ah Kung would remain at the head of the table after dinner with Ah Por by his side and, surrounded by his grandchildren and sometimes a few adults, he would begin his storytelling.

Stories of the monkey god Sun Wukung were his favourites, especially those episodes of the monkey god's many rebellious acts against the hierarchy of heaven, in particular his sacrilege and mischievous act in peeing into the palm of the Buddha. This was strange considering Ah Kung's own animosity towards monkeys and their wanton and destructive ways. But then perhaps not, as he was

Children of the Monkey God

himself born in the year of the monkey.

Relishing the rebellious and irreverent nature of the monkey god seemed to be of particular delight to him. Could it have something to do with the Hakka characteristic of rebelling against established authority? Could it also be that they find in the monkey god a soul mate, always having to live on the fringes of society, outcasts whenever they may be, in China and in the Nanyang? Yet, he was equally delighted when the monkey god was tricked by Kwan Yin to wear around his head a magical gold circlet, which when magically tightened would cause him considerable pain on the recitation of a particular sutra by his master, Tripitaka. Thus was Sun Wukung subdued by a trick. A trick worthy of the one he himself employed years ago when he painted a young careless monkey with bright garish paints to rid him and his mates from his estate.

Ah Kung's stories of the monkey god and Tripitaka's quest in search of Buddhist scriptures in the west were more than just mere stories. A large part of Ah Kung's telling involved detailed analysis of the various characters and of the merits or lack of them in certain courses of action adopted by master and disciples. The inept and whining ways of the master and leader of the expedition, Tripitaka, were constantly singled out by Ah Kung for criticism as lacking leadership qualities. As far as he was concerned, characters like Tripitaka were weak and cowardly, panicking at the first sign of a crisis and completely at a loss on the course of action required in getting the group out of a dire situation. Scholars and monks had a tendency to turn out that way, said Ah Kung. To him the real hero of the piece was Sun Wukung, not Tripitaka nor the shadowy Sandy and, least of all, Pigsy, ever indolent and lecherous. For him, Sun Wukung with his irreverent and mischievous nature, his courage, resourcefulness, tricks and strong magical powers was the character to emulate. His seventy-two transformations, his ability to ride the clouds, and his aerial skills in taking somersault leaps that would carry him thousands of miles through the air, were marvels to behold.

Through these stories and many others were we introduced to the Chinese world of myths, legends and magic, as well as to its history.

On myths and magic we heard stories of gods and goddesses such as Kwan Yin and the eight Taoist immortals, in particular Li T'ieh Kuai, the limping and hunchbacked immortal, with his crutch and wine-containing gourd. We also heard about the moon goddess, Chang-erh, and her flight to the moon, and my two favourites, Nacha and Red Boy, the boy gods, plus many more.

On history, we heard of the exploits of the various emperors who ruled China at different times; of Chin Si Huangti, the first emperor of the country, who through the waging of numerous bloody civil wars unified it by the simple expedient of annihilating all opposition. We also heard about his single-minded ambition to build the Great Wall even if it meant the loss of hundreds of thousands, if not millions, of lives; of the adventures and exploits of the most renowned and loyal servant of the Ming emperors and China's greatest mariner, Admiral Cheng Ho, deified to the status of a god and given the name of Sum Poh Kung, the Lord of the Three Treasures, and many more besides.

From Ah Por I heard stories of her favourite historical and literary character – Hua Mulan, who took her father's place in the army as a conscript and how she excelled in various brave and heroic campaigns, even bettering the deeds of her male colleagues and counterparts.

It was also on evenings like this that we heard tales of

Ah Kung's struggles in life; of the earlier years of poverty that he and his family went through; of his survival for existence as a hired farmhand and, at times, as a lowly-paid shop assistant to Teochew towkay; also of his endeavours to educate himself. He never had the luxury of going to school, he said. What Chinese characters he had learned were picked up from his father and from others who were more literate and educated than himself. He never learned to speak Mandarin, and the characters he learned were read and written by him in the Hakka dialect. He was also able to read more than he was able to write. The book that he used mainly for learning his Chinese characters was the Tung Tsu from whence he also cultivated a great fondness for it as well as becoming adept at using it. In his young days he was the drummer in a lion dance troupe in Batu Kawa and learned Kung Fu from his stint there, as was the traditional practice. How as a head-strong young man he, together with members of his troupe, would get into numerous physical scraps with the members of other lion dancers of other dialects, in particular the Cantonese, in their refusal to bow and to pay respect to the Hakka lion (a mythical creature called a Chi-lin), a superior and higher-ranked beast in the celestial hierarchy of the Chinese gods, he said. He told us of his trek to Indonesia in quest of a wife and of finally finding Ah Por. He also told of how his father gave him a mere three hundred dollars to enable him to make his purchase of his first plot of land and of his first and ever appearance in a court case to claim what was rightfully his. It was on nights like this he related to us his first encounter with a giant sea turtle - looking back at the incident and laughing at himself for his ignorance - and of his battle for supremacy with the crocodile, as well as his battle of wits with the monkeys in the coconut plantation. The account of the trip he made to Kuching with Ah Por, when she nearly lost her leg to gangrene, was a story jointly told by both of them, as were the many trials and tribulations that they went through together in building up their farm and in bringing up the family.

It was also during evenings like this that we learned of our family heritage and what it meant to be Chinese, and above all what it meant to be a Hakka. Yet our family did not start off as people of the Hakka dialect group, he said. According to his father, our ancestors were northern Chinese who had to flee from Manchu persecution. They were people who were associated with the Ming Dynasty, which in the mid-17th century was overthrown by Manchurian invaders from the north-east of China, and who later went on to establish the last dynasty of China - the Ching Dynasty. For the Ming rulers it was an inglorious end to what Ah Kung claimed was a glorious chapter in Chinese history. Our ancestors' fortunes went the way of the Ming rulers - spiralling downwards into poverty and near oblivion.

The Ming Dynasty, according to Ah Kung, was the greatest of all the Chinese dynasties. His statement was undoubtedly made with a large degree of parochial and family bias but in the context of his other claim that we were related to the Ming rulers, quite understandable.

Chu Yuan Chang, the first emperor of the Ming Dynasty and, therefore, its founder, was a beggar, a vagabond and a brigand before he finally succeeded in gathering together a big enough force to rid China of its Mongolian rulers and, with them, the short-lived Yuan Dynasty. To my grandfather, he was the greatest of the Ming emperors - a people's emperor who rose from the lowest rank to overthrow a foreign dynasty. He was fond of telling us that, as a beggar, Chu Yuan Chang was covered in dirt for most of the time, his head a nest for lice and his clothes all rags, rather than silken robes. Yet, this lowly person went on to inspire hundreds of thousands of loyal followers to take

Children of the Monkey God

arms against the unpopular rulers of the Yuan Dynasty.

Nothing is beyond anyone, he would say, not even a beggar, as long as you are willing to work hard for it. Although it was not in Ah Kung's character to compare himself to an emperor, he was in his own way drawing a parallel between his own life and that of the "son of heaven", referring, of course, to the years of hardship and poverty he had to endure before finally reaching his goal of adequately providing for himself and his extended family.

There was little doubt that the rule of the Ming Dynasty was a popular one in its early days, having rid China of the ruthless and unpopular Mongol rulers. Like most dynasties of China, the Ming rulers started off well with a legitimate claim to rule the country with a newly-acquired 'mandate from heaven'. And, like all the other failed dynasties, its later-day rulers gave up their right to this very mandate by becoming increasingly divorced from the people and consequently losing their support and trust due to their repressive policies. Its courts were a mere shadow of their predecessors in both ability and skill, being full of corrupt officials – most of them eunuchs – as well as self-indulgent noblemen and their concubines. A mere shadow they might have been, but it nevertheless cast a long shadow, placing an unduly huge burden on the people. What made it worse was the size of the emperor's court. The later Ming rulers and their relatives and court supporters would by themselves amount to thousands, as a result of nearly two hundred and fifty years of rule.

The emperor's extended family system, augmented by the numerous concubines and children that a rich and powerful relative of the emperor would be able to support, would mean countless members of a single patriarch with the surname of Chu being accepted within the fold of that system. Such was also the case with an ancestor of ours who, according to my grandfather, served in one of the Ming courts. We knew for a fact that he had at least seven concubines, for we were the descendants of this gentleman by his seventh concubine. In all likelihood, he would have had even more.

It was a mind-boggling thought, to say the least, as we sat on hard rough benches in a thatched house thousands of miles from China pondering this fact. A touch of surrealism was added to this scene with most of us males half-clad and making the odd attempt now and then to swat the few mosquitoes drifting into the house amidst the kerosene flames that cast flickering shadows over our faces.

Although my grandfather was fond of citing the first emperor as a fine example of what could be achieved if one were to put one's mind and effort into what one was doing, he was equally emphatic in pointing out the lessons that could be learned when debauchery and decadence took over one's lifestyle.

The later emperors were nothing compared to the first emperor, he said. Complacent of their own situation and uncaring of the peoples' needs, while wallowing in the luxury of court life, they were completely out of touch with the people and with reality. When the Manchu attacked, the Ming court was hardly able to put up any resistance - its remnant followers of court officials, eunuchs, concubines, palace guards, and hangers-on having to flee to the south in the face of the attack from the north.

The surviving members of the Ming court and some of their loyal supporters in their flight to the south established some sort of rebel headquarters there, particularly in the province of Fujian. These loyalists, though never really successful in their attempts to restore the Ming Dynasty, became a thorn in the side of the Manchu rulers for years to come. Fujian province as well as Guangdong, its neighbouring province to the southwest, became hotbeds of rebellion for Ming loyalists, riff-raff, mercenaries, triad members and anyone who had a grudge against the Manchu rulers. Our forbears and other Ming survivors with the family name of Chu most probably became the galvanising force behind some of the movements for Ming revival and for ridding the Manchu invaders from China.

Their defiant acts, which they hoped would take only years to accomplish, however, stretched into decades and then into centuries. Over that period of time, they became absorbed by the local cultures and languages, becoming, for all intents and purposes, people of these southern provinces. While they were a magnet to Ming loyalists and other dissidents - for there were many Chinese who saw the Manchu rulers as a foreign invading force - they were invariably regarded as a constant threat by the Ching rulers.

Many acts of reprisal were carried out by the Manchu rulers in response to their defiance in the time-honoured, albeit dubious, Chinese practice of seeking out and exterminating all the members of any family suspected of disloyalty to them. Whole families, including women and children, would be wiped out in this manner, and anyone who carried the family name of Chu would be an immediate suspect, for, in theory, if not in reality, he would be taken for a relative of the Ming emperors.

Caught in a cultural tangled web of their own weaving, generations of Chinese rulers had come to the realization that it was necessary for their own survival to exterminate a whole family when only a single member was the real culprit. The Confucian edict of filial piety made certain that this would be the outcome for both the warring factions in any violent encounter, whether large or small, for it dictated that their descendents were duty-bound to seek out their enemies and destroy them and their families. Aggravating the matter further, was another Confucian belief that Chinese of the same surname are the descendants of one common ancestor and are therefore related to each other. This, then, had the potential of escalating the feud between the warring parties further, casting an ever-increasing net on the number of people involved.

Trapped in a vicious cycle of violence and retribution and "guided" by the dubious dictum of "kill or be killed," these mindless acts of vengeance could last decades, even centuries. Thus it was that succeeding generations of Ching rulers sought to exterminate remnants of the descendants of the Ming Dynasty. On their part, these "remnants" did not help matters by holding on to their dream of a Ming revival and participating in numerous revolts against the Ching rulers. Sometimes reactive and sometimes provocative, these acts of rebellion had the consequence of inviting and provoking retaliation, reprisal and repression from the rulers.

Thus it was that our forbears found themselves being constantly hounded by the Manchu in their place of "sanctuary" in Fujian province, which is why they found themselves once again on the move after a "sojourn" that spanned three or four generations in that province. And for that period of time when they were in Fujian our forbears were Fujianese or Hokkien people.

The journey out of Fujian this time would take them farther south into the neighbouring province of Guangdong; not into the better developed areas populated by people speaking the Cantonese dialect, nor into the larger towns and cities, but into the poorer and less developed areas populated by people of the Hakka dialect. These were the very descendants of the people of northern origin who had to flee from Mongolian persecution in the 10th century. Dubbed the "guest people"- for that's what the name "Hakka" literally means - they were the gypsies of China, as well as latecomers to areas that had already been taken by earlier settlers, and were able only to work on lands considered too poor to farm even by the local Cantonese. These were unwanted and infertile lands situated far from the towns and cities; isolated, remote, hilly and highly inaccessible - a sort of haven for outlaws and outcasts. Many of the inhabitants had no choice but to abandon farming and turn to mining in the hope of eking out a living from land so barren that nothing much would grow on it.

And it was here among the Hakka that our forbears made a new home for themselves. And like the Hakka who had settled here long before them, my forbears started their own clan settlement and, in time, became assimilated into the Hakka way of life. After the lapse of time spanned by that of a few generations, they not only became Hakka themselves, they had their own Hakka clan with their own clan villages and hamlets.

Attacking forces going into these Hakka-dominated areas went at their own peril, for their villages were reputed to be heavily fortified and fiercely defended. These settlements were, in fact, more fortresses than villages and its inhabitants close clansmen, who saw in their united and continued resistance against external attacks their best, if not their only means of survival. From this bonding of clansmen and villagers there developed a whole host of social and cultural practices that placed the ideals of clanship and brotherhood as paramount and inviolable principles.

These practices did not remain confined to China for long, as later generations of overseas-bound migrating Hakka would take them along with them to countries far beyond the shores of China. In regions like West Kalimantan and Sarawak, where they were left relatively on their own, these practices of the Hakka took root. In taking root, they also took on concrete shape and became more structured in the way they used these doctrines of clanship and brotherhood in organising themselves into strong, independent self-governing bodies hitherto impossible in China or anywhere else in the world. With more resources available to them than were possible elsewhere, including China, in terms of manpower, finance and other favourable conditions, these organizations grew into the big, powerful Kongsi houses of the West Kalimantan and Sarawak gold fields. Anywhere else, including mainland China, they would, no doubt, have remained as small village benevolent or triad societies. This would appear to be the case in USA and Australia, where stifling and restrictive policies of racially motivated governments tended to encourage the formation of benevolent societies at one end of the spectrum, and triads at the other end.

Although in decline, these Kongsi houses in West Kalimantan were well-established organizations by the time that my great grandfather and his youngest brother left China to join them around the year 1850. They joined the Kongsi house of the Shum Tio Kau in which clansmen by the surname of Chu played a dominant role in its affairs. And they left at a time of great upheaval in China.

In the period of the Opium Wars between 1839 to1842, the Ching regime had been severely humiliated by Britain, being exposed as being weak, corrupt and inept. The decade of 1840s also saw widespread floods and famine in China. Hundreds of thousands drowned. Many more were displaced and left homeless. Millions of people were affected, resulting in huge numbers dying from malnutrition and poverty. Discontentment and anger with the government were widespread among the people. Civil wars and unrests broke out everywhere, especially in the south.

The most significant of these revolts was the one led by

Children of the Monkey God

Hung Xingquan, a Hakka from Guandong province. The son of a poor peasant, Hung was perhaps psychotic in his conviction that he was the younger brother of Jesus Christ charged with a godly mission to rid China of its heathen Manchu rulers and to establish heaven on earth. His rebellion, called the Taiping (the Great Peace) Rebellion, from 1842 to 1864, was to span more than twenty years, having within its ranks at least two million followers at the height of its popularity, most of them recently converted protestants and drawn from the southern provinces of China, in particular Hakka from the Guangdong area. Although the rebellion didn't succeed in overthrowing the Manchu, it nonetheless shook its tenuous foundations. The cost was high though, the direct and indirect result being the death of twenty million people.

Although it was not unthinkable that my great grandfather would have been involved in some form of uprising against the Manchu rulers - given the social and political climate of that time and the intense animosity that our forbears seemed to have against them - it was highly unlikely that he was involved with the Taiping rebels. There was no hint that he was at any time a Christian or that he had shown any inclination to become one. Furthermore, the Taiping rebellion was already in its seventh or eighth year of revolt when he left the shores of China, gathering momentum and more supporters as it engulfed the country. It was not likely that my great grandfather would have left China if he had been involved with it. To me, his action in leaving the country of his birth was more that of a person desperate to escape the clutches of the authorities, not that of a person who was a member of an organization big and strong enough to offer him concealment and protection.

On the other hand, he and his brother might simply have left China for the lure of the gold fields of Kalimantan, most probably encouraged into it by Kalimantan old-timers' tales of the fabulous fortunes that could be made there. Being young, impressionable and poor, they would have recklessly jumped at any opportunity offered by either relatives or fellow clansmen to join them in sailing southward on a junk.

While story telling by Ah Kung and Ah Por would constitute the main activities of most evenings in the plantation, it would sometimes be interspersed with the use of the hand-wound gramophone. This was, arguably, the most expensive, if not the only, concession made by Ah Kung to modern inventions of luxury on the plantation. Songs and music of Chow Shuan and of the Teochew opera would be played from a collection of some highly scratchy, worn–out records. The former were bought by my youngest uncle because Chow Shuan was his favourite singer and he enjoyed listening to her sometime sweet and sometime melancholy voice. The latter were bought by him as a bribe to encourage Ah Kung, tight-fisted as he always was with his money, to buy the gramophone and the records. My youngest uncle felt that having to listen to the high-pitched and whining arias of the incomprehensible Teochew opera singers was a small price to pay in exchange for records of his favourite singer. He also took the view that just because he lived and worked in a coconut plantation did not mean he had to forego some of the luxuries provided by life.

He would also very soon afterwards persuade Ah Kung to purchase a used-pickup, which he literally ran into the ground in less than a year. The rough tracks of the plantation, the high salt content present in the beach and the general environment, together with the mildly saline well-water he used to wash the small truck with, were also contributory factors in its early demise due to rust corrosion and lack of maintenance. Abandoned and permanently parked next to the pig-stye, it was an eye-sore and a constant reminder of the folly of utilising any mechanically-propelled machines in the plantation, without at least having first acquired the knowledge and skills necessary to service and maintain them.

My daytime activities at the plantation were filled mainly with playing with my cousins, watching coconuts processed and transformed into copra at the smokehouse, and looking for ripe fruits, such as mangoes, mangosteens, rambutans and young green coconuts. Other activities included swimming, catching crabs with rattan traps, hauling in prawns with a cast net and hunting large beach clams and cockles buried a mere foot from the surface. The latter activities of gathering fresh crustaceans for food were sometimes carried out with some of my young cousins but mainly with my eldest aunt, a widow from a very young age, who showed me all the best spots for catching these succulent creatures. These were small-scale activities involving at the most a few people.

Fishing however, was something different, especially the plantation's style of fishing with a dragnet of a few hundred feet long. Nearly all the members of the extended family system would be involved. A bullock cart would be used to carry the fine, but bulky, fishing net together with its accessories of ropes, poles and rattan carrying-baskets to the beach.

Men, women and children of all ages would join in the fishing with gusto, some, especially the stronger and bigger ones, also pulling the net. A few would be given the task of harrying the fish at strategic points of the net. Others were allotted the duty of picking and gathering the catch of wriggling, twisting fish, prawns, shellfish and other crustaceans as the net was slowly but surely dragged to the shore. The same process of dragging the net would be repeated a few times at different spots along the beach and very soon a sizeable catch would be the end result of a highly enjoyable two hours' work in the waters of the South China Sea.

Back on the farm, the catch would be cleaned and gutted. The discarded parts were to be used later on as fertilizers by Ah Por in her garden, together with her egg and crustacean shells of clam, cockles, crabs and prawns. In the meantime, some fish would be deep fried in the giant kitchen wok with the rich and fragrant home-made coconut oil, while assorted shell fish of prawns and crabs would be grilled and poached.

The dinning table would be nearly covered with the finished product of fresh fried fish, prawns and crabs, both grilled and poached, as the whole family would descend on it without ceremony, their hunger exacerbated by having to work in the sea for two to three hours. Very little rice would be served as there was no necessity for it, plus the huge meal would take place soon after each catch, which might be at any time of the day or night. The determining factor, and thus the final arbitrator of these fishing expeditions and, consequently, the meals that followed, was the time of the daily ebb and flow of the tide. It determined the optimum time to fish, as calculated by Ah Kung from the chart provided by the Tung Tsu, his Chinese almanac. And these could happen anytime.

Thus it was that at one time we were all loudly woken by a keen grandfather at two o'clock in the morning, calling on all his children and grandchildren to hurry up and get to the beach, as the fish were waiting to be caught. I didn't mind these early morning trips, as I found them exciting, to say nothing of a novelty. My cousins and uncles, who had gone through it so many times already, did not share my enthusiasm, however. Grumbling and muttering that it was too cold, they would reluctantly trudge down to the beach with Ah Kung in the lead, the sounds made by their hands smacking their bodies loud and clear in the darkness as they tried desperately to swat the hundreds of mosquitoes and sand-flies milling around them.

"Why are we out here in the middle of the night as food offerings for these tiny insects?" they muttered sullenly and irreverently.

These were the main activities that my brother and I were involved in, on those holiday periods we spent with our paternal grandparents in Sedungus. While they were not exactly boring, they would at times be quite monotonous. That monotony would be lifted, when on an apparent whim, my grandfather would decide to go visit his second and favourite daughter at a place called Sungai Buah (Malay for "Fruit River"), located five or six kilometres south-east of Sedungus. While I have described these parental visits on the part of Ah Kung as a mere whim, it would perhaps be more correct to call it a craving for his favourite fruit – the durian. Yes, that king of all fruits, the durian - spiky, creamy, sweet, delicious and pungent. And my second aunt together with her family, were the proud and lucky owners of a durian plantation of an area of a hundred acres, more or less. There were other fruit trees there as well, such as mangoes, mangosteens, rambutans and "langsats" or cateyes but the durian trees were the dominant crop covering this small hill not far from Kuching. She and her husband were lucky to have bought this plantation - not long after their marriage - from a Kuching towkay, who had neither the inclination nor time to tend it properly; persuaded into selling it to my aunt by him, my father would claim in later years. The plantation had been good to my aunt, yielding for her and her family a more than steady income over the years.

Our trips to the durian plantation were made on a small out-boat powered by a small Johnson engine. The river leading into the plantation was too small to take a cargo-launch like "Lizzie". The out-boat was too small, however, to take more than six or seven people but luckily for my brother and me, as "honoured visitors", we would be the youngsters chosen to accompany the visiting adults consisting of grandparents and two or three other uncles and aunts. We were also lucky that these visits somehow or rather coincided with the durian season at the end-of-the year school holiday period. My second aunt, perhaps out of a strong sense of hospitality and filial piety (to her parents), would only let us eat and take back the best durians. It was harvest time and there were small mounds of durian of different grades and sizes everywhere, ready for loading and transporting into her small cargo-launch for sale to the middle-men in Kuching. It was a family business with her three sons and two daughters the only farm-hands involved in picking and carrying the fallen fruits in two fairly large rattan baskets slung across an ironwood shoulder-pole. They were the strongest and toughest of all my cousins. And it was not difficult to see from where they got their strength and toughness. Bullock carts could not be used for transportation on this hilly plantation and the harvested fruits had to be carried manually. The rough terrain of small rocks alternating with numerous outcrops of roots, both large and small, also made it more practical for them to go about their work bare-footed, especially during the wet monsoon season with its slippery surfaces. They didn't believe in wearing either shoes or sneakers and the end result was the development of thick calluses on their feet. I had never seen thicker calluses on feet than those of my cousins'. Her second son - in between bouts of demonstrating his skill in maintaining a classical kung-fu's horse stance - was not at all modest in showing off his thick calluses by balancing his whole body on a large spiky durian. Needless to say, I was impressed. Not quite twenty yet, he was solidly built and with a body weight of perhaps eighty-five to ninety kilos he did not seem to have been hurt in the slightest by standing on the durian. There was no indication that the sharp long spikes of the durian had been able to penetrate the sole of his feet.

I was equally impressed by her two daughters whose strength would have put many a strong man to shame. Doing the same work as their brothers, they were just as strong as them. From what I could see there was no discernible gender barrier getting in their way in the performance of their farm works. This was demonstrated to me in one memorable incident when the older of the two daughters, Ghian, in her early twenties, was asked by her mother to pluck some fresh langsats for Ah Kung and Ah Por. These tropical fruits, sweet, yellow-skinned and about the same size as loquats, grow on trees that on maturity can reach up to more than one hundred feet high. This particular tree she was going to climb was perhaps a hundred feet in height with a trunk more than three feet in circumference. I remember that particular day to be slightly overcast and while it was not raining heavily the light drizzle had made the trunk quite wet and therefore slippery as well. Yet, Cousin Ghian had no hesitation in harnessing her waist to the trunk of the tree with a rope and, barefooted and all, was very swiftly moving as nimbly as a macaque on the branches of the tree, plucking bunches of its fruit and dropping them into the rattan basket she had strapped around her waist. I was told later on that she was the best climber of the family, better even than her brothers.

Our arrival back home at Sedungus was received with keen enthusiasm by the other relatives who had been left behind out of necessity. There was no lack of helping hand in the unloading of the small pile of durian given by my second aunt to Ah Kung and Ah Por to take back with them.

The allure of the durian was simply irresistible. And inevitably, a subversive and un-filial thought would creep into my head after one of these trips to my second aunt, and that was how much nicer it would have been had Ah Kung owned a durian farm instead of a coconut plantation.

TOWN LIFE

Two years after the end of the Second World War, Ah Kung and Ah Por made the decision to move to Kuching to live a life of semi-retirement. They were in their early sixties and had decided that they were entitled to a 'bit of soft living'. They also had the funds to support such a change in lifestyle, the result of a fairly large windfall that had fallen onto Ah Kung's lap after the war. This was in the form of the skyrocketing prices of copra, pepper, rubber and other cash crops and commodities, in huge demand from a world hungry for them after an enforced deprivation of nearly five years.

Ah Kung's windfall came mainly by way of the stockpile he had built of his own copra. The sale of hundreds of tons of this cash crop after the war had made for him a small fortune – enough for him to buy two shop houses in Kuching. It was thus a time of celebration and great relief for the family to be able to finally sell their stockpile for such princely sums.

Yet there was a time when they felt anxious as to whether the war would end before their stockpile started to go bad and rot. The lull in the world market for commodities and cash crops during the war years had meant that Ah Kung was unable to sell his copra to the merchants of Kuching. Economic life, as was the case all over the world, had practically come to a standstill.

The number of shopkeepers still in business in Kuching during the war years was reduced to a handful, the vast majority having already fled mainly to the coastal areas to seek refuge against the Japanese occupation, at the start of, or even before, the arrival of Japanese troops on Borneo Island. With their shops closed and boarded up, these, and other urban war refugees and their families, survived as best as they could by growing yams, sweet potatoes, tapiocas and other rice-substitute crops rich in carbohydrate and also by rearing chicken, ducks, geese and pigs on their own lands or that of friends' or relatives'. For those who sought refuge by the coast, the sea offered a bountiful supply of fish and crustaceans - obtained with the help of traps, drag and cast nets - such as whiting, anchovies, herrings, sprats, small white baits, shrimps and prawns. Although these catches were of the smaller species, they were, nevertheless, rich in protein.

Although the Japanese military authority, the "Kempeitai", tried their best to encourage local businesses to carry on as before, there was still widespread fear of the Japanese invaders among the town's Chinese merchants and traders. Reports of Japanese atrocities in China and other parts of Asia had preceded their arrival in Sarawak, and the monetary donations that many of the merchants and traders had made in the anti-Japanese war efforts in China had led them to believe, quite justifiably, that they might be treated quite harshly by them.

Not only were normal economic and commercial activities in Kuching and, indeed, other parts of Sarawak, brought almost to a standstill; a thriving black market took its place. New and ingenious ways to survive were devised by the local people and barter trading became a way of life with very little faith placed in the official currency of the Japanese military authority. Dubbed the "banana money" by virtue of a prominent picture of that same fruit plant on every denomination note, it was treated with near-contempt and widely rejected as an exchange currency.

International trading had all but come to a complete halt with the non-operation of nearly all cargo ships plying the waters of the South China Sea linking Sarawak to Singapore and the rest of the world. Fearful of the naval battles conducted between the allied forces and the Japanese navy, the owners of these ships had wisely decided to weigh anchor until the end of the war. Import and export trading became virtually impossible and cash crop farmers like Ah Kung found out that the ever-reliable overseas market for their products had vanished overnight.

The few shopkeepers who continued to carry on trading in the town would not buy his copra. However, coconuts growing and maturing on the trees still had to be harvested, processed and turned into copra whether or not there were buyers for them. Ah Kung was not one who could bear to see his coconuts turn brown, drop from the trees and rot on the ground. That would have been so wasteful. He was also not one to stand idly by, even though there were no buyers for his finished products. He continued to harvest and to process the ripe brown coconuts with his family, as if there was no war going on.

"Besides, what else was there to do?" he would ask rhetorically.

Fortuitously for him, processed copra, when smoked and dried, could last for quite a while and stockpiling it would not be a problem. He knew that the war had to end eventually and copra and other commodities, such as pepper and rubber, would surge in price after the war. He also decided to stockpile these items by buying them off other farmers in the neighbouring areas. The bulk of his stockpile, however, remained his own copra, processed from his own coconuts by him and his family. Some of it he turned into extremely thick, rich and pungent coconut oil, an essential item very much in demand as cooking oil, in exchange for other needed produce in the black market such as rice, sugar and salt. The conversion of coconuts into cooking oil during the war years hardly made any inroads into his stockpile, which continued to grow with each passing year.

The end result was that he had a rather huge stockpile of copra on his hands by the time the war ended. The prices of copra and other cash crops continued to surge, even after the sale of this stockpile, and Ah Kung took full advantage of this fact by carrying on with further production of his plantation's copra and selling them as fast as they were grabbed up by a world hungry for more.

Thus was Ah Kung able to purchase two shop houses in Kuching – one in 1947 in Padungan Road for $7000 and another in less than a two years period in India Street for $29,700, quite princely sums in those days.

And so it was that my grandparents took up residence in Kuching in the year 1947 - more specifically in No. 70, Padungan Road. It was also my home for the first nineteen years of my life.

Although Kuching in 1947 was not yet the busy city it is now, it was still a vastly different environment from the plantation that Ah Kung was used to. Overall, Sarawak was undergoing some changes and Kuching, being the capital of the country, was going to be the centre of it all.

The end of the war also saw the end of one hundred years of Brookes' rule. The arrival of the Japanese invaders had been a rude awakening to the Brooke family, who had hitherto run the country along lines that would have been more appropriate for an English manor, albeit a very large English manor. Extremely paternalistic in their ways, the three Brooke rulers, one in succession after the other, sought to shelter and protect the country from the rest of the world

Children of the Monkey God 117

and, while that had worked in the earlier years of their rule, it had proven to be woefully inadequate and extremely antiquated in the later years of the last rajah. This was particularly so in the area of national defence, which saw Sir Charles Vyner Brooke leaving the country ahead of the invading Japanese forces. He was never to return again, and this was perhaps an admission that he had failed his people at a time when they needed him most. Moreover, it was an admission that the sun had set on the Brooke Dynasty and that the people of Sarawak needed something more than what the Brookes had hitherto been able to provide them.

The British colonial government took over the country after the defeat of the Japanese, starting with the administrative structure of the Brooke government but, instead of a rajah occupying the Astana, the people of Sarawak now had a Westminster-appointed governor.

In households all over the country, as was the customary practice with every change of ruler, the portrait of the last white rajah was taken down to be replaced by that of King George. While the portrait of Sir Charles Vyner Brooke was also taken down in Ah Kung's house in the coconut plantation, the portrait of the rebellious republican Sun Yet Sen, who had been dead for more than two decades, would continue to occupy his honoured place in the living room, side by side with the portrait of the newly installed Royal King of England - newly installed as far as Sarawak was concerned. Like the rajah, his portrait was also taken down when Elizabeth II ascended the throne in 1953. Sun Yet Sen - the first president of the Republic of China – however, maintained his position on the wall, but this time he had a new partner in the person of Elizabeth II. As far as Ah Kung was concerned, English monarchs might come and go, but Chinese heroes would always be there. It also mattered not that he had on his wall the portrait of an

English monarch next to that of a Chinese Republican.

For my grandparents, moving to the town was a transition from farm-life to town-life that they were looking forward to. It was, however, never a complete transition. Although the coconut farm was now more than capably run and managed jointly by my eldest widowed aunt and my third, fourth and youngest uncles, Ah Kung would still make two and three trips a year there, ostensibly as "inspection tours" of a few weeks' duration, but perhaps more because he still missed the farming life. However, the rigours of the past thirty to forty years of hard work had taken their toll and he craved for the "soft" living of the town and, because he could now afford it, he would make the choice of living out the rest of his life in the town together with Ah Por.

A few favourable factors conspired to make that choice an easy one.

First, those adult children of his who had chosen to remain on the plantation were able to carry on in his footsteps without any disruption in its copra production. It was not a difficult transition, considering that they had been working with him on the farm for quite a number of years and knew what was required of them. Furthermore, an agreement was put in place whereby they would pay him a fixed levy on the copra produced from the respective plots assigned to them and which would later be passed to them in his will.

Second, the purchase of the shop house in India Street provided him with an alternative source of income after its conversion to a low-budget hotel or lodging house consisting of fifteen small bedrooms.

Third, was the decision of my parents to stay with him and my grandmother. With my father's assistance in the

Children of the Monkey God

running of the lodging house in India Street and my mother's help in keeping the house in Padungan Road, especially in cooking for them, Ah Kung and Ah Por were more than happy with the set-up.

This was especially so because of the two big passions of his life, both only available in Kuching.

One was Teochew opera. The other was good food. And there was little doubt that my mother was a good cook. In actual fact, she was the best cook among his daughters-in-law, he would claim. While the other four of his daughters-in-law were Hakka of farming background, my mother was a Hokkien from a modest family background in Kuching. It was common knowledge, and my grandfather was always the first one to admit it, that Hakka fares were rustic and lacked the refined qualities of other dialect groups such as the Teochew, Hokkien and Cantonese.

More importantly, my mother was not only a Hokkien, she was also a Nonya Hokkien, one of those Straits Chinese who could trace their roots to the first groups of Hokkien Chinese to settle in the Malacca and Singapore region, as well as the general area of the Malay Archipelago. Preceding other Chinese dialect groups by a few hundred years, they were the first and, therefore, the oldest Chinese migrant group to have settled in the Nanyang region. This also meant that as a group they were more successful in their integration with the local Malay and other indigenous peoples than any other Chinese dialect group. Their men were called "Baba" and their women "Nonya" by the local Malays.

One of the results that emerged from this blend of cultures was the birth of a new and mixed cuisine called Nonya cooking. With the use of local spices, a new dimension was added to Chinese cooking and, of all the dialect groups, the Hokkien were the most adept in the application of these local spices to their dishes.

It could also have been the socio-economic position that the Hokkien occupied in the Nanyang that made such good cooks of their womenfolk. Involving themselves mainly as merchants, traders, shopkeepers, and later on as professionals and civil servants, it was an accepted (and well-known) fact that they were the better-off members of the local Chinese community. There was also little doubt that these socio-economic positions they occupied were mainly the preserve of the male members of the Hokkien group for unlike the women of the Hakka and Foochow groups who, for some of the times, had to work alongside their menfolk on the farm, Hokkien women did not involve themselves as much in the chosen trade or profession of their husbands. The kitchen was thus the domain of the Hokkien housewife and that was where she would rule as a matriarch.

The Hokkien matriarch oversaw a domestic kingdom that was fairly large by modern standards in term of the number of family members that had to be catered for. This was especially true of the merchant class - the towkay who had become rich and successful not only as businessmen, but as shopkeepers and landowners.

In Kuching they were the families of the Chans, Lims, Ongs, Tans, and Wees and, at a time when the extended family system was still very much in vogue, the large size of the family made it a certainty that food and its preparation were taken in all seriousness. They were wealthy families who could afford to spend a fair amount of their resources on food and with a fairly large retinue of servants to help her, the matriarch of such a household saw it as her task to provide a lavish meal at least three times a day for her family, especially dinner which would see seven or eight dishes, even on a normal non-festival day, on the dining table.

Most of these matriarchs only reached that status in their middle age after the death of their mother-in-law, her predecessor and therefore the previous matriarch, and although they were not expected to do the cooking themselves, they were expected to at least oversee the smooth running of the household and kitchen duties. Having earned the right to retire from carrying out further scullery duties, these Hokkien matriarchs normally saw to it that there should be at least one competent kitchen successor in the person of a daughter-in-law or a daughter, usually the former.

In those days a daughter-in-law was expected to live with her parents-in-law, especially if her husband also happened to be the eldest son of the family. She was expected to cook and care for them and to attend to their every need; one could even say that it was the principal unwritten clause of a Hokkien marriage covenant.

It would not be an exaggeration, therefore, to say that most Hokkien matriarchs took extreme care to make certain that the young maids who would eventually end up as their sons' wives were not only filial in their outlook and behaviour; but must be good cooks as well. By the same token, they would expect nothing less of their own daughters and, although these offspring of theirs would eventually get married and, therefore, "belong" to someone else's family, she must still see to it that they were properly trained in the art of fine cooking. This was not only to increase their marriageable worth, and perhaps the marriage dowry as well, but also to ensure she would not lose face.

My mother was the daughter of one such matriarch, who saw to it that her daughters and daughters-in-law were the ones to do the cooking, while she would spend most of the day playing mah-jong and other card games with her friends and relatives. My mother was one of my maternal grandmother's three remaining daughters who had to start her kitchen duties at a very early age, unlike her other seven brothers who, as the privileged male members of the family, were not required to do any housework. Also, unlike her brothers, she never went to school. The long hours she had spent in her mother's kitchen saw to it that she was an accomplished cook by the time she married my father as a young woman. It was, therefore, no surprise that she was a much better cook than any of my grandparents' other daughters-in-law. She was the daughter-in-law who would not only cook for them, but was also the one who would look after them for the rest of their life, a true sense of filial piety demanding nothing less of her.

Ah Kung might have gone into semi-retirement, but he was not one to stay idle. He still wanted to carry on working, although not as hard as before. The windfall that he had made from the sale of his stockpile of copra, rubber and pepper had provided him with options he didn't have back in those days when he was a poor landless farmer. He had now the money, not only to buy a shop house to be used as a home, but also enough to start a small business. What he was looking for was something small and safe that did not entail too many risks. Ah Kung was not one who liked taking risks, nor was he over-ambitious in his business endeavours. His approach towards investment was more tempered by prudence than fired by any inner ambition to make it big in the business world. He had been a farmer all his life and he conducted his business affairs like a farmer – conservative and cautious. He decided on running a small hotel or lodging house. It was not a difficult decision for him to make and, furthermore, it was a project he had had in mind for quite sometime.

Children of the Monkey God

"I remember the days when I had to go to Kuching to sell my copra and buy provisions for the plantation. I could find hardly any hotel or lodging house where I could stay overnight. It was particularly difficult for Hakka farmers from the coast or countryside. They had scarcely any relatives or friends in a town dominated by Hokkien. That point was painfully driven home to me when your grandmother was sick with that infected leg. For some of the nights when we couldn't find a room in the local lodging house, we had to sleep on the five-foot walkway like a couple of homeless people. I resolved to start one when I could afford it." Ah Kung was to relate to his grandchildren in later days on his decision to purchase the shop house at India Street.

Although it was only three storeys high, there was little doubting that it was the tallest building when he bought it in the late 40's. Well, at least as far as the eye could see from its third floor until the 60's when other taller buildings started to sprout all around it. He bought it from a Hokkien towkay who most probably had made use of the ground floor as a shop. The other levels would have been put to use as store-rooms and living quarters for himself and his family as was the practice with shopkeepers in those days.

After carrying out some minimal renovations, Ah Kung managed to get fifteen bedrooms out of it and these he rented at the cost of three to five dollars per night. It was a price that was affordable to poor travellers from either the coast or the countryside. For the very poor lodgers who were not overly concerned with privacy, there were single foldable canvas beds costing one dollar each and which were placed in a big recess area on the first floor. These canvas beds were folded up and tucked away in a corner under the first floor staircase during the day and were only taken out at night when hired by a customer, who would then be provided with a blanket and a pillow. I rather suspected that some of the regular hirers of these canvas beds were homeless folks who also took the opportunity to make use of the common bathrooms and toilets situated at the rear end of each floor.

I loved it whenever Ah Kung asked me to accompany him on one of his regular nightly trips to the lodging house. Although he had employed the husband of his youngest daughter to work there as a full time receptionist and booking clerk, he would still drop in on it most nights of the week, not only to oversee things, but mainly to have a good chat with some of the customers. Other than a few Dayaks and the odd travelling salesmen from Kuala Lumpur or Singapore, most of the guests were Hakka farmers who, together with Ah Kung, would invariably embark on extremely long arguments on current affairs, the pros and cons of Brookes' and British rule, the rise and fall of the various dynasties of China, the merits and demerits of the current touring Teochew opera troupe, etc.

These discussions, taking place in the lounge area next to the registration and booking office, with the participants sitting on long hard timber benches, and lasting for several hours, were, for a ten year-old boy, quite incomprehensible. It was a discussion among equals and no class barriers were apparent, even though some of the participants might have come from vastly different social backgrounds.

I enjoyed it particularly when, in the midst of one of these discussions, Ah Kung, in one of his rare, unguarded moments – his usual instinct against unnecessary expenditure caught unawares – would, on my prompting, condescend to give me twenty cents or so to buy some tit-bits from the many food vendors plying their wares around India Street.

Children of the Monkey God

There is very little doubt that my grandparents indelibly left their imprint on me as a youngster. I would even venture to say that they had a bigger influence on me than my own parents.

That influence began when I was only one year old, the time when our family moved in to live with Ah Kung and Ah Por in Padungan in 1947. However, one year before that, my father had already moved to Kuching from the coconut plantation to resume his duties with the Sarawak Government's Department of Post and Telegraph as a Morse code operator. He took with him my mother and their first two sons, my elder brothers; I was not born yet. Their days of refuge of five years in the coconut plantation were over.

Not senior enough to be assigned even the smallest government housing quarters, the whole family had to stay with my maternal grandparents at the first floor of a shop house in Main Bazaar. It was a temporary arrangement until alternative, although not necessarily better, accommodation could be found.

My maternal grandparents were not the easiest people in the world to live with and I am certain my parents, especially my father, dreaded every moment spent with them. It was at this time that my father took up mah-jong, a nocturnal habit that would keep him away from his mother-in-law's home for most of the evenings. I am certain that he had also had a big influence on the decision of Ah Kung to buy a shop house in Kuching with the idea of setting up permanent residence there. In this way he and his family would be able to move in with his own parents to avoid the wagging tongue of a nagging mother-in-law. The arrangement must have also suited Ah Kung and Ah Por who had by now had more than a taste of my mother's cooking during her wartime stay with them in the coconut plantation.

My mother would also have been happy to move out of her mother's house, whom she also considered to be a terrible nag. Unfortunately, my father continued with his nocturnal outings, even after our move to Padungan Road, and so it was that my paternal grandparents had such a big impact on me during the formative years of my youth; more so than my father.

Ah Kung might have decided to take up residence in the town but he would always remain a farmer at heart, more particularly a Hakka farmer - earthy and frugal, disdainful of all things flashy or showy, and highly intolerant of anyone with wasteful habits. There is a saying in the family that Ah Kung's one cent was larger than a bullock cartwheel. Being frugal was a way of life for him, as it has been for millions of Chinese peasants from time immemorial. It was a way of life that made certain they survived the lean years of hunger and poverty, for there would always be lean years in the lifetime of a farmer.

In our family, Ah Kung saw to it that food on the table was treated with a lot of reverence and this was particularly the case with rice, which was given a special place and elevated to the status of quasi-sacredness. Not even a grain of it must be left on the plate or else the kitchen god would see to it that the offender be punished by being turned out into the street, made a homeless beggar and remain hungry for the rest of his life. Such stories abounded of the dire consequences suffered by uncaring offenders, should they fail to treat food, especially rice, with the reverence and respect it deserved.

One favourite tale of my grandparents that made it to the storytelling sessions quite often was that of a rich man who had fallen on hard times, become homeless and, while begging on the street was, one day, taken home by a good Samaritan and given food, being later told that the rice served to him was actually his very own. The benefactor then proceeded to explain that he was the poor neighbour who used to occupy a small hut next to the big mansion of the rich man. Unable to stand the waste practised by the family members of the rich man and their servants the poor neighbour and his family began to save their discarded food, in particular, the rice thrown out after every meal. The rice grains, even though they were already cooked, were put out to dry in the sun and through the years the poor man and his family managed to store sack-full of this discarded cooked rice to be recycled and re-cooked.

It was from stories like these that Ah Kung sought to impart to us his philosophy of life. It was never going to be an easy task. For one thing, the financial circumstances of the family had changed, and for another, Ah Kung was not operating from his farm any more. This was for him one of the disadvantages of living in the town - the distractions and influences of town life that tended to draw his grandchildren away from time-honoured traditional practices of frugality.

There were, of course, advantages to town life. The proximity to all types of shops and restaurants and the consequential availability of most variety of consumer goods was one such advantage. The other was the availability of most forms of amenities, such as electricity and piped water, as well as the accessibility of various places of entertainment, in particular the cinemas and Chinese theatres.

Not that Ah Kung was overly fond of the types of music available from the radio and gramophone at the turn of a switch, a luxury that was denied to the family on the farm. He found modern music, whether Chinese or Western, too loud and incomprehensible. And it would be an understatement to suggest he would even deign to step into a cinema screening a Hollywood movie. I recall the only time he was persuaded to go to a film. It was a black and white movie made in Hong Kong on the adventures of Wong Fei Hung, a renowned martial arts master from the province of Guangdong. He told me after the movie that he found it impossible to follow the plot – the soundtrack too loud for his liking, the Cantonese dialect hardly comprehensible to him and the switching of scenes extremely confusing. He never went to another movie again.

My grandmother, on the other hand, became an avid movie-goer, even though there was only one type of movie she would go to – the great Hollywood musicals of the forties, fifties and early sixties. Like Ah Kung she found the plot of most movies, even the Chinese ones, difficult to follow, especially those "dialogue" movies or "movies with a lot of talking" as she would call them, whether it was Mandarin, Cantonese or English that was spoken. Hollywood musicals were a different matter, however. The colours, the glamour and the splendour on the big screen would bring a big smile to her face and lasting cheer to her heart, especially when Gene Kelly did his famous number with the umbrella in "Singing in the Rain." She never tired of seeing that particular movie or others of the same genre. The elaborately choreographed swimming numbers of Esther Williams were also a favourite with her. Dubbed the "swimming" movies, these earlier films of synchronised swimming were a big hit. Howard Keel and Jane Powell in "Seven Brides for Seven Brothers" remained one of her old time favourites. She enjoyed the gusto and energy put in by the performers just as she enjoyed the grace and slick dancing of Fred Astaire and Ginger Rogers.

These "singing and dancing" movies, as she would call them, were one of the great joys of her life and her standing instruction to me was to inform her of any such movies being shown in the huge 1000-seat Odeon cinema, a big cinema by any standard and scarcely a hundred yards from where we lived at No.70. For some reason or other, she considered me the most literate of her grandchildren in English and, therefore, the grandchild she could rely upon for information of any such films being screened at the Odeon. She also knew that I shared with her the same love and enthusiasm for these movies and that I would be more than eager to accompany her.

I was also chosen because of her need for someone to explain the plot, her full range of the English vocabulary being restricted to three or four words of "yes," "no," "hello" and "amen." I could understand how she had somehow managed to pick up the first three words of common usage but the last one presented a bit of a mystery, a word not at all secular and not so common, until she explained to me one day that she learned it from her youngest sister-in-law. Although this sixth and youngest sister of my grandfather became a Christian convert after her marriage to an Anglican textile shopkeeper in India Street, much to Ah Kung's disapproval and chagrin, she and Ah Por remained fast friends with regular visits exchanged between them. To Ah Por, this beloved sister-in-law was an "amen" person like all other Christians, just as people of the Buddhist faith, of whom she was one, were the "omitohfood" people (Hakka for "amitaba" and meaning "boundless light" in Sanskrit and is a reference to the "Buddha of the Immeasurable Light").

It was always an adventure going with Ah Por to the cheap Saturday morning shows of old Hollywood musical re-runs at the Odeon cinema. The inevitable and unfailing tussle with the Malay doorman was an event not to be missed and was perhaps even more entertaining than the movie itself. And it all happened because Ah Por, equally as thrifty as Ah Kung, refused to buy more than one fifty-cent admission ticket but yet demanded the doorman to admit three persons on that single ticket – for herself and her two grandchildren. Most of the cinemas in Kuching in those days had a liberal policy of allowing a child to go into the cinema with an adult on one ticket but they put their foot down when it came to two children with an adult on a single ticket. Ah Por, however, saw no reason why she had to buy two tickets when she could get in with one, let alone three, which, strictly speaking, was the number she should have purchased.

Hustling, cajoling and threatening, she was always able to get the better of the Malay doorman. She would state her case, arguing that we were only small children who would sit on her lap and, since all of us occupied one seat, one ticket was all that was required. Or the theatre was nearly empty and a couple of small children would not make any difference to the other patrons watching the movie and, the coup de grace:

"The cinema is not yours anyway, so why should you bother?"

And with that she would boldly stride into the cinema with her arms over our small shoulders. And, of course, we never restricted ourselves to a mere single seat once we were inside the cinema, Ah Por quite contented to let us roam within the huge theatre.

I always felt quite safe as a small boy in the company of my grandmother and that was not merely because of the confidence she exuded, but perhaps also because of a small secret weapon she carried in her purse. I call it a purse, although it would be more correct to call it a small pouch. Roughly 4 by 5 inches in size, it was a highly fashionable item among the older sarong-clad women of those days. Constructed from either thick crude wool or colourful local beads, it would be worn hung from a broad silver belt, another popular item with women of that age, and strapped around the waist.

Other than the fact that it was a popular fashion accessory it was also, because of its size, a useful thing to carry around in the days before the widespread use of the European ladies' handbag among the local women. Although the pouch itself was not even half the size of an average handbag it was, nevertheless, large enough to carry useful items (other than currency notes and coins) such as a small comb, a lipstick, a facial compact, (although these latter two pieces would not be part of Ah Por's inventory), a few lucky charms and a medium's or shaman's ward and, in the case of Ah Por's pouch, a small piece of bark. I knew of this because she pulled me aside one day in our living room in Padungan and said almost in a conspiratorial whisper:

"Come here. I have something I want to show you."

She then reached her hand into her pouch, slowly and carefully pulling from it a small piece of dark brown bark, barely one inch thick and about two inches long. Sharp at one end, it was also extremely old.

"Do you know what this is?" she asked.

I shook my head.

With a glint in her eyes and a slight smile on her face, she then proceeded to explain that the piece of ancient timber in her pouch was plied from an extremely poisonous tree in Sambas and given to her by her mother for use as a weapon against any would-be sex-molester or attacker. One scratch of it on an attacker's body would kill him, she claimed.

She had carried it with her since that day, keeping it

next to her person for more than fifty years, ready to use in case of any attack either on her or her grandchildren. There was very little doubt in my mind that she would not hesitate to use that innocuous-looking little piece of bark should she deem it necessary, especially after that gun-shooting incident with a lecherous neighbour in the coconut farm many years ago.

Ah Kung never went to these Hollywood movies with Ah Por or with any of his grandchildren. He had no great fondness for the way they "pranced about on the screen", as he would put it, nor for the stars whom he considered to be too heavily made up and still calling themselves "miss" when they were either already married or in their middle years.

For him, the greatest form of entertainment was, and always would be, the Teochew opera. Any other Chinese opera performed by street performers or amateurs from the local Hokkien and Cantonese benevolent societies, (who would put on a show or two during festival times) hardly counted. In contrast, the performers of the Teochew opera were professionals drawn from places like Singapore and Kuala Lumpur, whose troupes would, on the odd occasion, include Kuching as part of their itinerary. The owners and sponsors of these touring troupes would seek him out as one of the local financial backers and, in return for his contribution Ah Kung would be entitled to free passes to all their shows, which would run for a few weeks at the Odeon Cinema. Ah Kung never refused their request for financial assistance and, although he would incur a loss of few hundred dollars with each investment, he continued to support them, perhaps with the knowledge that financial support from patrons like him was needed to help keep this art form alive. It was quite out of keeping with his usual prudent approach to money matters.

Children of the Monkey God   133

I made a number of trips to the Teochew opera with Ah Kung and Ah Por in my earlier years as a boy growing up. The Odeon Cinema would be turned into a theatre, its big white screen taken down and replaced by stage props of Chinese pavilions, gardens, palaces and natural landscapes, depending on the play that was being staged.

There was no doubt that my grandparents enjoyed every moment of the opera staged, although Ah Kung was better versed with most of them than Ah Por. He had an advantage over Ah Por in that respect; his stint as a shop assistant with the Teochew in his young days had inculcated in him a love and understanding of their opera, which he believed was the most refined of all Chinese operas. He would follow closely every gesture, every movement and every aria and, more often than not, would comment on the interpretation given by the players.

The stance taken by an emperor, an army general or a great hero was crucial in conveying their authority or defiance, depending on the circumstances. The stare they gave to an adversary was all-important in conveying to the audience their contempt for their enemies. The simulated horse riding style of the players on stage had to be well done to help the audience place them in a scene of rolling plains and hills, and the exaggerated swaying hips of a female match-maker or that of a mistress of a brothel - both roles invariably played by an overly-plump male actor – had to be executed in such a way as to bring light comic relief in between scenes that could be quite heavy going at times.

Thus, by their singing and body language were these players judged. Tales of the rise and fall of the various Chinese dynasties; the trials and tribulations suffered by talented scholars in their endeavours to achieve success for themselves and their poverty-stricken families; the many tragic romances of young couples seeking to escape family-imposed arranged marriages; the heroic deeds of legendary and historical figures; the many goings-on of the gods, deities, fairies and spirits and many more would come to life on stage amidst the clashes of cymbals and the beating of drums. It was noisy, it was colourful but it was also another world. It was a world I could not relate to; a world far beyond my comprehension. It was also a world that held no relevance to the many answers a growing teenager sought. Marlon Brandon and James Dean with their on-screen mumbles held more relevance than these ghostly, albeit colourful, figures of the past.

STREET FRIENDS & CLASSMATES

My grandparents' decision to live a life of semi-retirement in the town may appear odd in the eyes of some people, especially those urban dwellers whose view of retirement is that the countryside surely has more to offer by way of providing a more relaxed and quiet lifestyle; an opportunity for the retiree to unwind far away from the hustle and bustle of the city. But Ah Kung and Ah Por were not your normal would-be urban retirees. They were a pair of hard-working coconut farmers who had devoted nearly fifty years of their lives eking out a living in a near-remote plantation devoid of all modern amenities. And in all those years spent there, the farm was representative of a life of toil. It was thus a reminder of a harsh life with very little opportunity to enjoy the finer things of life such as eating good food, watching Chinese opera and movies, taking a ride in a car, listening to music and having light at the turn of a power switch, plus running water and all the amenities that town dwellers often take for granted.

Town dwellers they might have become, but both my grandparents still refused to compromise when it came to their Hakka ways of doing things. Fiercely proud and independent, they still clung to their Hakka dialect and refused to learn Hokkien, and this in a town where that dialect was the lingua franca of the streets. This was particularly the case with the street of Padungan, which was predominantly Hokkien with a few families of other dialect groups, such as Teochew, Cantonese, Hainanese, Foochow, Chow-an, Hakka, Shanghainese and Henghua thrown in.

We were the only Hakka family within a stone's throw of our house and we stood out - inviting taunts of "here come the Hakka monkeys, with their red, red bottoms" from the neighbourhood children. Ah Kung taught us from an early age to be proud of being Hakka and to stand up to any insults thrown at us from the neighbourhood kids, which usually meant getting into quite a few scraps. My mother was none too pleased whenever she learned that we had been involved in these fights. While she would be admonishing us for what she felt was our disgraceful behaviour, Ah Kung and Ah Por would be proudly smiling away in the background. As for the children who taunted us, they learned very soon not to do it anymore.

Ah Kung's recalcitrance toward the Hokkien dialect and his animosity toward them were not too difficult to fathom. It was made clear to us, whenever he related the fight for sovereignty carried out by the rebellious Hakka miners in the Bau Rebellion of 1857, on the part played by the Kuching Hokkien towkay in siding with the rajah.

Kuching Town in the 1950's and 1960's was a far cry from the Kuching City of today. Unlike today, inner city living was still very much a vibrant way of life. The shop houses from one end of the town to the other – from the Brooke Shipyard in the west to the small clock tower in Padungan in the east – were designed as a complete family unit with the ground floor put to use as a shop by the owner himself or by the lessee, if it was rented out. The first and subsequent floors would then be used as storerooms and as living quarters by their family members and servants.

Although suburban living was starting to become more popular, largely because of the demand of an expanding population, as well as the broadening and increasing availability of amenities such as paved roads, public transport, piped water and electricity, inner city living still remained the preferred way of life for some of its residents. It was not, however, most people's idea of ideal living, as

Children of the Monkey God

the extended family system tended to turn a lot of these shop houses into extremely cramped living quarters, with family members of at least two, if not three, generations living under one roof. It was not uncommon, therefore, to find some houses with fifteen to twenty members living in one shop-house or even occupying one floor.

With so many people living in such close proximity to each other, however, the resultant street life was active, colourful and noisy.

Kuching was not only a predominantly Chinese town in the 50's and 60's; it was also a Chinese town outside of China in a British colony. The few Malay families who lived there were confined more to the Sekama and Satok Roads areas and the occasional Dayaks and Indians that one chanced to come across on the streets lived more on the peripheral outskirts of the town, rather than in the town centre itself. The latter were mainly migrant workers brought over from southern India to be used as the lowest paid menial labourers of the Public Works Department.

Yet, paradoxically, there resided right within this very Chinese town a few British families belonging to the chairman, directors and other executive officers of the Borneo Company. The company was the owner of the northern slope of Bukit Mata Kuching, a small hill facing the Sarawak River. The property was about three quarters of a kilometre in length, running parallel to the full stretch of Thompson Road (renamed Tunku Abdul Rahman Road), from whence it joined Main Bazaar at its western end and Padungan Road at its eastern side. The company's main building of offices, storerooms and godowns were located at the foot of the hill, while the houses - English-style country mansions and bungalows – were strategically located either on top or on the side of the hill, with the higher-ranked officers presumably occupying the higher-located and bigger buildings. These houses with their well-kept lush green lawns and fruit trees of mangosteen, durian, rambutan, papaya and banana and flowers of magnolia, bougainvillea and hibiscus were, collectively, an anomalous enclave, situated as it was between the rows of Chinese shop houses of Main Bazaar and Padungan Road. Perhaps this anomaly could be explained by the fact that the Borneo Company was already there before the subsequent construction of the shop-houses surrounding it. Formed in the early years of the first rajah' reign, it was already occupying this site when Padungan was still a small Malay village.

Of all the streets, lanes and roads of the town, Padungan Road was, with little doubt, socially and perhaps also culturally, the most active of them all. Part of the reason might have been the manner in which the street was laid out. It is doubtful that the original planners of the town intended it to be so, but this is how it eventually turned out. It was made up of grass islands in the middle of the roads; the Sarawak River running along its northern border, with its southern side merging into a football field, a youth club and a few adjoining playgrounds. This big open area became a hive of activity in the cooler hours of the evening when scores of children, big and small, would get together to play games of badminton, football, marbles, rounders, hopscotch, hide-and-seek and to fly kites. Also, the completion in the 50's and 60's on its southern boundary of several blocks of three and seven-storey low-cost municipal council flats at Ban Hock Road next to the site of an old Malay kampong or village had the effect of increasing the residential population of this general area somewhat, thus adding to its already busy and energetic street life.

These, then, were factors that helped to make Padungan Road a much more socially vibrant area than the smaller and less densely populated older parts of the town, such as India or Carpenter Street or Main Bazaar. They also made it a noisy street.

The cacophony of sounds that greeted me every morning came from those of street vendors plying all types of foods and drinks, calling out their specialities of yam and Chinese radish cakes, deep fried breads, all types of porridge, noodles and buns, glutinous rice dumplings, sweets made from red and green beans, hot and cold Soya bean drinks, coconut and other fruit juices, etc. It also emanated from the clanking noise of cooking vessels and utensils coming from the numerous coffee and teahouses dotting the streets, and from the shouts their waiters made as they called out their patrons' orders. Added to this, was the sound of shopkeepers of grocery and other stores, preparing for the start of another day, pushing their squeaking and heavy metal grill-guards to open their doors in readiness for their first morning customers. There was also the din of numerous black and white-feathered swiflets emerging from their nests built into the corners of the first floor rafters of the shop houses as they went about their parental duty in search of food for their young, making trilling sounds as they skilfully dodged pillars and other concrete structures. Above all, there was the sound of songs, music, daily announcements, news and commentaries that would come pouring out from the radio sets of almost every house in the street, merging with, and sometimes dominating, this daily street noise.

The radio set was not only the prized possession and centrepiece of every living room in the street; it was also the most advanced and popular form of home entertainment before the advent of television. Costing virtually next to nothing to run and an electrical wonder to behold, especially with a gramophone attached to it, the radio set was the main perpetrator of street noise. It started from the very early morning and did not end until quite late in the evening. It was comprised mainly of songs, news, announcements, drama and comedy sketches from the local station, Radio Sarawak, the BBC, the Voice of America, Radio Indonesia and from stations of other commonwealth countries such as Malaya, Singapore and Australia.

There was little doubt that the people of Kuching were zealous in the use of their radios; some would even call it over-zealous. Each household would treat their radio sets like weapons and would unleash their daily volley of shots from their Phillips or Telefunkens, the two most popular brands, into the street. In the days when air-conditioners were still a thing of the future, the open doors and shuttered windows of the street's houses allowed such volleys to be fired with maximum effect.

The radio set was, therefore, more than just a mere weapon of war; it was also an instrument of free and wild expression. And more than anything else, this daily battle of the airwaves not only defined the town, but also the residents who took part in it.

It was a battle to show who had the better and more expensive model and who had the better aerial to receive clear signals from far away countries. Undoubtedly, the crème de la crème was the Telefunken, especially its top of the range radio and record-player combination set that produced such crisp, clear stereo sound. It was, arguably, the second most important status symbol of the street after the car. A person's popularity or unpopularity, as well as his social standing in the street, soared or dipped with its acquisition and use.

It was also a battle that defined where you were culturally and socially, depending on whether you had a preference for Chinese or English programmes. Those listeners of English language programmes were looked upon as show-offs and traitors by their Chinese counter-parts, who were, in turn, looked upon as backward and out-of-touch traditionalists by the listeners of English programmes. On top of that, one or two rascally pranksters would sometimes - for the sheer pleasure of it - decide to throw a spanner in the works by tuning into some Malay or Indian stations playing songs of those nationalities.

Padungan Road was not only a street of vendors, traders, shopkeepers and businessmen, it was also a street of their children; children whose parents, or the parents before them, were migrants from China. They were the children I grew up with - my mates on the street - and whose five-foot shop-house pavements became part of our playground in our games of hop-scotch (also known as dog's head in Chinese), marbles, card games, dice, rope-skipping and even roller-skating. For games of hide and seek, rounders, football and kite-flying, the open area next to the Song Kheng Hai Football Ground at the southern boundary of the street, provided ample space for these activities. With the exception of kite-flying, they were games we played all year round.

Kite-flying not only required space, it required wind and, the stronger the wind the better it would be. This could only happen during the monsoon season between the months of September and February, when the north-eastern breezes of the Himalayan monsoon would be at their fiercest. And our kite-flying was not mere ordinary kite-flying. They were battles of the sky and our kites were line-guided aeroplanes used to swoop on an opponent's kite.

However, before these battles could take place, a kite that could glide swiftly through the air must first be made, and this began with its frame or backbone, which would be fashioned from young green bamboo splints, finely shaved, whittled down and tied together with cotton threads. This provided the structure on which either wax or rice paper would be pasted. It was important to get this framework right, as it would be a crucial factor in determining the kite's aerodynamic abilities. Heavy reliance was, therefore, placed on the skills of the kite-maker in shaving and whittling the bamboo rods to their correct shape, size and length. As for the paper, most kite-flyers preferred rice to wax, not only because of its porous quality - thus making the kite easier to guide and control in the air - but also because all sorts of designs and colourful paint-works could be created on it.

The next thing that had to be taken care of would be the line used for flying and controlling the kite. It had to be gelatine-coated with a fine powder of glass to make it razor-sharp, thus turning it into a lethal weapon of war. This could only be obtained from hours spent pounding thin shards of discarded light bulbs. An extremely fine muslin cloth was then used as a sieve to filter out any minute lumps of glass splinters still present in the powder. Lumps, even the size of a tiny grain of sand, and any incorrect consistency of the gelatine used for coating the powder onto the line would cause blobs to form. These blobs or knots along the line were points of weakness, interfering with its ability to flow smoothly as it made contact with an opponent's line which could then slice through the flawed line with ease.

Extreme care was, therefore, needed to make certain that such blobs would not be formed along the stretched line when applying the mixture of glass powder, wet gelatine (obtained from long hours of boiling beef tendons) and colouring agents with a piece of rag. These colouring agents, of bright red or yellow, were food colours 'borrowed' from my mother's kitchen with the latter extracted from the juice of her turmeric roots. A further application of the sticky mixture was often necessary to get rid of any remaining blobs, as well as having the added advantage of making it stronger. It was tedious work but it made it all worthwhile when we finally launched the kite, now decked with colourful designs, into the air and, eventually, high up into the sky ready to do battle with any taker.

Although the kite gliding high up in the sky would be taking part in aerial battles as a sole combatant, it would be controlled on the ground by a team of two or three members with one of them holding a medium-sized empty can of Milo or Ovaltine. These oversized cans were our spindles around which the gelatine-coated glass lines would be wound. Meanwhile, the main player, the kite-flyer, would carry out all the various manoeuvres of swooping in to attack or veering and swinging away to evade a sortie and finally releasing the line when contact was made with that of another kite. The timing of the release was crucial, as too much tension on the line at the moment of contact would result in an immediate cut-off. Too little tension would result in a battle that would last indefinitely, ending in an indecisive stand-off.

Kite battles were exhilarating events, with each team having their own support group to cheer them on, and could be carried out against an opponent standing merely a few feet away or against one who could be a few hundred feet either downwind or upwind from us.

Kite battles were combats of skill with the eventual losers accepting their loss with good grace. Perhaps it was the acceptance by both warring parties of the inevitability of the outcome – that there could be only one victor - that helped to mould and shape this attitude towards each other. Whatever it was, I cannot recall any single moment when there had been a loss of temper or any harsh words exchanged after an aerial fight.

The battle was soon over, with the losing kite adrift and floundering in mid-air, sometimes dipping its nose and, at other times, wagging and swaying its bottom as it made its descent back to earth.

A fallen kite drifting slowly downward toward the ground would be looked on with excitement and anticipation by the huge group of spectators waiting to pounce on it. Now a spoil of war and free from any claim of ownership by the loser/owner, (for he lost that right when he lost the fight) it would set the scene for another battle – this time on the ground.

Armed with long bamboo poles, the crowd waiting on the ground was more interested in fighting for possession of the fallen kite than in any combat of skills, such as the one that had taken place a few minutes ago in the air. For one thing, they were more like vultures swooping onto a carcass and for another, rough and raucous mercenary tactics of pushing and shoving were frequently employed in an undignified free-for-all to get hold of the highly sought-after war trophy. More often than not, the kite would end up all torn and tattered; a sorry end for an exquisite and beautiful glider, which only moments ago was proudly gracing the sky.

I spent many an hour with my brothers, cousins and street friends in the making of kites, in the preparation of their lines and in the battles of the sky. The peak period for kite-flying was December, the month when the monsoon breeze was at its strongest, as well as coinciding with the long school holiday-break at the end of term. On any given fine day in that month, scores of kites would dot the sky in the still open space stretching from Padungan Road to Ban Hock Road, some doing battle, others merely happy to show off their aerodynamic gliding skills. This, then, was our main battleground and air space.

Or so we thought.

Until one day when a solitary kite appeared on our side of the town from across the Sarawak River in what we considered to be a cheeky intrusion into our aerospace. Flying at a height of perhaps a hundred feet higher than any of our kites, it came from the general direction of the Malay villages of either Kampong Gersik or Surabaya. Carried by the north-easterlies of the monsoon wind with a line capacity of a few thousand feet, it was not only a blight to our eyes but a testimony to the skills of those people operating it. It was obviously a champion kite on its own home turf and, more likely than not, picked by some of the boys of the villages as its audacious representative to carry out a sortie on the other side of the river, i.e., our side of the river. This was, without a doubt, a challenge to an aerial battle, which we could neither ignore nor back down from.

The challenge having been made, a group of us proceeded to the northern side of the street, i.e., the very edge of the southern bank of the river, and once stationed there, one of our better teams of kite-flyers sent their kite into the air to do battle with it.

It soon became apparent that the battle would be a lost cause for us. The invading kite was superior to ours in all aspects, despite its disadvantage of having to tow an inordinately long line behind it. This handicap notwithstanding, it was able to glide, swoop and manoeuvre in the air with far more ease and flexibility than our own champion kite. The battle was over in no time at all and another of our kites was sent up to take it down. It was to no avail. We lost a lot of kites in the days to come to the villagers of either Kampong Gersik or Surabaya with not even a single victory to our name.

We became extremely curious as to the reasons for

their invincibility and consequential victories. Speculations were soon rife among some of us as to whether it might have been the design of their kites, their skills in handling and flying them, especially the slight advantage they had in flying them upwind from us, or the line they used. The general consensus, after days of discussion, analysis and speculation, was that it was most probably their line that did the trick. Continuing on in this vein, we became quite convinced that they must have used very fine, durable nylon fishing line for coating with their glass powder instead of the cotton thread-line used on our side of the river; an unfair and unsporting advantage, we said to ourselves.

Spurred on by the desire to gain at least one victory, and taunted into further action by the mixture of humiliating cheering, jeering, hooting and clapping sounds made by our cross-river rivals whenever one of our kites fell, even though this was barely audible, it soon became the quest of the kite-flyers of Padungan to take down one of their kites. The enemy's fallen kite with its line intact, landing on our side of the river would definitely reveal the secret of their success, we reasoned. There was even a plan devised to entice their kites, while closing in on ours to do battle, to come as close as possible to ours and as low as possible to ground level to enable a few of the boys carrying long bamboo poles to reach them and bring them down to earth. This was not an honourable tactic but we were a bunch of desperate people looking for desperate solutions.

Again it was not to be; for try as we might, whether by means honourable or dishonourable, we were never able to bring down a single kite of our worthy adversaries from across the river.

The monsoon season was not only a time for flying kites; it was also a time for playing football. Cool air and wet ground were ideal conditions for sliding long distances along the ground and for turning the game into a water sport. The wetter the ground the better and it was best when it was water-logged. This meant having to wait for a day when there was a heavy downpour, when my street friends and I, after having successfully evaded our respective parents' attention, would somehow meet up in the playground located behind our houses, which on a dry day would have seen us flying kites.

Playing football in these waterlogged conditions with heavy pelting rain was never going to be easy. Kicking the heavily soaked leather ball of thick cowhide became a task of near-impossibility. That hardly bothered us though, for our intention was not to play football. Our real intention was to play in the rain. Splashing in ankle-deep water and sliding along as we chased after the ball, we were not at all concerned about scoring goals. We just wanted to be out there in the rain, feeling the impact of its gigantic drops as they hit our backs and faces as we stumbled and fell, lying there and not wanting to get up again. It was pure joy and it did not matter that we would suffer the consequences later on in the night from the numerous fine scratches caused by the sharp blades of grass. An allergic reaction would develop, making the skin go warm and itch, resulting in prolonged periods of scratching, discomfort and sleeplessness.

Although my street playmates were my friends for the greater part of my youth, they did not attend the same school as I did. Most of them went to Chinese schools. I was one of the few children in that street who were sent to an English-medium school by their parents. Although it was not an impossible situation to be in, it was, in more ways than one, an incongruous one.

For a start, there was definitely within my family an unspoken tussle between my father and my grandfather as to which school we children should be attending. Ah Kung was a proud Chinese who saw no other way of bringing up his grandchildren than as Chinese, and to him this meant making certain we went through the Chinese education system; in his opinion, the most superior and therefore the best of all systems.

Ah Kung managed to have his way for a while with my two older brothers. They were both sent to Chinese schools with my eldest brother achieving the equivalent of a middle school or the "O" level grade of an English school at the age of seventeen. Following this, he was, on the intervention of my father, transferred to St Joseph's School, an English-Catholic school where he completed a further three years of English-medium education. In the case of my second brother, he had to spend the first two years of his education in a Chinese school before being switched, again at the behest of my father, to St. Thomas's School, an Anglican school about a kilometre away from our house.

My father had managed to win his tussle with Ah Kung by the time I was of school age. My education and that of my two younger brothers were all at St. Thomas's. He had decided that an education in English from an early age would be of tremendous help in laying the foundation for a better future – that English education in a British colony was the best preparation he could provide for his children.

This tussle between father and son was in more ways than one an odd one; a conflict in which the seeds of discord within the family were undoubtedly sown by my grandfather, who for pragmatic reasons had sent my father, his second son, to be educated in St Joseph's as a young boarder. In the meantime he had already, in line with the traditional Chinese practice in the Nanyang, sent his eldest son to be privately tutored in one of the Chinese schools in Kuching in Chinese arts, literature and history, effectively making him the anointed one or heir-apparent of the family as far as Chinese cultural heritage was concerned.

Thus it was that at the same time my father started his schooling in St. Joseph, his eldest brother was nearly halfway through his education in Kuching at one of the Chinese schools. He would eventually finish with a Chinese middle school grade. While Ah Kung saw that as important in preserving the Chinese culture within the family, he felt it was also necessary that at least one of his other sons should be educated in English for the purpose of dealing with government applications and other similar matters that required the expertise of an English-educated son. That son happened to be my father.

It was a decision that would have far-reaching consequences; a decision that not only laid the foundation of his conflict with my father over the type of education that I and my brothers should have, but it also sowed the seeds of a far more serious discord between my father and his eldest brother, resulting in a irreparable break-down in their relationship. It was a clash of two strong-willed personalities, exacerbated by their differences in outlook and culture, one that was cultivated by the different medium-schools they had attended in their youth through no fault of their own.

Thus it was that I went to St Thomas' kindergarten at the age of six.

St Thomas' did not have enough classrooms to accommodate all of its students and the kindergarten classroom was actually situated at St Mary's School on the other side of McDougall Road from St Thomas' proper, and I became one of the few 'privileged' boys permitted to enter the premises of an all-girls' school to study. In reality it was more a case of both the school authorities deciding that the admission of six year-old boys onto the grounds of St

Mary's was not such a serious infringement on their common policy of gender segregation.

There it was that I was introduced to the English language by way of the alphabet song (The 'ABC' song) by a fierce teacher with a pock-marked face. In St Thomas' proper, in primary one the following year, I learned by monosyllabic rote for the whole year a book from the Longmans' series called "A Man and a Pen". This was done in faithful recitation after the teacher – Chinese school style, albeit not with the same discipline.

Being English-educated, my brothers and I thus stood out in the extended and Chinese-educated family system of Ah Kung's, just as we sometimes stood out in the predominantly Chinese-educated neighbourhood of Padungan. It was a fact that I was constantly reminded of, surrounded as we were by families with nearly all of their children attending Chinese schools.

On top of that, our house was situated next to a couple of classrooms run by the Chinese-medium Chung Hua Primary School No.3. These classrooms on the ground and first floor of No. 72, Padungan Road were part of the school's complex and whose main building was on the other side of the street, a row of riverside lumber warehouses converted into makeshift classrooms. This, and the shop house at No. 72, belonged to a wealthy timber merchant who had generously allowed the school to use them charging little or no rent.

For some reason or another, Chinese schools in Kuching did not keep the same session times as the English-medium missionary schools and, while our school and that of the other missionary schools would complete our lessons by one o'clock in the afternoon, the Chinese schools would still have their lessons until late in the afternoon.

Children of the Monkey God 151

With time available on my hands on these late afternoons, and with many of my Chinese neighbourhood friends still at school, I would, as a curious small boy, peek into one of the open windows of the ground-floor classroom at No.72, watching and listening to the lessons conducted inside. It was akin to looking into an alien world, watching fifty very well-disciplined children of about my age reciting line after line in sing-song unison after their teachers from passages read out in Mandarin from a book. In our house, Hakka was the dialect we would use to speak to each other, and out in the street Hokkien was the preferred dialect. At school, on the other hand, English was spoken more than any other languages. Mandarin was seldom used, except on radio programmes and in movies at the cinema. Listening and watching these students in faithful recitation after their teacher, it struck me that it was not merely the language which sounded so alien to my young ears – I got used to its sounds and tones in later years and was even able to speak a few words– it was also the sight of seeing so many of them, so well-behaved and disciplined in what they were doing. It was quite a far-cry from the scene I was used to in my own classroom where we would, for most of the time, whisper to each other and even, sometimes, throw crunched-up balls of paper, origami planes and pieces of chewing gum at each other the moment the teacher had their back turned. And what were those girls doing studying in the same classroom with the boys? Shouldn't they be segregated from the boys and put in their own school like St. Mary's (run by the Anglican Church) or St. Teresa's (run by the Catholic Church)?

In spite of their show of discipline, one or two of the students could not help but stare back at me, hostility and envy contained in those looks. Hostility, for I was obviously a turncoat English schoolboy, for why else could I be that free to look through their class-room window? And envy, because I could roam about the street while they were still sitting in a hot, stuffy classroom with fifty other children, faithfully reciting word for word and line for line from passages read out by their teacher.

I learned to lead a double life from an early age. It was a life forced on me by the circumstances of living in two different worlds. There was the Chinese world of the home and the street, and there was the English world of St Thomas's school, just as there were street friends and schoolmates. Both groups of friends lived in worlds that were at the same time separable and distinguishable, yet also inseparable and indistinguishable.

Most of the street mates were mates in the afternoon and evening, the after-school friends that I roamed the streets with. These were the neighbourhood kids. They were not only the kids I spent a lot of time with; they were the ones I grew up with. It was from them I learned to play soccer and ping-pong, to swim, fight, fly kite with and play various types of card games, as well as to gamble. It was also from them that I discovered how flexible and dexterous the hands and fingers could be when used as tools of obscene gestures, as well as instruments of anger. And from them it was that I learned the full vocabulary range of the English equivalent of four-letter words; not from my schoolmates who, while not openly disapproving, would be rather uncomfortable with such crude and uncultured behaviour.

I learned at an early age to behave differently in each circle – the well-mannered English-educated boy when I was in school, well, as well-mannered and well-behaved as I was able to master, anyway, but the rough and spontaneous street urchin in the company of my street friends. In the school I was known by my given name of 'Fah Sen' but out in the street of Padungan I was known by my nickname of

'Kang'. None of the members of one circle ever knew the name I used in the other circle. It was not so much that I chose to deliberately keep them in the dark about my other name, as the fact that it never entered my head to tell them about it. It was something that just happened naturally.

It was also an indication of how separate each group was from the other. Above all, it happened because of the different types of activities I was involved in with each respective group at different times. There were those activities that I took part in at school from early morning until early afternoon, and there were those that I took part in on the street from early afternoon until early night.

The lack of extra-curriculum subjects at St Thomas's also helped me keep these two groups of friends quite separate. It did not cause me too much concern that our school had very few extra-curriculum activities, as my experiences in some of them had not been that pleasant. Thus, a series of non-mandatory afternoon mandarin classes conducted by our Chinese-educated physical education teacher - who was not at all trained in that particular area - had the disastrous effect of turning all of his students against that language. Also, a few football games I played with my school friends had them accusing me of "rough play". They were, apparently, not highly impressed with my sliding technique to gain possession of the ball from an opposition player or intercept a cross for the purpose of scoring a goal. What some of them had failed to realize was that what I had done was second nature to me, playing football the way I had always done with my street friends, especially on rainy days, when the temperature had dropped to a comfortable degree, and when we were able to slide an immensely long distance along the wet and slippery surface. After a few such accusations by schoolmates, I remembered to temper my style of play. Although this was not to my liking, I felt I had to accommodate them, even though this might prove highly detrimental to my own techniques, to say nothing of clearly restricting my spontaneous and exuberant approach to the game. This concession, however, robbed me of much of the fun of playing football and I did my best not to play any more games with them at school or for the school house team.

Going by some of the things I have written so far, some readers might think that I did not have as much fun with my schoolmates as I had with my street friends. Far from it. I had fun with them, all right. They just happened to be different types of fun; different because of the social and cultural divide that separated the two groups.

Take for instance, recreational dancing, especially the latest craze of rock n' roll, and the twist, which were considered by most of my street friends as something both repulsively alien and derisively quaint. The idea of young unmarried teenage boys and girls holding each other in the act of doing the waltz, the foxtrot, the quickstep or the rumba was, to some of them, socially unacceptable and morally reprehensible. In the traditional, conservative world of Chinese propriety and strict social mores of that time, taught to them both at home and in schools, dancing and going to parties were near-forbidden activities carried out by shameless English school students, who had turned their backs on traditional Chinese cultural values. If anything else, these were acts strictly within the preserve of married adults only, to be carried out within the confines of their homes; not for flaunting and openly parading at parties, as the boys and girls of the English missionary schools were wont to do. They found it outrageous that these schools even went to the extent of organizing such functions within their compounds for their already culturally-subverted students. As far as I knew, none of my street friends went to any dance parties or,

Children of the Monkey God 155

if any of them did, I never heard about it.

My own involvement in that area was reserved for my school friends and I was discreet enough not to talk about it with my friends in the neighbourhood. Not that I felt I had to conceal such activities from them. As far as I was concerned, these other activities were my own affair, not theirs. They were my involvement in the other circle, one that included my schoolmates and friends and didn't include them; the other world, so to speak. A world where tight pants, long pointed shoes and Brylcreamed Elvis Presley hairstyles for the boys and bouncy circular skirts, high-heeled shoes and pony tails for the girls were the fashion, in contrast to the drab, loose outfits and the short, flat hairstyles of the boys and girls from Chinese schools. The boys and girls of one world played records churning out songs of American and British artistes, and those of the other world, that of Taiwan, Hong Kong and Old China(not of the New China for they were communist-orientated and, therefore banned). The former were in English, the latter in Hokkien, Cantonese and Mandarin.

If truth be told, I did not live in these two different worlds out of choice. As I have said before, it was an existence forced on me by circumstances beyond my control. I would even venture to say that I was not aware of living in two different worlds until many years later when I had the chance to reflect on my youth. I am certain that my experience is not in any way unique. No doubt there are countless others who have gone through and, I imagine, will continue to go through the same experience. I would venture to say that perhaps it happens to all of us but in varying degrees and, like the chameleon who does it all the time unawares, we are not even conscious of the switches we automatically make to our persona as we move from one environment to another, whether it be physical, social or cultural. It is a survival skill that I feel Mother Nature has equipped us with and which I learned to use from very early on as I transited between the respective environments of St Thomas' School, Padungan Road and sometimes even the suburbs of Kuching, where most of my schoolmates lived.

Kuching, in the 50s and 60s, was continuing to expand and the ever-growing suburbs, now increasingly serviced by piped water and electricity, were becoming attractive to a growing middle class consisting of civil servants and professionals. Included in this growing number were those shop-keepers, merchants and traders who had traditionally been living in shop-houses in the town with their family. Some of them were beginning to succumb to the allure of the suburbia life-style.

Also, Sarawak seemed to have put behind it those early pioneering days of unrest and rebellion and, with the peace that came after the Japanese Occupation, there was a sense of security and confidence with living "out of town". Thus it was that more tradesmen, itinerant workers, vegetable and fruit gardeners, civil servants, professionals, businessmen etc., were starting to populate the areas surrounding Kuching. Houses, big and small, single and multi-storey, detached, semi-detached and terraced, as well as hovels, huts and sheds, were starting to sprout up everywhere.

Although I spent quite a number of years with these suburban residents, in, and sometimes even out of school, I still find it difficult to fix a gauge on them. Linguistically, they spoke at least one Chinese dialect, particularly Hokkien, for they were mainly children of that dialect group. Mandarin was not only out of reach for most of them, but out of the question for the simple reason that it was not a dialect that was widely spoken in the streets or at home, and could only, for most people, be learned formally at the Chinese schools. Except for those few whose families had converted to Christianity, the bulk of them were members of families who still practised ancestral worship and were, therefore, theoretically at least, followers of the Buddhist and Taoist faiths. Yet it was an extremely difficult task to gather together more than a handful of my school or classmates who would share my interest in the rich multi-god belief-system of Chinese culture, let alone the heroes and other colourful characters from Chinese folklore and literary classics.

Perhaps, unlike them, I was fortunate enough to have grandparents who loved telling their grandchildren stories, not only of heroes and gods, but also tales of the Chinese nether world of ghosts and spirits; stories of animals and other creatures with abilities to assume human form. Also tales of cunning foxes carrying out magical acts of shape-shifting transformations to beguile innocent human beings. And of the tale of the white serpent who took on the form of a beautiful woman to lure young men into her lair and other stories of romance and love between human beings and the spirits of the woods and netherworld.

Out on the streets with my mates from my neighbourhood, stories were told of the outlawed heroes of the marshlands, taking up arms as fringe dwellers against the established order of society, and of tales of the heroic struggles of the monks of Shoaling Temple and many more. These were further added to and embellished by the films that were starting to come out of Hong Kong. The early years of the black and white versions were mainly available through the few cinemas operating in Kuching, in particular the Cathay, formerly the Lillian and the Sylvia, now the site of a government office building. The Capital was another cinema showing these movies, only a stone's throw from my house and on the opposite side of the road from the Odeon as was a nameless open cinema on the site of the former

Happy World's ground at the start of Pending Road, a mere kilometre from my house. Oral renditions from my grandparents, relatives and neighbourhood friends of the stories of gods, spirits, ghosts, heroes and villains would come to life on the big screen, and I spent many enthralling hours in these cinemas, most of the time without the permission or knowledge of my parents, or sometimes even that of the cinemas' doorkeepers.

This, then, was the world that not only occupied a large part of my boyhood life, but also my imagination. Yet it was a world that I had to keep separate from my school friends. As for the latter, I shared with them the literary world of the west; the world of Robin Hood and his merry men, ace pilot Biggles of the RAF, Dr. Doolittle, and Long John Silver. I also shared with them the works of Charles Dickens, George Bernard Shaw, Jane Austen, Robert Lewis Stephenson, Somerset Maugham, Shakespeare and many more from our school's English Literature classes and through the courtesy of the public library run by the British Council at Rock Road.

It was an Anglo-Saxon world to begin with but, through the years, American infiltration, especially through the agency of its comic books, began to make itself felt. This was how we got more and more drawn into the world of Buck Jones, Kit Carson, Roy Rogers, Gene Autry the singing cowboy, Davie Crockett, Hop-Along-Cassidy, Tom Mix, Captain Marvel, Superman, Batman and Robin, Tarzan and many more.

So successful was this infiltration that the school hierarchy decided to do something about it. Father Keen, the school principal, and Miss Foss, the primary school headmistress, decided to join forces in the issue of an edict - under threat of severe punishment – banning the reading and possession of all American comic books in the school compound. This was followed up by the further declaration

Children of the Monkey God

that the use of American slang words such as "gee," "yeah," "hi," "lousy" and even "okay", as spoken by the characters of these subversive materials, would do irreparable damage to our grammar and spelling and were, thus, also banned. This ban was ineffective in stopping the reading of comics outside the school compound, however, and the swapping of these forbidden articles became a favourite pastime with many of the boys of St Thomas'.

In actual fact, American infiltration and influence became more intensified with the introduction of more celluloid heroes through the big screen, and cinemas like the Odeon in Padungan Road, Rex, Cathay, etc., were soon showing the latest movies from Hollywood. Actors like John Wayne, James Steward, Errol Flynn, Marilyn Monroe, Jayne Mansfield, Doris Day, etc., became household names.

To their credit, the British administrators of the government-owned Radio Sarawak were still holding out as much as they could, and its weekly episodes of the Goon Show, Doctor Findlay's Casebook, Hancock's Half-Hour, Round the Horn and the Clitheroe Kid continued to be regularly aired to a listening public that seemed to be shrinking with each passing day. And this in spite of the brilliant performances of talented artistes such as Peter Sellers, Harry Seacombe, Spike Milligan, Tony Hancock, Kenneth Horne and a few others. Not that it was, by any stretch of the imagination, a very big audience to start with, its listeners consisting mainly of people from the small British expatriate population who resided in the hillier and therefore cooler, quieter, greener part of Suburbia Kuching; namely, in that exclusive enclave on the outskirts of the town formed by Bampfylde, Crookshank, Golf Link (now renamed Budaya), Reservoir Roads and part of Rock Road and whose air daily reeked of chlorophyll scent, discharged from freshly mowed lawns. They were the heads of departments and the senior officers of the Sarawak civil service, the chairmen, directors and other top executive officers of the various British commercial houses and merchant banks of Kuching. The Sarawak Club – located at the top of the hill of Golf Link Road – was the exclusive, all-white European enclave, where members would get together for their daily rounds of gins, whiskeys, ales, beers, tennis and golf. Their wives would shop only at Joo Chan, India Street, for its imported hams, bacons, cheeses, butters, sauces and other choice delicacies, unavailable from the other grocery shops of the town. They were in a world of their own and quite oblivious to the American infiltration taking place outside their fortress.

In no time at all, the American infiltration became something akin to a tidal wave that could not be stopped, and even Father Keen and Miss Foss eventually succumbed to it by agreeing to a special outing for the whole school to a morning matinee of the "The Ten Commandments" starring Charlton Heston. Undoubtedly, it was an American movie, but which missionary school could resist the temptation of bringing its students to watch a motion picture that brought to "life" the story of Moses and the deliverance of the people of Israel from Egypt? It was a fun day for the students and in the line formation regularly and unfailingly referred to by the teachers as "two-by-two", we marched like troopers, some of us - the younger children - hand in hand, to Rex Cinema, barely two hundred yards from the school. The parting of the Red Sea by Moses was impressive and unlike any special effects we had ever seen before. Although it wasn't easy, we managed to hold back our ecstatic screams of "Hee-low lai!" ("Here comes the hero!" in Hokkien, an expression freely used when viewing movies involving cowboy heroes such as the Lone Ranger and other great Hollywood characters such as Tarzan, Superman, Batman, etc.) when Charlton Heston performed that particular miracle. The presence of the supervising teachers in the cinema, with their ever-watchful eyes, saw to that. In spite of that enforced restraint, I am quite certain a number of non-believers were converted to Christianity that morning when we went to see Charlton Heston do his bit for the faith.

The American cultural infiltration did not stop with Charlton Heston. Although Radio Sarawak remained a staunch bulwark of British programmes – there was hardly any airing of American documentary or comedy shows by the station – American pop and rock n' roll songs were starting to overwhelm the country, and, as the only radio station in the country, it could not help but reflect that trend. Annie Tan's weekly Saturday afternoon request programme, appropriately entitled "From me to you", became the most popular programme in the country and, although there were requests for songs of British artistes such as Cliff Richard, Tommy Steele and the Shadows, the overwhelming demand was for American singers such as Elvis Presley, Ricky Nelson, Pat Boone, Connie Francis, etc.

Although I have used the term "infiltration" to describe the American cultural influence, (an influence, I may add, that was to have a long-lasting impact not only on Sarawak, but all over the world), it was not a term openly used by the British and Australian schoolteachers to express the feelings they had against American popular arts and culture. It was more or less implied in the disdain and contempt most of them felt towards it. As far as they were concerned, American culture and literature were almost, if not equally, as extraneous as any other non-Anglo-Saxon culture and literature. The only time I can recall any reference made to American literary works was a passing remark made by one of the English literature teachers to that of Mark Twain.

British imperial power might have been waning after the Second World War, but its cultural and literary fortress still had to be defended at all costs. Neither American nor any other alien influence was permitted to mount an assault against it; particularly American, which represented the biggest threat of all. King Arthur and his knights of the round table and Robin Hood and his band of merry men were the finest examples of the classical legendary heroes, according to some of the teachers. More than ever before, they were held up in contrast to the crass comic book 'heroes' in the shape of Superman and Batman, recently-created and technologically superior, but lacking all credibility. King Arthur and Robin Hood might continue to hold sway in the court of St Thomas's School, but outside of that Anglo-Saxon world they were fighting a losing battle.

Perhaps it was not a coincidence that British influence in the field of popular arts, culture and music was beginning to wane in the late fifties and early sixties, although the Beatles did provide a temporary reprieve in the mid-sixties. Globally, British colonialism was on the retreat with British Prime Minister Harold MacMillan's "Wind of Change" speech before the South African Parliament on February 1960 marking a major turning point in British history and colonial policy. It was an inevitable recognition by the then Prime Minister that "Mother England" could not hope to hold on to the colonies indefinitely; such was the impact made by the post-war independence movements. Scores of countries across the globe made known their desire to be freed of European colonial rule. Sarawak was no exception, and together with Sabah, its sister state in Borneo, it would be allowed to gain independence by joining the Federation of Malaysia in September 1963.

Undoubtedly, the numerous movements for independence by the colonies were starting to have a profound effect on British administration everywhere. Changes, some subtle and others not so subtle, were beginning to take place in all aspects of colonial life.

And, in keeping with the times, for they were a-changing, the Sarawak Club was beginning to open its doors to non-whites, converting their initial admissions into its premises as select guests to token members, and although the club's white members and their wives continued to shop at Joo Chan, they could also be seen at the newly-opened Ting Supermarket. There were even talks in town that they were beginning to screen Hollywood movies within its private compounds. And, although they still carried with them an air of aloofness, it was noticeable that their façade was starting to wear thin.

In St Thomas' School itself, the last batch of expatriate teachers contracted to teach at the school was definitely of a different breed to that of their predecessors. Father Keen, our school principal, and Miss Foss, our primary school headmistress, had both retired during this period of impending changes. In their places, the school had obtained the services of Father Wellington and a small group of fresh young university graduates who were more accepting of the fate of the British Raj in the colonies and of the relentless and inevitable march of world history. This latest batch of teachers were not only young, they were also less concerned with keeping up the appearances of a ruling colonial master. For one thing, they were less formal in their lifestyle and garb, and for another they did not feel the need to maintain a detached attitude – the hallmark of the white man in the colonies.

Messrs Saunders, Plowright and Robertson, our teachers in History, English and English Literature, respectively in Forms Five and Six behaved with far less decorum and formality than their expatriate predecessors, perhaps even less than some of the locally-trained teachers. And, whether they knew it or not, it also left a lasting impression on a teenage schoolboy growing up in the colonies.

Perhaps the most poignant moment for me was the sight of our stout-looking English Literature teacher, "Bulldog" Robertson, waiting for his local take-away meal one weekend evening.

Standing next to the now-defunct "Tiger Garden" noodle hawker stall in his casual short-sleeved shirt and shorts and cheap rubber Japanese thongs ("flip-flops" was the contemptuous name given to these banned items by the austere Father Keen), he had no idea of the "damage" he had done to the image of the British Empire. Perhaps he knew but didn't care. Or perhaps he was merely that new breed of Europeans who had grown weary of having to keep up appearances and conduct themselves in the reserved manner of their predecessors. It was an ostentatious behaviour that I am sure would have been extremely tiresome on the perpetrators, and not dissimilar to the physical discomfort they would also have suffered in having to wear at all times a tight and cumbersome neck-tie in the high humidity of the tropics. Whatever it was, such a casual and seemingly innocuous behaviour of an expatriate teacher would been something quite unthinkable a few years earlier.

For my part, I can't recall with much clarity any of the ceremonies heralding Sarawak's independence from Britain, or of the handing over of the reign to the local governor, or of the last remaining days of Her Majesty's government in Sarawak. But one thing is for sure; the sight of "Bulldog" Robertson standing next to a noodle stall in the dying days of British colonialism made a bigger impression on me than all the country's combined colourful pageants and ceremonies ushering in a new era of independence.

This period of impending political change in the early

sixties saw us, students of St Thomas' School in our teenage years with most of my English-educated middle class classmates living mainly in the sprawling suburbs of Kuching. Many of them had parents, more particularly fathers, who were either civil servants or professionals and encouraged by their parents, they too wanted to have a career in the civil service or in one of the professions.

For those who aspired to be civil servants, it was the life-pension provided by the government that most attracted them. No other form of employment, with the possible exception of the Sarawak Shell Petroleum Company and other quasi-government bodies, provided its employees with anything similar – a pension for life after the retirement age of fifty-five. It was a secure future to look forward to and many government employees could not wait for the day when they would start to "eat their pension", as it was known in local colloquial terms.

Nine years of education up to the level of Form Three (Cambridge's Junior School Certificate), involving six years of primary and three years of secondary, was all that was required to secure the lowest clerical position in the government service. This was provided that you could endure being moved around from one remote rural outpost to another while outlasting some of your colleagues - as a few of them would drop-out after a few years - till the age of fifty-five, then you would have withstood the system rather well. And for these survivors, like my maternal grandfather, they would be awarded a long service medal in recognition of their long and loyal service to the colonial government, together with the life pension.

This system of recruiting people into the colonial civil service by the Brookes and the British was in many ways similar to that of the Chinese Imperial Government that had prevailed in China for centuries. They shared in common the following characteristics – the necessity to pass the prescribed public examinations, the posting to remote parts of the country, the gradual promotion up the bureaucratic system, the prestige, the official recognition, the security and the financial rewards that went with the job.

Unfortunately, though, the embracement of this system – one that links public grading examinations to entry into the civil service - had the undesirable side effect of making some of their followers think they had somehow become members of an elite group. In Kuching, it also had the further ironic effect of making them turn their backs on their own Chinese literary heritage. People from a Chinese school background were looked upon as quaint and outdated and of somewhat inferior quality, and their inability to speak, read or write English and their refusal to appreciate the jazzy and crooning styles of Bing Crosby, Frank Sinatra, Dean Martin, Nat King Cole, etc., and all other things western or Hollywood, would see them branded as backward country bumpkins.

Such an attitude had the tendency to make worse a social and cultural chasm that had already existed between the Chinese and the English educated. Within my own extended family of paternal and maternal relatives there existed differing views on what types of education the children should have and I often found myself in the middle of these opposing camps.

There was no shortage of advice by my mother's relatives on the choice of a career for her young fledglings, in particular from her six surviving brothers and their respective spouses. All six of them had followed the footsteps of their father in joining the Sarawak civil service and, having endured all the trials and tribulations thrown at them by the system, were models of success, which we, as children, should do well to emulate, as my mother was fond of constantly reminding us. Only one brother didn't make it into the civil service, having lost his life at sea as a young man after having fallen in with bad company. This, in itself, was proof of how important it was for all her sons to enter the public service, as she was wont to point out.

I would dread it come Chinese New Year, a birthday celebration or a festival get-together, when the same advice would be proffered over and over again by the many assorted maternal uncles, aunts and older cousins gathered together under one roof. It was, perhaps, this very same pressure to join them in the same career that put me off the Sarawak civil service and I became convinced at quite an early age not to lead the life of a staid public servant.

While my father's side of Chinese-educated relatives had nothing much to say about Chinese education, career-wise, - the political reality of living in a British colony made certain of that - they had plenty to say about its importance in preserving the Chinese heritage and culture. My Chinese-educated street friends shared the same view, maintaining that there was no comparable literature in the West to Chinese classics such as the "Romance of the Three Kingdoms," "The Water Margin," "Dreams of the Red Chamber," and "The Journey to the West" as well as the works of Confucius and his followers, just to name a few.

My suggestion that I was able to have access to some of these materials by reading their respective English translations, as I had already done with a couple of these classics at the British Council's Library (of all places), was brushed aside as a lame effort on my part to appreciate their literal contents, insisting that I must read these works in Chinese to be able to really appreciate them.

There was little doubt in my mind that they were aware that it was a feat beyond me, but it was their way of telling me what I had missed out on by not having a Chinese education. More than that, it was also their way of saying how superior the Chinese education was in comparison to that of the English or of any other nationality. And while they conceded that a Chinese education would not gain them entry into the British colonial civil service, it would be of tremendous use to them when they went into the world of trade and commerce, as there would be available to them the vast network of overseas Chinese business connections.

I kept my school friends separate from my street friends by making certain that they never met, not in my presence, anyway. Not that they were likely to, given their diametrically opposed interests in social, cultural and other events. For instance, I would not bring any of my street mates to a school function, be it a fete, fun fair, concert or sports event. Conversely, whenever any of my school friends came to visit me in my home, I would make certain they didn't come into contact with my street friends. I didn't want them to meet because I was certain they would not only be uncomfortable with each other's company, but possibly hostile to each other as well.

My school friends from the outlying suburbs of Kuching rode expensive Raleigh bicycles, which were looked upon with some resentment by my street friends, most of whom could barely afford a bike and, for the few who could, it would be a cheap China-made model passed down by an older sibling. My school friends' clothes, hairstyle and fashion sense stood them apart from my street friends and announced them to be kids from English schools. They stood out with their Hollywood-inspired tight trousers and jeans and their Elvis Presley hairstyle – "the Mt. Santubong on top of their heads" was the derisive description of my street friends.

These cross-cultural differences and misunderstandings

Children of the Monkey God 169

between the English-educated, my school mates, and the Chinese-educated, my street friends, would run deeper than mere physical appearances. This was particularly so in the use of spoken English. While the missionary schools felt that it was important that their students should speak English at all times – no doubt to help them to have a better grip on their school subjects – they had no idea of the deep resentment such a policy would cause among some of the local residents. No doubt some of my school mates felt that they were merely following school rules in speaking it wherever they happened to be, blissfully unaware of the resentment such acts would cause with the mainly Chinese-educated residents of the town. It was a subject I found difficult to broach with my school friends, not having yet acquired the necessary social skills at that young age, but some of them found out for themselves the feeling of the town residents towards English school children's inability to read Chinese in one memorable, albeit forgettable after-school incident.

It occurred one early morning at an end of term's outing to Santubong, involving nearly thirty of us from either the third or fourth form at the old Tan Boon Tian Jetty while waiting to get on board the motor launch.

Walking toward us was a Chinese newspaper boy of barely thirteen or fourteen doing his morning round with a thick wad of Chinese dailies slung across one of his arms. He must have thought we were potential customers who might make his morning paper load lighter. He couldn't have been more wrong.

On reaching our group standing at the end of the jetty, he asked whether anyone was interested in buying any newspapers. Before I had time to react or, at least, give a warning of the type required, one of our classmates blurted out that we could not read Chinese. It was an honest and spontaneous reply, albeit naïve and given without any thought, let alone realization that it might cause an adverse reaction or be offensive. And the reaction was prompt and instantaneous.

"You call yourself Chinese", the boy almost screamed, "yet you can't read Chinese. What sort of Chinese are you?" he asked as he turned to walk away, anger and disgust written all over his face.

There were nearly thirty of us there on that morning, boys a few years older than him, but such were his feelings of righteousness that he didn't feel at all daunted that his remarks might provoke the group into giving him a beating. Perhaps, being a member of the young underground and banned communist movement helped, for it was a widely-held belief in the town that newspaper boys of the Chinese dailies were their young recruits responsible for the widespread writing of anti-British slogans on the walls of mainly public buildings in the early sixties. This was a task not difficult for them to carry out under the cover of darkness in the early hours of the morning, with hardly a witness to their deeds. On our part, a sombre mood descended on the group which, fortunately, did not last too long, and the incident was all but forgotten by the time we reached Santubong.

Most of my classmates did not grow up in the streets of Kuching and had hardly any idea of the feelings that the town residents had towards British-style institutions, which had helped mould them in the likeness of British public school boys. And, like the boys of those exalted institutions thousands of miles away in dear old Mother England, we were made to feel that we were something special. More than that, we were made to feel like an elite group, occupying a scholarly, if still not fully academic status, high and above that of everyone else's.

Children of the Monkey God 171

We were constantly reminded that we were the boys of St Thomas', Sarawak's oldest and one of the top schools in the country, especially in our achievements in the yearly Cambridge's Senior School (the equivalent of the English 'O' Levels) and Higher School (the equivalent of the English 'A' Levels) examinations. We would have been the top school, but, for quite a number of years, that honour, unfortunately, had been "unfairly" usurped by the boys of St Joseph's, a catholic school scarcely a mile from where our school was situated. Yes, "unfairly" because their teachers spoon-fed their students and gave them well-prepared notes tailored to gain top marks at the examinations, or so we were told by our teachers.

Several of these teachers said this, I felt, to excuse their own laid-back style of teaching, taking the view that they were more than justified with this approach and perhaps even turning it into an art form. Yes, they said, we might not do that well in the Cambridge exams, and they always seemed to beat us at the inter-school athletics championships as well, but our students grew up to be better leaders and were more successful at the universities and other higher institutes of learning than the boys of St Joseph's. Our methods of teaching equipped our students to study by themselves and to be independent of their teachers, they further claimed. It didn't escape the notice of many of us students that the teachers who regularly made this claim also happened to be the laziest of the teaching staff.

Inevitably, the students of St Joseph's became our biggest and most hated rivals - as had been the case from time immemorial - in all activities, both academic and non-academic, including sports. Our school's hierarchy was always fond of promoting the school spirit by pointing to St Joseph's as the school to beat. Not that we really needed any further spur along that direction.

The black and red colours of St Thomas' and the white and green colours of St Joseph's were always in contention with each other in sports meets, regattas, hockey matches and, above all, in the annual inter-school football match, the highly overrated and coveted McDonald Cup. Other schools participated as well in this knock-out competition, but inevitably the final match would always be fought out between St Thomas' and St Joseph's. Indeed, our headmaster, 'Tiger' Song's daily exaltation at morning assembly to the school football team to turn up for training every afternoon "rain or shine", (his very own words), appeared to have paid off.

Emotions would run high in these matches and, more often than not, would spill onto the supporters of both schools. While nothing more resulted from these highly charged affairs other than a lot of verbal taunts and abuses, there was one year when a huge fight involving twenty to thirty students from both schools did actually take place at Pending Road, a mere few hundred yards from Jubilee Ground, the venue of the match. I was not involved in that fight as I was with a different party of cyclists, consisting mainly of my own classmates, travelling ahead of another bigger party of older boys who were the ones involved – "taunted" into it by the victorious "Josephians," they later claimed. Apparently, the "Thomians" were victorious in that fight, which more or less compensated for our loss at the football field.

The incident was singled out for mention by the headmaster the next morning and, while he made it a point to admonish those students involved in the fight, he did not seem to be unduly keen on wanting to find out who they were. Many of us felt that he was actually quite pleased, albeit secretly, with the way that some of the "boys" were victoriously flying the colours of the school.

The subject of the fight was again taken up by our scripture teacher, Mr Gawing, later on in the morning. A no-nonsense man, a strict disciplinarian and a Dayak, he commanded tremendous respect from his students. Dark, stout, fierce looking and deeply religious, the bible was the only subject he taught and the only book he carried with him. He lived and breathed the bible and there was not a single moment that I can recall when he had drifted away from his favourite teaching subject – the Old Testament. Imagine our surprise, therefore, when he brought up the matter of the fight the moment he stepped into the classroom for the first period of the day.

"So," he said with what looked like a faint expression of a sneer on his face, "you boys must have felt quite proud of yourselves for beating up the boys of St Joseph's." He paused before continuing.

"In our days we would stand on the steps of St Joseph's Church with parangs in our hands," he demonstrated by dramatically moving his right arm to the left of his body to grasp the handle of his imaginary machete, as if in readiness for a battle to the death. Perhaps it was no surprise that Mr Gawing had such a great love for the Old Testament with its tales of great battles, sacrifices, blood, vengeance and retribution. Old Mrs Wong, our New Testament teacher, on the other hand, wept whenever she read the part on the crucifixion of Jesus.

The upholding of the school spirit and its embodiment in nearly all aspects of our lives was all-important in St Thomas'. Hardly a day passed by without some mention being made of the pride we should carry as boys of St Thomas' and of the way we should conduct ourselves as students of that great institution. Although there were no special classes set aside for the teaching of ethics and morals, no effort was spared by some of the teachers in imparting to us the importance of upholding the principles of fairness, honesty, responsibility and integrity. Leading the way was our headmaster of many years, Mr. Song Thian Eng, or "Tiger Song", as he was more popularly known. As evidenced by his nick-name, he was re-known in the way he enforced strict discipline in the school. He was not only a good teacher of mathematics, but also one of the most fair and honest people I had ever come across. Perhaps it was because of his strong influence that the school, at least during the time I was a student there, did not have a strong bully culture. If it existed at all, it was minimal in its impact with very few being affected by it, both as perpetrators or victims. This was particularly the case with the school's prefect system which had the unfortunate result in turning a few of its senior members into "little Hitlers."

Neither was there a so-called "popular group" culture. If anything, in our school there was an anti-popular group culture, whereby any boy wanting to show off or place himself above his peers after having excelled in either sport or study, would quickly find himself isolated, unpopular and without friends. This was, perhaps, again the influence of our headmaster who, in his choice of school captains, always made certain that they were students who were not snobbish or aloof, but, instead, were widely accepted and loved by the main student body. I will always remember his pet instruction to his students in the need for them to be punctual on all occasions, as this would be a yardstick by which their politeness and consideration for other people's time and feelings would be measured. He was also insistent that we should observe the school rule of wearing our school badge with its symbol of the set square and the motto "Aim Higher" at all times during school hours, together with our school uniform of white shirt and dark blue shorts.

My street friends did not have a similar tradition of

Children of the Monkey God

"school spirit" in the Chinese schools they attended - how could they have the same passion as the boys of St Thomas', when they attended schools with names like Chinese School No.1 or No.3? Whenever they chanced to see me wearing my school badge, they would tease me, calling it a "dog tag". This would happen whenever I had forgotten to take it off within the vicinity of Padungan. They made it a point not to wear dark blue shorts, in case they got themselves mistaken as boys of St Thomas', and I made it a point not to wear khaki shorts, the school shorts of the Chinese schools, and most of all, neither I, nor any of my classmates, would ever be caught wearing grey shorts, the school uniform of the boys of St Joseph's.

While the boys of St Joseph's were the bitter rivals of our school, the boys of other streets became the rivals of our street. Padungan and its surrounding area was our domain and, together with my street friends, we roamed its side streets and lanes in groups, big and small, when we were not going to school or doing house chores, although the time spent on the latter activities was minimal.

Although we were not gangsters, we came quite close to becoming like them and the bigger the group we happened to form at any one time, the more brazen and bold we became. Woe unto those owners who had fruit trees by their house or in their orchard. Rambutans, guavas, sugar canes, durians, pomelos, coconuts and all types of fruits became the target of our juvenile raids.

The caretaker of the Henghua Temple at Padungan Road was none too pleased whenever these raids occurred, for we were not at all hesitant in casting rods crudely fashioned from tree branches at the temple's fruit trees. Although these rods were meant to hit and bring down the fruits - the actual targets - a few poorly aimed and carelessly thrown sticks would sometime overshoot, making loud clapping noises as they landed on the dark belian shingles of the temple's roof. I have little doubt that the resulting sounds must have caused no small degree of consternation to some of the devotees and worshippers deep in contemplation inside the temple. We would automatically scatter in all directions whenever that happened, sometimes even before the sticks made contact with the roof, for we knew for sure that the caretaker would appear. Sure enough, there he would be, standing at the back door of the temple, wielding his own rod, a Chinese carrying pole made of hardwood - bigger, heavier and uglier looking than any of the ones we had been using. Shouting and swearing at us in his incomprehensible guttural Henghua dialect he would try to pursue us. Middle-aged and quite heavily-built, he was no match for our young swift legs, and we were often out of his sight before he could even descend the temple steps to give chase. Perhaps, the rolling and awkward gait he had acquired after spending long years out at sea as a fisherman – as most male Henghua were known to do – might have contributed somewhat to his bow-legged style of lame pursuit.

Having the caretaker of the local temple coming after us with a carrying pole was not a surprise; it had happened many a time before and it was something we were prepared for. However, having the wife of one of the officers of the prestigious Borneo Company coming after us during one of our fruit orchard raids was a complete surprise. The sight of a screaming middle-aged English woman - with eyes a-blazing and nostrils a-flaring - charging at us with a big, sinister-looking parang at full speed down the slope of Bukit Mata was something not only unexpected, but unthinkable. They were people who lived in a world of their own, a world apart from the locals and devoid of any involvement with their mundane affairs, a world of privileges and elitism far above the hustle and bustle of the inferior residents of the streets below their hill. These were things best left to either the gardener or the caretaker of the house, one would have thought. She didn't seem to feel that way, judging by her actions, however.

Admittedly, we were trespassing and raiding her fruit garden while her own retinue of domestic servants (which most probably would have been a housekeeper, gardener, chauffeur, cook and their family members) were standing back and looking on from their servants' quarters, unconcerned at our marauding behaviour. Their laid-back attitude was transformed into one of amusement, however, at the sudden appearance of a rather undignified and extremely irate 'mem' (meaning the matriarch or mistress of a European household) chasing a bunch of street urchins over a few stolen fruits with an ugly parang in her hand. Maybe it was their inaction or complacency in not stopping us in the first place, which spurred her to take action herself. She was definitely angry with us. There was very little doubt about that. Whatever it was, we didn't wait to find out.

Although we were more than taken aback at the sight of this parang-wielding 'red-haired' person (a generic local term for all Europeans, for the woman in question was in actual fact grey-haired) we could not help but laugh and giggle as we scattered in different directions, some toward Thompson Road (now Tunku Abdul Rahman Road) and others toward Padungan Road.

The chase didn't last long, however. She gave up the moment we were out of her property and onto the public roads. She was probably aware that her machete-wielding antics might not have gone down that well in preserving that iron-clad veneer of dignified stoicism and placidity that the British prided themselves on – perhaps a momentary lapse on her part. That was the first and only time we ever raided that garden.

As I grew older, I became increasingly aware that some of the activities of my street friends were starting to take on the characteristics of delinquents and even gangsters. Awareness that something is bad for oneself does not always lead to actions being taken to correct it, especially when one is young and reckless, but in this case it did, and I began to gradually extract myself from these activities, and even from socialising with some of my street friends. This became particularly the case after the appearance in the neighbourhood of a character by the name of "Ah Soh".

Although he was not even a resident of our street – for he hailed from one of the south-eastern suburbs of Kuching - Ah Soh was able to establish himself as a leader of the "Padungan Gang" after only a short period of time.

A swarthy, muscular young man of about twenty years', with large piercing eyes, Ah Soh was a firm exponent in the art of kung-fu and, using the skills he had somehow acquired, he soon gathered around him a group of street boys interested in martial art training. Older than these young boys by at least a few years and physically stronger than them, it became an easy matter for him to establish himself as their leader.

There was little doubt Ah Soh was trained in the art of kung-fu, for I, personally, witnessed him once in action in his intervention in a fight between two young men. With skilful and well-timed hand-blocks he was able to stop both of the protagonists from raining blows on each other, while at the same time admonishing them with words such as "Chinese should not fight Chinese" and "We are all brothers" - words that could have been borrowed from the pages of the "Water Margin" - words from someone who was still honourable in his actions and who had not yet begun his own reign of terror. I could see why some of my street friends had such a strong belief in this man and how

Children of the Monkey God

they would be enticed to join his gang.

By tradition, the instructor of a kung-fu class is also the master of the pupils he teaches and Ah Soh made it clear from the start that he was not only their master, but would not tolerate any challenge to his authority. Although charismatic in his own way, as most strong leaders are, he was not at all lacking in unscrupulous means of exacting loyalty and obedience from his band of followers. Cajoling, bullying and beating his followers into submission - with the aid of newly-appointed and trusted lieutenants and right-hand men - became the daily practices of his kung-fu class. Any of his followers showing unquestioning loyalty would be rewarded with promotion and treated with favouritism, whereas, conversely, dissension by any member would see them punished and ostracised.

Transition from being the revered master of a martial art class to being the absolute leader or 'elder brother' of a street gang became a mere formality for Ah Soh, and the thin line demarcating the two different organizations became blurred to the point of non-existence. My street friends' interest in football, kite-flying, ping-pong, swimming and such like started to wane as they became more and more involved with Ah Soh and his criminal activities, making complete their transition from kung-fu students to fully-fledged street gang members.

Initially, the group declared itself to be a band of heroes and outlaws similar in vein to the honourable and chivalrous characters of the Chinese Classics and complete with the laudable and altruistic objective of helping the poor and less fortunate. There was even a secret triad ceremony to formalize the birth of the gang involving the slaughter of a rooster, the drinking of its blood and the swearing of allegiance as loyal and trusted blood brothers at Teluk Karang, a small coastal hill a few miles north-east of Mt

Santobong. However, unbeknown to the gang members, the Sarawak Police's Criminal Investigation Division (the CID), following a tip-off, were lying in wait for them, and all the participating gang members, including Ah Soh and a cousin of mine, were arrested and charged with illegal triad activities.

The arrest was a big story, not only in our street, but throughout the town and the whole country, capturing the main headline in the Sarawak Tribune, the country's biggest circulation daily newspaper. Sarawak had not seen such brazen acts of illegal activities from the Chinese community since the Hakka Rebellion of 1857, more than a hundred years ago. My family elders of grandparents, parents, aunts and uncles, used the occasion as a timely reminder to us of how fortuitous it was for my brothers and me that we were not involved with Ah Soh and his gang, and how bad it was that my cousin was arrested. What a terrible boy he had become since joining Ah Soh, lamented my poor aunt.

The arrest failed to act as a deterrent to the gang's activities, however, and, if anything, it added to their dubious reputation as a gang that deserved to be respected and feared. Their subsequent release, following a short stint in jail, saw them bolder and more brazen in their behaviour, as the neighbourhood looked on them with awe at their new-found reputation. Their initial aim of helping the poor and less fortunate became quickly forgotten as they embarked on various projects of operating illegal cock-fighting, gambling dens, extortion schemes and 'protection' rackets, while at the same time taking on and defeating other smaller rival bands of the town in nefarious gang war-fare. For all intent and purpose they seemed to be unstoppable in their criminal activities as they went about their objective of expanding their operations and increasing their sphere of control.

It caused me no small degree of pain as I watched some

of my long-time friends taking on the persona of Ah Soh as they bullied and terrorised the neighbourhood. They became almost strangers to me and the best acknowledgement I could get out of them was a mere nod if we happened to come across each other on the street. They knew my dislike of Ah Soh and his activities and, while they would not ask me to join them, they preferred to keep their distance from me and from those others who were not gang members. They had become members of an exclusive club, it would seem.

Not all my friends from the street joined Ah Soh's gang, however. Some, like me, decided this was not to their liking, and while we managed to get together sometimes for games of football, cards and dice, particularly during Chinese New Year, things were never the same again, especially with so many of our former friends missing.

Ah Soh's reign of terror in the neighbourhood ended with his death scarcely a few years following that infamous initiation ceremony near Santobong. His death was not, ironically, at the hands of any rival gangs, but rather from two of his trusted lieutenants. Sick and tired of the physical and mental abuses meted out to them, they made the bold decision to ambush their much-feared 'eldest brother' at a cock-fighting pit. Even his high skills in kung-fu were not good enough to protect him from the surprise vicious bludgeoning carried out with a couple of heavy hardwood shoulder poles, an instrument much favoured by Chinese coolies for lugging heavy goods. To his credit, Ah Soh bore himself like a true hero of the Chinese Classics, standing his ground and refusing to flinch or bolt, perhaps subscribing to the Chinese motto of "though you may beat me to death, I will never run," despite the pleas of many of the spectators at the cockfight for him to flee.

This eye-witness account of Ah Soh's last stand might

have served as an inspiration for his posthumous deification by his remaining followers, who, in the months following his death, regularly paid their respects to his portrait with prayers and offerings of food before a shrine they had created in his honour.

His gang was never the same again however, breaking up quite soon after his death and, for my part, I was glad not to have been involved with either them or their activities.

RELATIVES

"Look at her buttocks. She would be excellent for child bearing – that one. She is going to bear some lucky man lots of children," said Tai Pak, my eldest paternal uncle.

The subject of his admiration was a rather large Indonesian woman of Chinese Hakka descent, a member of the third or fourth generation of the Hakka gold miners, who had sought their fortunes in the once rich gold fields of south-western Kalimantan. Generously endowed, she was not at all shy in flaunting herself in front of the men with a sarong gathered at chest level. She had just finished taking her bath and, coming out of the washroom, she must have known the effect she would have on the men lounging in the sitting room of our house in Padungan Road. The air reeked of the heavy scent of the cheap Indonesian soap she had just used on her body. She was single, unattached and in her early to mid-thirties.

"I wouldn't mind having her as my second wife," said my youngest uncle.

"You shameless lot. Look at you. Salivating like dogs," said Ah Por in great annoyance at the reaction that the Indonesian woman had had on her two married sons.

The Indonesian woman left our house later on in the evening and I never saw her again. She had just arrived the night before with Uncle Chang from Bau after having trekked through the watershed dividing Sarawak from the Sambas region of Indonesian Kalimantan a few days ago.

Although we were all told to address him as such,

"Uncle Chang" was not really an uncle in the true sense of the word. He was, in truth, a distant nephew of my grandmother but it was enough to make him an uncle in the extended family system of the Chinese. In any event, he carried the same surname as my grandmother, and that in itself qualified him to be called "uncle", in line with the traditional belief that all persons of the same surname are descendents from the same male ancestor.

I can recall Uncle Chang making three or four visits to our house when I was a boy and each one of these visits would invariably lift Ah Por's mood. His appearances at the doorsteps of the house were always unannounced. This was the result, in those days, of a non-existent telephone service between Sarawak and Kalimantan, and, indeed, any postal service, even if it existed, would have seen the letter arriving many weeks or even months after it had been sent, if at all.

My grandmother looked forward to the visits of Uncle Chang, for he would bring with him tidings of her family from across the border, a family she had not seen for nearly fifty years after her marriage to Ah Kung; a family she would never see again.

This latest visit of Uncle Chang proved to be no exception. She was initially pleased at seeing him after the lapse of a few years, but her pleasure soon turned to ire, as she was none too happy with Uncle Chang's travelling companion, whom she felt had a disruptive influence on the male members of the family. There was little doubting that she was elated to see Uncle Chang, but there was more than a touch of annoyance toward him for what she saw as his irresponsible behaviour in bringing to the house a woman she considered a bit too free with her body language.

Although Ah Por was not a prude, she was also not too well disposed towards any tendency by the male members of her family to take a second wife, a concubine or even a mistress, as was the customary practice with some families. As she could see that this travelling companion of Uncle Chang's was starting to give such a subversive idea to a couple of her sons she made it known she wanted her out of the house as soon as possible. It must have been quite painful for her even to hint of her displeasure with the woman from Kalimantan for Uncle Chang had come a long way from her home village and custom dictated that he must be accorded all the hospitality and welcome that a visiting relative deserved. There was also the possibility that she might never see him again, for every trip that he made could possibly be his last, as Uncle Chang's visits were not only very rare, but also fraught with dangers.

Up until the 1960s most local people took the view that traders and merchants crossing the borders were merely following the footsteps of the various Dayak tribes and other indigenous people. From time immemorial, these tribes considered themselves free to roam the whole region unfettered by any sense of national boundaries. The British authorities had a different idea, however. People like Uncle Chang were treated as smugglers to be prosecuted if caught, and put into jail if found guilty.

Dried python, crocodile skins and dried tobacco leaves were the main items that these people dealt in, although the occasional request from a young, marriageable woman or her family to cross the borders with them to seek a husband in return for a commission was a welcome bonus. This would have been the case with the latest travelling companion of Uncle Chang, although I rather suspected that because of her age she would have been equally happy just to end up as the mistress or concubine of an older man, rather than as the bride of a young bachelor. Perhaps my grandmother suspected that this was the woman's intention as well. She had no wish for any of her sons to take her as mistress or concubine; hence her edict to Uncle Chang. I never found out what happened to her after her departure from our house the following morning, except that one of my cousins saw her working as a waitress in one of the town's many coffee shops a few months later.

Uncle Chang made only one more trip after that. This was after a lapse of a few years and, unlike his previous trip, this last trip had a happy ending, for his travelling companion this time was a young woman who eventually was wedded to one of my cousins, a son of my eldest uncle. Ah Por was very happy with the outcome, as this young maid proved to be a likeable and hardworking granddaughter-in-law. Uncle Chang, in turn, was forgiven for the perceived lapse committed on his previous trip.

The border between Sarawak and Kalimantan became a battle zone shortly after that last trip of Uncle Chang's. Official hostilities between the British and, later on, the Malaysian government on the one side, and the Indonesian government on the other, lasted for nearly five years from 1962-1966. This was the period of the so-called "Confrontation" policy of former Indonesian President Sukarno, with the effect of making the border and its surrounding area a dangerous place for anyone. Cross-border operators and traders like Uncle Chang were virtually forced out of business as a consequence, and we never saw him again, thus breaking any link my grandmother had with her relatives living on the other side of the border.

Although the ousting of President Sukarno in 1968 practically spelled the end of his policy of "confrontation" against Malaysia, regular patrolling of the border area by troops of both sides - introduced during this period of mutual aggression - continued to be carried out for the next few decades. The days when the border could be freely crossed without any passport or other form of travel documents were over; and consequently so was our contact with my grandmother's relatives as well.

Ah Por, however, was not the only Indonesian member of our extended family in Sarawak. One of her older brothers, a widower, crossed the border to join her some years after her marriage to Ah Kung, hoping to seek his fortune in Sarawak, as it was generally recognised that more opportunities existed on this side of the border. He joined Ah Kung's workforce in the coconut plantation at a time when my grandfather was going through a period of expansion. He was "Kiu Kung," our beloved kite-making grand uncle. He came with only the shirt on his back and, with no property to pass on to his only son, he secured the latter's future by letting Ah Kung adopt him. This required his changing his surname from "Chang" to "Chu" in accordance with strict customary requirements, thus making him eligible to inherit my grandfather's property on a par with Ah Kung's natural-born sons.

Although practically all the relatives of my grandmother's were on the other side of the border and, therefore, Indonesian in nationality, they were still Hakka, and in terms of social and cultural practices, as well as speech, it would be extremely difficult for the casual observer to detect any difference between them and us. The parents of my grandparents might have been members of opposite warring clans during the period known as the "Wars of the Kongsi" between the 1770s to 1850s, but they were still Hakka originating from the same region in China and, although they were not clansmen, they had become kinsmen through marriage.

Not so with the relatives on my mother's side, who were Hokkien people. Generally speaking, a meeting of Hakka and Hokkien in the days when I was a young boy tended to create an uncomfortable situation, if not quite a volatile one. Perhaps that was why there were not that many gatherings between my paternal and maternal relatives.

There was little denying that there were common denominators shared by these two groups. Both were, after all, members of the huge pool of Chinese people, Han and non-Han. Those who had not yet been converted to Christianity, celebrated the same festivals, worshipped the same gods and followed the same principles of ancestral worship and filial piety. Yet, significant differences in attitude and practice existed between them on quite a wide range of issues.

For a start, they spoke different dialects. This could present quite a problem in the days when I was a boy, because of the unwillingness of most members of either side to learn the dialect of the other. The Hokkien took the view that the Hakka dialect was a crude peasant dialect unworthy of their attention, while the Hakka saw the Hokkien as city upstarts. If they were unwilling to learn the Hakka dialect, why should they be bothered to learn theirs? It was at a time when the social line between the two groups was still quite clearly delineated, and very few members from either side had yet managed to cross that line. Most of the Hakka in Sarawak were the descendants of miners and farmers from China and subsequent generations of these original migrants tended to follow in the same footsteps as their forebears. The same pattern occurred in the commercially-inclined Hokkien community, with later generations of their members ending up as shopkeepers, traders, businessmen, civil servants and professionals in line with that of their forebears.

Thus it was that on my father's side of the family I had relatives who were coconut, rubber, pepper, durian and fruit farmers. They were rustic and earthy and not at all hesitant about using strong terms to convey their likes and dislikes. On the other hand, my Hokkien relatives were people of more genteel calling. They were civil servants, professionals and businessmen, and hardly a swear word passed their lips, not even in anger.

I had to be a social and cultural chameleon as a boy, growing up as I did in these two different and sometimes quite contradictory worlds of paternal and maternal relatives. At home and in my Hakka world, I would not only be speaking Hakka, but would be very much at home with its rustic and earthy style, where the equivalent of the English four-letter word would flow freely. With my Hokkien relatives, on the other hand, I had to take care not to use words that would be considered unacceptable in polite company. It was not difficult to switch from one style of speaking to the other, although the occasional slip of the tongue would occur, much to the chagrin of my mother.

These minor "cross-cultural" differences between dialect groups were not uncommon when I was a boy, but, in my case, they were more pronounced because of the "cross-dialect marriage" of my parents. My father was the only child of his family to have married a Hokkien woman, with his other four brothers and four sisters all marrying Hakka. Conversely, my mother was the only child in her family to have married a Hakka, her other brothers, of whom there were six, and sisters, of whom there were two, all marrying Hokkien. This was compounded by the fact that my extended family was, by anyone's standard, massive. My immediate relatives, counting only uncles, aunties and cousins from both sides, would have numbered nearly two hundred.

The relatives on my mother's side of the family were "exterior" relatives, as opposed to my father's relatives who were our "interior" relatives, a distinction based on whether they were relatives of the male or female bloodline. Thus, Ah Kong and Ah Mah, meaning grandfather and grandmother in the Hokkien dialect were my "exterior grandparents", while Ah Kung and Ah Por, meaning the same thing in the Hakka dialect, were our "interior grandparents". Translated into political term the word "interior" in Chinese has the same meaning as "domestic" while that of "exterior" has its English equivalent word, namely "foreign". Put another way, "interior" relatives had the same status as people of the same nationality, while "exterior" relatives were regarded as having the status of foreigners. To further distinguish these statuses, different titles would be used for calling senior relatives, such as aunts and uncles, depending on where they stood in the "interior" or "exterior" category, as opposed to the use of generic terms of "uncles" and "aunts" in western culture. Thus an "interior" uncle (a father's brother) in the Hakka dialect would be called "ah shook", while that of an "exterior" uncle (a mother's brother) would be referred to as "ah kiu". Theoretically, one was supposed to treat the interior relatives with a greater degree of closeness, respect and affection than the exterior relatives, although it didn't always work out that way.

Most of my "exterior" relatives lived in and around Kuching, and plenty of opportunities, therefore, existed for me to keep on seeing them, especially with the numerous festivals and birthdays that seemed to occur with such frequency in the Chinese calendar.

The biggest celebration in the Chinese lunar calendar was without doubt the Chinese New Year and, although it did not involve a gathering of the clan in the way that a grand or a great grand parent's birthday would, it was a customary requirement for us to call on all my mother's Hokkien relatives, in particular her parents and her siblings.

Children of the Monkey God

My Hakka relatives, however, did not attach as much importance to these New Year's visits as my mother's, and I can only recall a few visits made on them.

Although these New Year calls on my maternal relatives appeared, on the face of them, to be just that, certain protocol still had to be observed. The first involved the seniority in rank of the relatives, especially that of my mother's parents, who had to be called upon before her other older brothers and sister. These visits symbolised the respects she must pay, not only to her parents, but her older siblings (not dissimilar to the tribute system that Imperial China used to insist on from vassal states and countries) and, vice versa, the siblings and those relatives such as nephews and nieces younger than her, had to pay her a visit before she would reciprocate. Thus, an older relative would make a call on you only after you had carried out your duty in paying your respects to them.

My mother's first and mandatory New Year visit to her parents, made before anyone else, was not only out of respect for them as the elders occupying the pinnacle of the family hierarchy, but perhaps also out of fear that if she failed to do so, words of her dereliction of filial duty would reach them. There was little doubt of that eventually occurring in the grapevine of the complex extended Hokkien family system, as there would always be someone who would proffer information to my grandparents that so and so was at "her house early this morning"; and if it happened that that person had failed to call on them beforehand, the rule of protocol would have been broken. Words of admonishment would then be issued to the alleged offender. Such was the Hokkien way.

Rules of protocol regarding filial piety had to be strictly observed, as my mother never failed to remind us, as we trotted after her on our way to pay our respects to her parents on the first day of Chinese New Year.

"Don't shame me in front of them. Speak only when you are spoken to. And don't run around the house. Sit properly and be very still in your chair. Otherwise they will think you didn't come out of me; don't be like Sun Wu Kung, the Monkey God, who came out of a boulder with no parents to guide him. You are not the Monkey God and you didn't come out of a boulder, so make sure you don't behave like him."

I accompanied her on these visits each year with mixed feelings. While the "ang pows", or the money that came wrapped in red paper, were certainly something I looked forward to, having to sit very still and quiet at all times was something I didn't enjoy one bit.

Sitting quietly like a mouse and not saying a word unless spoken to, was merely our second act of obeisance. Our first was to pay our annual homage. Our maternal grandparents, like the Chinese emperors of old, would be sitting upright in their stiff wooden chairs, in readiness for us, while we would go down on our knees, starting with the oldest to the youngest. Clasping our hands together as in prayer, we would then wish them a happy and prosperous new year.

"Why must you go down on your knees and pray to elders who are not yet dead?" Ah Kung would provocatively ask us without fail every year at either the start or the end of our annual pilgrimage to our maternal grandparents' home. In an assertion of his senior ranking as an "interior grandparent', he would sometimes add for good measure the following statement:

"You don't bend your knees to me, so why should you do it to them?" or "I never ask you to kow-tow to me, so

Children of the Monkey God

why should they ask it of you?"

My mother was never too pleased with this statement of Ah Kung's and, while she never said anything in response, I could see the anger simmering just beneath the surface. For, filial piety with her and her family was a big thing, perhaps even the central, guiding principle of their life, and my grandfather's statement struck at the very core of that belief-system. As far as she was concerned, Ah Kung's statement was an act of sabotage, which would only encourage us to commit further acts of filial disobedience. Yet to openly defy her own father-in-law, or to show any sign of dissension, would, in itself, be un-filial, something she would never bring herself to do, although there were times when I thought she would burst out with some strong remarks of her own against Ah Kung's statement. But - a credit to her mother's training – she never did.

On his part, Ah Kung's statement should not be taken to mean that he deliberately tried to encourage us to be un-filial to our elders. Far from it. No, Ah Kung was merely being Ah Kung and a Hakka, a proud, dignified man who had, throughout his life, held firmly to the belief that he would never bend his knees to any man. For us to kowtow before another human being, even though they were our maternal grandparents, was something abhorrent to him.

Ah Kong and Ah Mah lived on the first floor of a small townhouse in the heart of the commercial area of Kuching in Main Bazaar. Ah Kong had already retired for more than twenty years from the Sarawak civil service when I would call on him as a six or seven year-old with my mother and brothers. A frail old man who had difficulty remembering the names of his grandchildren, he existed on his civil service life-pension with Ah Mah by his side, albeit with the help of a domestic servant to cook for them and to look after their other daily needs. No other family member lived with them, all their sons and daughters having already married with homes and families of their own. He had an ancestral home once, a grand Chinese mansion on the outskirts of town, where my mother was born and grew up. This house, having already been sold a number of years ago, and his children having left home, would mark the beginning of the decline of the traditional Hokkien extended family system in Kuching.

Although my maternal grandfather was not a "towkay" in the generally accepted sense of a rich merchant or businessman, he was still able to live the life of one during the time he was with the Sarawak Civil Service. However, the funds that were available to him as a civil servant would have limited his ability to keep up with this lifestyle, while also putting a tremendous strain on his efforts to properly keep the big house that he had inherited from his family.

By its very nature and size, an extended family required a lot of money to run. The first, and sometimes even the second generation of migrant Hokkien towkay from China were generally able to do this, for example, Song Kheng Hai and Ong Tiang Swee, a couple of big-time local towkay in Kuching. Their children and their children's children would have found this an extremely difficult act to follow, however. This was especially so when these later generations decided to venture into the not-so-traditional area of the colonial civil service and the professions. While the movement into this new ground might signal the gradual demise of the traditional extended family system, it also signalled the emergence of a new Chinese middle class in Sarawak.

My maternal grandfather was a member of this newly emerging middle class. Educated in English, Ah Kong joined the civil service as a young clerk and stayed there until his retirement at the mandatory age of 55, his long and faithful service with the government having earned him a long service medal and lifetime pension. A large framed portrait of him wearing this very chunky, heavy-looking long service medal formed the centre-piece of their small living room. While it served to remind his visitors of his achievements in the civil service it was, at the same time, an object of incongruity, especially in the cramped living room of their small townhouse. It seemed especially so in the absence of a support cast, consisting of his previously large extended family of six surviving sons and three daughters, numerous grandchildren and servants. It would not have been out of place in its previous home, however, large and ornate as it would have been and hanging proudly from the wall of the guest room of the mansion where my mother grew up as a girl. Sadly, the huge upkeeps of the place proved to be too much of a burden on his small pension, and what was an ancestral home for a few generations was eventually sold off. I remember some of the memories my mother told me she had of her ancestral home – the bustle, the noise and the energy generated by so many people living under one roof and their constant interaction with each other.

Following our yearly prostration before our two elders and our wish that they had a happy new year, Ah Mah would respond to our salutations by giving each of us her customary new year's gift of $1.20 wrapped in a piece of red paper – the "ang pow". This was invariably followed by her annual and unfailing admonition to us to study hard and pass our exams for qualification into the civil service.

In the meantime, Ah Kong, too weak to speak, would merely smile and nod his head in agreement, while my mother rendered her "annual" report of our "doings" and "misdoings" to her parents, although there were more of the latter than the former. Like a schoolgirl before her school mistress, she would relate all our deeds of the past year - the more important ones, anyway. At such times, we became part of the furniture of my grandmother's house – bare and spartan as it was.

True to my mother's instruction not to say anything unless spoken to in the presence of my grandparents, I would try to keep very still and be "invisible". As I have said before, this was not an easy thing to do. The stiff wooden chairs we were sitting on were hard and uncomfortable. For the best part of an hour – for that was how long the visit normally lasted - I found myself shifting and fidgeting, for it was the only movement I was allowed without inviting hard stares from my mother. It was at times like this that I was grateful for the freedom of movement I was allowed to have when I was with my "interior" grandparents.

There was little doubt we were very much in awe of our maternal grandparents, especially our grandmother. My mother saw to that. Other than her admonishment to speak only when spoken to, a few other warnings would also be issued before we mounted the narrow staircase leading into their living room.

"You must accept her new year's red packet with both hands - not one hand. You must remain seated in your chair and you cannot run amok and scream at each other, like you do at Ah Kung's house. Otherwise, you will upset Ah Mah and Ah Kong. Worse still, they will think that I have not brought you up properly. And don't grab at the New Year's cakes and titbits like so many ghosts of the seven-and-a-half moon (hungry ghosts)"; that last instruction of my mother's was, with little doubt, the most difficult to carry out.

Being the first house we had to call on, and having to hold back from attacking these festive delicacies so early in the morning before breakfast was never going to be easy. Fortunately for us, Ah Mah was only human and, after the mandatory prostration and kowtowing were over and done with, she was more than happy to see our faces light up when the delicacies were passed around by either her or her domestic helper.

Yes, there was a human side to her. I saw it on a few occasions when my mother's side of the family came together for a wedding or birthday celebration. She was, undoubtedly, the strict old dowager toward most people around her – harsh, severe and unsmiling - but there was one person who was always able to break down her Confucian armour – her youngest daughter, or See Yee, my fourth maternal aunt, one of the two surviving sisters of my mother.

For either one of her parents' birthday celebrations, my mother would spend nearly the whole day at her eldest brother's three-storey house at Ban Hock Road. Centrally located and bigger than most of the other relatives' houses, it was in a better position to accommodate the fifty or so people who would gather there. Perhaps, his seniority in rank as the eldest sibling might have had something to do with it, or perhaps it was simply his affable and accommodating nature.

At these gatherings of the "clan", the older female members of the extended family were the ones responsible for the organizing and the cooking. My mother, together with most of the other women, young and old, would disappear into the kitchen to prepare the many main dishes, cakes and titbits that the Nonya were famous for, with recipes passed down from Ah Mah. I would, again, be assigned to sit on a hard chair with the usual admonishment from my mother to behave myself. Somehow or other, my two older brothers had always been able to manage to wheedle their way out of accompanying my mother on these trips by making some excuses and, since these functions were not of the same nature as that of the mandatory new year's homage, my mother would somehow relent to their pleas.

I was left on my own for most of the time, in spite of the huge number of relatives gathered there. The din was quite deafening, for, although the house was three-storey, the kitchen was situated on the ground floor and nearly all the activities - the chopping, and cooking, chatting, shouting and playing of the children – were also carried out on the ground floor. Some of the more lonely times of my life were spent amidst these crowded gathering and noise.

There were a lot of children present at these parties - mainly "exterior" cousins. Most of them were of my age; the post war baby boomers of Sarawak, so to speak, yet I felt isolated. They were my relatives but, without the benefit of getting ourselves better acquainted, other than the two or three times we came together to celebrate the birthday of our elders each year, it was practically impossible to get close to each other. But, above all, I was to them not only a Hakka boy, but also an "exterior" relative. Sitting there with nothing to do and no one to play with or talk to, I would feel extremely bored, when someone would loudly proclaim the arrival of See Yee.

"See Yee," or my fourth aunt in the Hokkien dialect, was the youngest sister of my mother. She was, also in my mind, the most colourful of all my relatives, paternal and maternal included. Being the youngest of all the daughters, she became the child most doted upon by her parents and older siblings, as was commonly the case in Chinese families. In most cases, this would have a negative effect and the youngest child would, more often than not, turn out spoilt and unruly. Not so in the case of See Yee. The love, attention and affection showered upon her seemed to have a positive effect, and those people around her were rewarded with this wonderful person, who was able to light up the place the moment she arrived. Confucian protocol, requiring proper behaviour from its women, was thrown out of the window upon See Yee's entrance into any house. How she managed to do it will always remain a mystery to me. She was an electrifying person in every sense of the word and the party always livened up with her arrival. Extroverted, eccentric, vivacious, lively and cheerful, no one could resist her charms or her earthy humour, not even her strict mother. She would announce her entry with a shout, a call, a scream or a laugh, depending on her mood.

"See Yee is here," someone would always call out, as soon as she was spotted approaching the house.

That call not only announced her arrival, it also meant that a licence had been granted to anyone who was willing to participate with her in all sorts of tomfoolery. With See Yee as the ringleader, mayhem would ensue. Anyone within reaching distance of her would be pulled in to do the mumbo or the cha-cha or any of the dances that took her fancy. It was not so much that she was not able to do the dances properly; the hilarity was provided more by her mimicking and mock actions. Tightly wrapped in her sarong, her exaggerated moves and twists would invariably bring the house down with grandparents, aunts, uncles and cousins collapsing in heaps of laughter. More fun and laughter ensued when she was joined in the dance by Tua Kim, her eldest sister-in-law. The two of them – Tua Kim, short, round, plump, bespectacled and in her sixties - and See Yee, only slightly taller and almost just as round and in her early forties – were truly a sight to behold, bumping each other's bottoms as they gyrated their way around the house.

That over, See Yee would turn her attention to her other favourite sport – tits-squeezing. Any woman, young and old, with the exception of my grandmother, was a target. It was pandemonium as the female members of the household scrambled to get out of her way, all the while laughing and squealing as they fled, either looking for a place to hide or someone to attack. Very soon nearly all the women would be involved in the tits-squeezing game started by See Yee. There was nothing sexual in it, as far as I could see. To the participants, it was perhaps an extension of the tickling game that children would occasionally indulge in, and all that was needed to extend it was for somebody audacious like See Yee to become the catalyst. If anything more could be read into it, it might be perhaps the women's way of expressing their dissension at the male-dominated Confucian society – their way of thumbing their noses at their men, for this was one game in which the men could not, and were not, allowed to participate. Everyone accepted her antics with humour and I had never seen anyone annoyed or angry at her outrageous behaviour.

My mother told me her youngest sister had always been cheeky and outrageous from as far back as she could remember. She was always able to get around her parents, in spite of their best efforts to contain her and impose some form of control. Perhaps being the youngest daughter had something to do with it, a lot of latitude being given to the youngest child as is normally the case within the Chinese family. But whatever it was, my grandmother was never able to get the better of my irrepressible aunt. Her strict insistence on the proper decorum being observed by her children at all times was not followed by See Yee and my grandmother preferred to collapse in laughter at her jokes and pranks, rather than get angry with her.

See Yee was not only the sole female member, or quite possibly the only member of the family, male or female, who was able to exact such concessions from her parents; she was also the only daughter of the family permitted to attend school. My mother and her other older sister never went to school, my grandparents adhering strictly to the traditional belief that, since they, like all women, would end up in the kitchen for most of their life, it would have been a waste of time and money to have an education.

But this view was starting to change at the time when See Yee was growing up as a young girl in the 1920s and 1930s. It was a Chinese school she attended, unlike her six surviving brothers, who all went to English missionary schools and who all ended up in the civil service. Going to a Chinese school meant that there was no expectation placed on her, other than to get an education.

But See Yee being See Yee, she got more than an education – she also got herself a husband. It was one of her teachers she ended up marrying, much to the chagrin of her parents, for he was nearly fifteen years her senior. There was, of course, a huge uproar from her parents, but in the end love prevailed and See Yee was the only daughter in the family whose marriage was one not arranged by her parents, a further break with tradition made by this strong-willed and "wayward" daughter.

There was no doubt that See Yee was one of my favourite aunts and I was always more than keen to accompany my mother when she decided to visit her. Unfortunately, these visits were too few and far in between. She would have loved to see her younger sister more often but See Yee's house was situated a few miles from where we lived and, with the bus service inadequate and her inability to drive a car a handicap, going there was always a constraint. However, those times when we managed to drop in on her were times that I treasure with a great deal of fondness.

See Yee and her family lived in an attap house at Crookshank Road made of timber and dry thatched palm leaves rented out to her family by a kind landowner for a very low monthly rent. She was the poorest of her brothers and sisters, all of whom had houses of their own built of concrete and bricks. Her husband had already retired as a school teacher (without any pension entitlement) even when I was only nine or ten years' old and, with a huge family of six or seven young children to bring up, most of them younger than me, she and her family survived on the little income she generated from selling home-made cakes, cookies and other tit-bits that Nonya women were renowned for.

Her house was fairly large and was always kept immaculately clean. Even without any air-conditioning it was always cool inside, much more so than the expensively built concrete houses that were springing up all over the suburbs of Kuching. The kitchen was necessarily large in comparison to all the other rooms, in view of the use it was put to by her family. It was her work place, in which nearly every member of her family was involved in the business of preparing and making cakes, cookies tit-bits and sometimes even vegetable and chilly pickles.

But what I particularly liked about her place was the chicken coops that she had next to the house. The house itself stood on a compound of perhaps half an acre from which she had somehow managed to turn the back portion into a small abattoir with numerous coops for her free range chicken, ducks and geese. There was even a small shallow pond in the middle of the fenced-in area for her ducks to play in. The chicken and ducks were for her family consumption but their eggs were mainly for use in her cake and cookie business. A few rambutan, guava and star fruit trees gave us the chance to pick as many fruits as we wanted. The chicken, ducks and geese provided us with a diversion when we were bored.

Children of the Monkey God

Above all, we loved it when she took out her full array of goodies for our consumption. She never failed to give us full encouragement to eat as much as we wanted. This encouragement was always in the form of a wish, a traditional practice that often accompanied a gift or present. To older people and on their birthdays, especially milestone birthdays, like a 60th, 70th or 80th, a wish for a long life was common, and in the gift of a red packet to young children during the New Year's celebration, it was mainly success in their studies and a quick and healthy growth.

"Eat, eat and you will grow big and tall," she would say to us.

To make her wish come true we always ate to our heart's content. And to her credit, my mother did not deem it necessary to stop us from doing so. Not in See Yee's house, anyway.

Going to See Yee's house was fun, not only because she was good company, but also because she never talked down to us, unlike most of my other maternal or "exterior" relatives. It was also one of those rare occasions when my mother found it unnecessary to tell us to behave ourselves or to remain seated in our chair and be still. We were free to roam about as we pleased, more or less. And we were always disappointed at the sight of my father's car coming down the driveway to take us home.

GHOSTS, DEMONS & MONSTERS

"Never point your finger at the moon," my mother used to warn us when we were little children. "It is a sign of great disrespect to the moon goddess living there, for you will never know whether she may take offence at your rudeness and decide to come down to earth in the middle of the night to punish you by slitting your ear lobes. If, however, you were to accidentally point at the moon you must apologise to her by rubbing your ear lobes with your hand. That way you will placate her and stop her from punishing you."

We didn't fancy the thought of having our ear lobes slit by the Moon Goddess and so we were always careful as children not to point our finger at her. Naturally, if we happened to do so by accident we made certain we made immediate amends by rubbing our earlobes.

"Never swear or reprimand the wind for being too light or too strong," said some of my elders "or else you will, for certain, invite the wrath of the Wind God, who will teach you a lesson for your rudeness and disrespect by giving you such a powerful slap across your face that your mouth will remain twisted to one side for the rest of your life."

Thus, it was by this and other means that as children we were gradually introduced to the mystical, and often, superstitious, world of the Chinese. And I doubt it is much different for children from other cultures. Folklore, stories and nursery rhythms are adults' ways to teach, punish, excite and frighten little children. They were also employed to entertain and romanticise, thus making them more interesting and palatable.

For most of the time they are merely the means by which one generation passes its knowledge and belief-system to the next - no matter how ludicrous some of these ideas might be. And thus it was a quite commonly held belief among some of our older folks that stroke victims, who had suffered some form of facial distortion, were actually people who had offended the Wind God. The force of the slap delivered to their face was such as to cause a permanent disability that could not be healed by mere conventional medicine. The only known cure was by way of appeasement in the form of prayers, gifts and sacrifices to be offered in the temples or on open ground – "to pray to the heaven" as they would put it.

Ghosts, spirits, monsters, demons and lost souls abounded everywhere and we were constantly reminded as children to take precautions to avoid colliding with them. Babies, young children, the sick, and elderly, with their weak or below-average 'chi', were particularly vulnerable. Extra care had to be taken by this 'class' of people in the participation of activities and events such as funerals and weddings.

The latter would no doubt cause some readers to puzzle over its inclusion, some of whom may well ask how anything disastrous could befall someone attending such a joyous occasion as a wedding. The answer is simple and there is really no mystery to it, according to the firm followers of this belief.

A bride is said to have very aggressive 'chi' and perhaps this powerful 'chi' of hers might have something to do with the fact that she is the main player in what, arguably, is the most important day of her life. Her boundless energy or 'chi' might just tend to get out of control at times, leading to a psychic attack on some unsuspecting guests. Or it might be a pure and simple case of the anger she feels at being forced into an arranged marriage, as was the case with most of the marriages in those days.

Personally, I prefer the latter explanation. The fact that she had to control her feelings by staying calm the whole time during the wedding proceedings might also make matters worse by adding more power to her 'chi'; all those repressed feelings would have had to express themselves eventually, zooming in on someone unfortunate enough to be in her path.

Whatever is the reason, it is not uncommon for relatives and guests to clear a pathway for the bride, especially upon her grand entrance into the groom's family home. More often than not, this practice of avoiding a head-on-collision with the bride would lead to hilarious acts of avoidance, causing old grannies, aunts and other relatives of the groom - upon learning of the arrival of the bridal car – to scatter in all directions in a desperate bid to get to the nearest available hiding place with as much alacrity as they could possibly muster in their tight–fitting sarongs.

It is said that this is the moment when the bride's 'chi' is at its most potent, for the entry into the groom's house is symbolically the last bridge she has burned in the path that she has taken, or in the case of an arranged marriage, the path that has been carved out for her by her parents. It is also accepted that these 'attacks' are the sub-conscious workings of the bride's psychic mind and nothing personal is attributed to them. Thus, she is not personally to be blamed if someone were to fall sick after attending the wedding, while on the other hand she is also required to understand and accept the reason for a close friend's or relative's failure to turn up at the wedding or the undignified manner in which some of her soon-to-be relatives and guests scatter at the sight of her.

"Well, you see," the friend or relative would regrettably inform the parents or sometimes even the bride-to-be herself, "I went to the temple the other day and the medium there told me my 'chi' is rather low at the moment and that I must therefore avoid going to any funerals or weddings in case I become the subject of a psychic attack."

It is considered bad form to question the validity of this claim and as far as I know it is the one excuse that seems to work every time. It is not uncommon for anyone who wishes to avoid going to a wedding to make a specific trip to the temple for consultation on this very point. And somehow or other the medium would invariably advise the devotee against attending the wedding function – a highly convenient way for anyone who wishes to get out of a function and one that seems tailor-made for the occasion.

For my part, I never seemed to have a low 'chi' where weddings were concerned when I was a boy and I can't recall having been left out of any such function that either my mother or grandmother wanted to take me to. They were the "red-lettered functions" and the bride's destructive 'chi' energy notwithstanding, were still safer outings to go to than funerals, labelled "white-lettered functions" by the locals. However, back home after the attendance of any funeral, my mother would make made sure that I washed my face from an enamelled-iron bowl of water with a fresh sprig of a local herb - grown in a pot by my grandmother - immersed in it. It was an aura cleansing solution that allegedly helped the person get rid of any spiritual "invasion" that might have taken place as a result of exposure to harmful ethereal energy – the local equivalent of holy water.

That enamel bowl was put to good use often. In the extended family system we were exposed to there were quite a few wakes or funerals that young children were compelled to attend; to show their family's respect and piety. Chinese

Children of the Monkey God

funeral ceremonies and the consequential procession were grand affairs in those days, unless the deceased was a young person or a Christian, in which case the deceased would be given a quiet send-off. However, if the deceased happened to be non-Christian, old and rich with a large extended family, his send-off would inevitably turn out to be a big, noisy affair.

A parade through the centre of the town was considered mandatory.

Led by a local brass band comprised mainly of retired remnants of the old constabulary band of largely Filipino and Malay members, the march would begin at the clock tower at the eastern end of Padungan Road and proceed into Thompson Road, now renamed Tunku Abdul Rahman Road. From there it would continue into Main Bazaar, where it would turn left at the end into the northern end of Rock Road, disbanding at the junction with McDougall Road, half-a-kilometre away, where it would proceed to its designated cemetery by litters, carriages, cars, trucks and coaches.

However, for its almost three kilometre procession through the centre of the town, it was a colourful and noisy affair. The remnants of the old police band were quite loud and uncompromising in their brass rendition of Chopin's Funeral March, perhaps necessarily so, as they were the vanguard heralding the arrival of the funeral procession. But then it might have been just out of force of habit that they continued to play in that manner, finding it difficult to adjust to a softer tone from years of playing as a police marching band. They were, in turn, followed by men carrying calligraphic banners, declaring in big proud characters for all to read, the age, the number of children and grandchildren, etc., that the deceased helped to bring into this world, plus his life-time achievements and any other relevant information that would help to elevate his social status in the eyes of those interested.

Exclamations of "Wah, what a long life he had," and "He had had plenty of grandchildren" could be heard from the crowd lining the street to watch the cortège. The garishly decorated hearse following the standard bearers would be pulled along by hired hands and the more there were of these, the richer he was adjudged to be. The mourners, consisting mainly of members of the deceased's extended family, other distant relatives and friends, would follow immediately behind the hearse.

To add to the cacophony, there would be another band of Chinese musicians with drums, cymbals and pipes together with a group of bell-ringing Taoist priests. To further add to the confusion, a group of sutra-chanting Buddhist priests would also be thrown in as a further precaution, making certain that the soul of the deceased would pass on from this world to the next – for at least one out of the two funeral rites performed, if not both, would be effective in seeing his ascension into heaven, as well as his reincarnation into a better life.

Living in Padungan Road made us regular onlookers of these funerals, as well as regular users of the herbal cleansing solution. It was an important ritual to carry out, as it helped to expurgate any possible intrusion by the deceased's still active spirit or ghost.

There was little doubt that Kuching was a 'ghost' town in the days when I was growing up as a boy. It was not so much a ghost town in the sense of it being deserted but more in the sense that ghosts, spirits and monsters seemed to lurk in every corner, waiting to pounce on the young and innocent.

All you had to do as proof that this was so was to listen to the howling of dogs and the hooting of owls in the middle of the night for they, like the cats, were endowed with luminous eyes that enabled them to see ghosts and spirits not visible to human eyes. But then these howls and cries of distress by the dogs might have been caused by our most popular local noodle hawker, "Mr Ong", on the prowl once again for free canine meat to be used for his "special dog soap" the following day. Fairly or unfairly, the residents of Padungan did tend to blame "Mr Ong" for the disappearance of their pet dogs, most of them mongrels.

Yes, our elders told us, these ethereal and dangerous beings are everywhere. Just because you can't see them does not mean they are not there. Dogs can see them and their howling is proof of it, they further claimed. Judging by the amount of howling we got every night, there must have been plenty of ghosts in Kuching in the days when I was a boy. For in spite of its name, Kuching, meaning 'cat' in Malay, had numerous stray dogs that roamed about the streets in the dead of night. While most of its inhabitants slumbered on peacefully, they would fight over scraps of food, barking and howling as they went about their business as street scavengers.

Graveyards, hospitals, old abandoned buildings, plus uninhabited buildings such as schools, cinemas and theatres, reputed Japanese execution grounds, lakes, reservoirs, rivers, as well as the sea and forests were favourite haunts of such ghosts, spirits and monsters. These creatures lived in trees, we were told, and if you didn't believe it, go to a banana grove and listen to the eerie cries of evil baby spirits who had made these trees their homes. It did not matter to these scaremongers that this screeching sound could only be heard on a windy night and was, in actual fact, caused by the closely grown, softly swaying trunks of the banana trees, rubbing against each other in response to the wind.

Stories abounded concerning numerous sightings of the weird and unexplainable kind. The night-watchman of the Rex cinema, a big, burley bearded Sikh, was once again, unexplainably carried down from his sleeping place in the cinema first-floor balcony to the ground floor. A young girl who had died days before the screening of a movie she had pledged to see before her death was seen attending it a few days after her funeral. Senior students of St Thomas', including one of the English teachers, told of the eerie sighting of a young female ghost in the main building of the school, a young girl who had reputedly hung herself there after a failed romance.

Certain acts were forbidden of us, as these would attract the attention of ghosts and evil spirits. The clipping of toe and fingernails must only be carried out in the daytime, certainly not at night. Likewise, whistling and the playing of certain wind instruments like the flute had to be confined to the day. Apparently, these nocturnal creatures find discarded nails appetising and the shrill sound of whistling and flute music not only tantalising, but inviting. Such imprudent acts would attract them to the offending perpetrators, who would then be opened to attacks.

It was also considered advisable not to call these creatures by their proper names, whether they happened to be devils, demons, ghosts, monsters or evil spirits. Such a thoughtless act would draw their attention to the person uttering their name. If it was really necessary to mention them, then they should be referred to as the 'impure entities.'

It was also forbidden to shout or call out at the sighting of unusual or supernatural occurrences. Any such sighting must be silently ignored and we were told to carry on as if nothing had happened; we should not speak to anyone about it, especially in the presence of the 'impure entities'. It was the equivalent of taking caution not to make eye contact with a ferocious beast. To do so would only attract its attention and make it angry, thus inviting disaster and sometimes, even death. It had been known to happen, we were told.

Our family have a favourite ghost story of how our great grandfather killed a ghost. It could well have been a demon. We would never know for certain. Whatever it was, it was something evil and definitely not of this world. More than just a story it also contains elementary instructions on how one should conduct oneself when confronted by such an apparition. It was a tale that was regularly told and retold with great pride and enthusiasm by some members of the family and listened to with a fair bit of scepticism by quite a few of us.

Ah Tai's strange but well-known encounter with a ghost happened in the coconut plantation in Sedungus not so long after the purchase of the first lot of land by Ah Kung. It occurred in the early hours of the morning before daybreak. We were never told what it was that he was doing roaming about the plantation so early in the morning. More likely than not, he was hunting wild boars, of which there were still quite a few in those early days of my grandfather's vocation as a coconut farmer.

It was on the western end of the then small plantation, a few hundred yards from the family home, when he chanced upon this legendary, but ghostly apparition. He came face to face with it with scarcely more than twenty feet between them. The encounter would have sent most people into a panic, so went the story, but not our great grandfather. After all, he did participate in the Bau Rebellion and that took a lot of guts. Although he had his hunting gun with him - for shooting at wild boars apparently - he did not straightaway fire at the ghostly apparition - again a rash act that most people in a panic would have done. He did not take flight from it either, for that would only encourage it to mount a deadly pursuit. He stayed calm, knowing what he must do to get out of the situation. He quietly turned his back on the 'impure entity' and assumed a kneeling position on the ground. He then turned the gun he had on his shoulder around so its trigger faced upward instead of downward, while making sure that it was aimed at the 'entity.' He then made a silent prayer to the gods and when that was completed he pulled the trigger of his gun. That done, he rose and walked quietly home, resisting the strong temptation to turn and look back.

He took Ah Kung with him to the spot where he shot the 'impure entity' after daybreak, having already told his family of the strange encounter he had had a mere few hours earlier.

"Your great grandfather pointed out to me the spot where the ghost stood. There was nothing there except hundreds of crawling maggots," was how Ah Kung described the scene to us.

As for the strange ritual adopted by my great grandfather in killing the ghost, Ah Kung explained that it had to be done that way because ghosts, demons and other similar creatures occupied the opposite end of the spectrum from humans. They were the yang to our yin or vice versa. That being the case, the opposite or reverse of everything applied to them. Only then was it possible for Ah Tai to make a lethal shot. My great grandfather should know. He was, after all, a practitioner of traditional Chinese medicine, which was deeply rooted in the Taoist philosophy of Yin and Yang.

Children of the Monkey God

Kuching, as I have mentioned earlier was not only a 'ghost' town; it was also a busy ghost town, especially in the 50s and 60s, with an inner town life, both vibrant and varied. It was, in many senses, a huge village or rural town, surrounded by nearby coastal and inland agricultural settlements, vegetable gardens, small-holding farms and a huge hinterland of tropical rainforest. A rural town it might have been, but it was still a growing town with its population constantly bolstered by migrants from the outlaying rural and coastal hinterland. Its busyness and its continuing expansion notwithstanding, there were still places – the town's nooks and crannies, if you like – that seemed to be the haunts of all sorts of demons and spirits. One such haunt, it was claimed by some of the local residents, was the Henghua temple located near our house.

Padungan's biggest temple was a dark and eerie place. It was a place of worship funded and built by members of the Henghua community, popularly referred to as the Chinese fishermen of Sarawak. Loud, gregarious, dark-skinned and guttural in their speech, this small community of southern Chinese had been the dominant force in the local fishing industry. Their patron deity was the goddess Machuo (also "Mazu" in mandarin), whom they looked to for guidance and protection when they went fishing out at sea.

To all appearances it was merely another temple, not much different from the few others in town. Although slightly larger than most of the town's temples, it was in itself very much a temple built in traditional style. The only thing that made it stand out from the rest was the rumour that it was built over a few graves containing the remains of deceased people of dubious reputation. It was mainly for that reason we were told by the elders to stay away from it. That in itself was an anomaly, given the fact that temples were supposed to be places of protection against ghosts, demons and evil spirits. Furthermore, it was also a very popular place of worship for the Henghua people. That may be so, retorted our elders, but do you know whose graves the temple was built on? The answer was given before we had time to say no. They were the graves of hardened criminals like murderers, rapists and robbers, whose souls were condemned to live in the nether world for all eternity. The temple was built over them to keep their evil spirits in their graves, rendering them harmless and making certain they could not cross to the land of the living.

As a boy, I had often wondered whether that was really possible, given the structure and architectural style of the building. Because of the area's susceptibility to the king-tide floods during the monsoon season, the temple was built on concrete columns of roughly two feet in diameter and three feet in height. The temple was therefore not exactly sitting on top of the ground or pressing down on anything, let alone any alleged graves, and it would seem quite an easy matter for any spirit to merely slip through the gap between the ground and the floor of the building to make good its escape.

There were graves there all right. Or what looked like graves. The concrete columns of the temple may have been only three feet high, but it left enough room for us small children to crawl under the building to play games of hide and seek or card games of poker, black jack and other games involving the use of dice with our meagre pocket money or with worthless pretend "banana money", the remnants of the old Japanese currency from the Second World War. It was dank and dark inside but it was an ideal place for our activities, especially the latter, for we would be out of sight of our elders and the police, neither of whom would have taken kindly to our illicit games.

Our card games were played on pieces of hard belian planks, which we found to be only half-buried in the compact clayey soil under the temple. There was little doubt that some of the exposed parts of these planks, randomly and sparingly scattered, did suspiciously resemble the high browed-shape of traditional Chinese coffins. We would spend hours within these dark, narrow confines, crouching over those planks without a worry in the world as to the consequences that might befall us, caught up as we were in the fun and excitement of gambling and trying to win money from each other.

But consequences there were, as I was to find out. As a boy, I had on many occasions broken out with a skin rash which would leave the best part of my body red and splotchy. It was a condition, which my mother claimed was caused by playing under or near the temple. For, right next to the temple was an old strangler's fig tree, which with its huge luxuriant and overhanging branches was also known as the small-leaf banyan tree. A parasitic plant, it had curled itself around a big durian tree and the two trees intertwined together had the combined effect of casting a huge and shady cool spot on their common base.

The tree was said to be the haunt of demons and evil spirits, but that in itself was not enough to deter the children of the neighbourhood from gathering there every afternoon after school to play marbles and other games. Late afternoon was the time when most of us would be found there - unless we decided to play soccer- for it was during that time when the setting sun would be behind the tree, casting a long shadow from a far distance. The Chinese school-classrooms in the building on its other side – the temple being on the opposite side - would also have broken up for the day, and we could make as much noise as we wanted without one of the teachers coming out to tell us to play somewhere else. We would play there until dusk when it would be time to go home to take our bath and have dinner.

On most nights, nothing would happen but there were some nights when my skin would come out in ugly rashes. Grumbling, muttering and accusing me of having played under the temple's demon tree, my mother would gather the necessary tools required to cleanse me of my affliction by an 'impure entity'.

According to her, as well as the other elders of the family, I had once again bumped into some sort of demon, an 'impure entity,' and I must be cleansed of its influence. Nobody thought to suggest that the rash I suffered might have been the result of an allergic reaction to either the tree or something else in the environment. An instant assumption was always made that the tree was the cause of it and the fact that it oozed a red sap was often taken as a confirmation that it was the home of some evil demon or perhaps even several demons. The red sap was their blood, we were told, and we were further warned to take care not to attempt to cut or chop it, as we might cause the injured demons living inside to retaliate against the offender. As an act of curiosity, I might have used a penknife on one or two occasions merely to watch the red sap oozing out of its trunk. That might have been enough to cause a rash to develop. It was also enough evidence for the adults and other younger members of the family to say "I told you so."

This sort of affliction, however, was a mere chance encounter, when it was said that the soul or "huon" of the person affected had been caused to depart from his body, and not as severe as a spiritual possession which would require the ritual of exorcism. It was something my mother was able to handle herself without the necessity of seeking expert help, not yet anyway. She would drag a box that she kept in the kitchen pantry and from inside it she would take three joss sticks, a couple of candles and some sacrificial currency notes, popularly known as hell's money.

Armed with these items she would proceed under the cover of darkness to a spot quite near, but not yet under the branches of the tree, for she must take care herself to avoid suffering from the same affliction as me. With the joss sticks and the lit candle, she would beg for forgiveness from whatever spirit I had offended, as well as for the travesties committed by a young, innocent boy in causing the temporary departure of the "huon" from his body. A plea would then be made to the spirit for my soul or "huon" to be returned to my body. As appeasement and as a gesture of sincere apology, the sacrificial currency notes were then burned as a compensatory offer.

An additional prayer was also made to Tu Ti, the Earth God, asking for his help in guiding home the wayward "huon" and he, the Earth God, would also be duly rewarded for his efforts with another gift of sacrificial currency notes and sometimes small servings of food. It was quite common to see such offerings by the roadside when I was a boy and we were told by our elders never to pick them up or desecrate them in any way, as we would end up offending the gods or spirits to which these offerings were intended.

For most of the time, my mother's pleas to the gods and spirits would appear to have done the trick and I would wake up the following morning with the rash cleared up. However, there were other times when this ritual demon appeasement failed to work, in which case a different type of cleansing was required.

This would involve the preparation of the 'water of seven colours'. A popular remedy among the locals of Kuching., it had its origin in the Taoist philosophy of the five elements of water, earth, wood, metal, and fire, collectively the elements that have come together to form the blueprint of life. For this preparation to work a large enamel vessel would be filled with clean water (the first element), and into it seven clean pebbles (earth) would be immersed together with the flowers (wood) of seven different colours, thus flowers from seven different plants. A pair of long scissors (metal) would then be placed astride the top of the vessel. The vessel together with its accessories would then be taken outdoors and placed under the sun (fire) where it would stay for an hour or so. Thus suitably infused with the energy of the five elements, the water would then be put to use as a cleansing solution to rid the body of the adverse influences caused by negative entities or energies present in the general environment.

This remedy was used when it was believed that a person's aura needed cleansing, when, for instance, he had had a string of losses at the racecourse, the mah-jong or poker table or after feeling unwell after attending a wedding or funeral. It was used by some fishermen before embarking on their fishing trips, a patient before surgery and sometimes even by students before taking a school examination or test. It was a simple, but effective, all-purpose solution to ward off evil and misfortune.

Not far from our home and just across the open ground from the Henghua Temple lived an old Hokkien matriarch whose Chinese house of some antiquity was situated on top of a hill overlooking the back of the houses in that part of Padungan, ours included. I do not exaggerate when I say that that old matriarch ruled her household with an iron fist. With her own husband dead many years ago, she had assumed the role of the head of the household like an old dowager.

Her extended family of sons, daughters and grandchildren was a large one, with most of them daily employed by her to rid the front part of her ground of weeds. Although I had never seen the old matriarch outside that house, I would see her almost every late afternoon sitting on the hard bench under the porch with her big heavy walking cane leaning next to her or on her lap. With the setting sun sinking on the horizon behind her house, she would sit there watching her daughters and grandchildren – her sons exempted from weeding duties because of their work commitments elsewhere in the town – like a sergeant-major supervising his troops. It was an activity we were able to see almost every late afternoon from our kitchen, except on days of heavy rain. The main part of their work consisted of clearing the frontage on the northern slope of their large compound. Thus almost daily, she would oversee the uprooting of every blade of grass, weed, moss, lichen or any other plant trying to set root there. These would all be so meticulously yanked out by her family workers under her supervision that there was hardly any greenery to be seen on that part of the hill. The grass and other plants were not simply mowed or cut down – every single stalk was uprooted. The old matriarch never took part in the weeding herself. She was too old and heavy for that. Instead she would sit on her wooden bench in her porch shouting out instructions and keeping a watchful eye on her team of relentless weed-pullers.

"Stupid old woman," said my grandfather. "Leaving her ground bare with all that unnecessary weeding; there won't be much soil left on that hill by the time the rains get through it."

There was little doubt that her family was in fear and awe of her. That much we knew because we were told of it by one of her grandsons and who was of the same age as us. His name was Ah Soon, or 'Big Testicles Soon' as we would call him out of his hearing because of his heavy lumbering walk. He was also the 'know-all' in our group of Padungan boys.

Although the grand old house that he and his family

lived in had seen better days and was badly in need of painting and repairs, it was still an eye-catching house, designed and built as it was in traditional Chinese architectural style incorporating an open courtyard in the centre of the building.

It was a fairly large building by Kuching standards, constructed of bricks and belian timber, the frontage of which was taken up by four huge columns supporting a large, open balcony on the first floor and a porch on the ground floor. The open courtyard in the centre of the building was used for washing clothes and as a kitchen. The bedrooms, of which there were quite a few, extended around the courtyard on both the ground and first floors. The entrance to the house was taken up by a huge alter of Kuan Ti, the god of war, whose uncompromising and fearsome aspect was reputed to be enough to put to flight all things evil and wicked. In spite of the open courtyard, it was still a house that tended to be shrouded in darkness and I dreaded it when I was asked by my grandmother to take some of our plantation's durians, mangosteens or mangoes for her old friend, the matriarch on the hill.

She was an old friend of Ah Por because when her husband was still alive her family took my eldest uncle in as a lodger for several years when he was a young student at a small privately-run Chinese school in Kuching. My grandfather had not bought the house in Padungan yet and, as my uncle had shown a certain amount of aptitude in academic studies, Ah Kung felt it necessary that he should attend school, even though it would mean losing a valuable farm hand.

We were looking out for the total eclipse of the sun from our wide kitchen window one day. It was announced over the radio and published in the newspaper that it was going to occur in the late afternoon. Ah Kung's knowledge

Children of the Monkey God

of it came from his current copy of the Tung Tsu. The position of the sun at that time of the day would be southwest and looking at it in that general direction would also mean looking toward the direction of the house of the old matriarch on the hill.

I remember it was clear and fine on that particular day and the old matriarch and her household subjects were as usual attending to their daily duty on the hill, laboriously digging and pulling out 'weeds' that had apparently sprung up overnight. The old matriarch was obviously unaware that the eclipse was about to take place, her house unequipped as it with any radio. I doubt whether anybody had informed her of the publication in the newspaper telling its readers of the impending eclipse.

The family were, thus, fully occupied in their usual daily routine of weeding when the sky began to slowly darken. And, as the shadow cast by the eclipse began to widen and spread, a transformation took place over the normally calm but authoritative old matriarch. Shouting and gesticulating excitedly at her household subjects, she soon whipped them into a frenzied state. We were not able to hear what she was saying from our position in the kitchen, but it was apparent that whatever it was had a lot of urgency to it. Her household members dropped whatever they were doing, some of them even dropping their tools. They rushed en masse into the house, emerging in a flash armed with all sorts of cooking utensils, including pots, pans and woks together with their lids. Panic and fear were written all over their faces. Once outside of the house and on the recently weeded slope, they began to beat these utensils with spoons, ladles, sticks and whatever instruments they were able to get their hands on, creating in the meantime a cacophony that was both unrehearsed and chaotic.

The old matriarch herself did not take part in this

utensil-banging activity but, with the aid of one of her grandchildren, she was now standing on the edge of her front porch. Leaning on the shoulder of her helper and looking up at the sky, she started to shout while pointing and waving her walking stick at some object up there. The normally stern matriarch was now a highly agitated one. It was a comical sight; yet at the same time a frightening one. Panic, at the best of times, has a way of spreading like wildfire and in this instance it spread from the top of the hill down to some of the onlookers in no time at all. I was one of those onlookers feeling a bit panicky. Why was she so frightened and why was she shouting at the sky? I turned around to my grandparents standing behind us and asked with some apprehension, "What is she doing?"

Ah Por replied, "Oh that! She is trying to scare away the heavenly demon dog with all that banging and shouting. She believes that it is trying to consume the sun and the way to stop it is to use a scare tactic to cause it to spit it out. The monster must not be permitted to succeed, otherwise it would spell the end of the world and life as we know it will cease to exist."

The cacophony of sounds created by the banging of kitchen utensils and shouting intensified in response to the inevitable near-total darkness covering the earth, especially with the matriarch's family joining her in her shrill admonitions to the demon dog to leave the sun alone. They were not able to stop it and we were covered in complete darkness in no time at all. This state of total darkness gave a completely different dimension to the panicky cries and chaotic dins still issuing from the hill, however. Noises, especially loud noises caused by unseen figures, had a way of amplifying themselves in what now looked and felt to be a vast empty space and to a young boy's ears they were frightening to behold, to say the least.

Children of the Monkey God

But then, just as inevitably as the moon's journey across the face of the sun would eventually run its full course, streaks of sunlight were now starting to stream through, causing the sky and the land to be covered in sunshine and brightness once more. On top of the hill the old matriarch in her porch broke into a huge and triumphant smile. She had, after all, played her part in the defeat of the giant demon dog of the sky. She had not been successful in stopping it from swallowing the sun but she had been successful in making it spit it out.

"Stupid old woman," said Ah Kung as he started to move away from the kitchen. Ah Kung, you see, knew all about eclipses from the diagrams and descriptions provided by his year book of the Chinese Almanac – the Tung Tsu.

There were two dramas acted out on that day, the eclipse of the sun by the moon and the impromptu and hectic performance of the matriarch and her family in defeating the demon dog. Looking back at the incident, I would have to say that the performance of the old matriarch nearly, but not quite, eclipsed that of the moon!

A treatment on the subject of ghosts, monsters and demons would not be complete without mentioning at least a couple of festivals devoted to the making of offerings to the souls of dead people and the gods, whether by way of honouring or appeasing them.

Technically, these offerings, in the case of foods, were meant for consumption by the gods and spirits of the nether world. This, however, did not mean that the humans of this world should refrain from having a hearty meal and enjoying themselves after the completion of the ceremony.

The foremost principle that must be observed was that the deities and spirits must be fed first, and the beauty of this practice, was that the same food could be used and reused to cater for as many, deities and spirits as the worshipper fancied.

Care must be taken, however, to ensure that those deities occupying a more hierarchical position must take precedence over those of a lower position by being the first to be invited, or that only vegetarian dishes should be offered to the bodhisattvas. Since our family shrine was that of Kwan Yin, my mother was always careful to include a few vegetarian items in her repertoire of dishes to be set aside for her.

Last, but not least, the spirits of our dead ancestors were then invited to join in the feast. They were included in all the festivals because it was the filial duty of their descendants to continue with the care and support to which they were accustomed when they were alive. That duty did not end with their death. It extended into death, with later generations carrying on the same duty, thus ensuring the continuity of a tradition that had survived for centuries. These were the lucky spirits, we were told, because they had descendants who still looked after them, even after death.

Thus it was during every Festival of Ching Ming (the first of the two festivals and an event specifically devoted to the worshipping of ancestors in Kuching) when extra efforts were made in providing a lavish meal for them and in replenishing their other provisions such as money, clothes, cigarettes, cars, household goods and luxury items, etc. The foods that were offered were more often than not the favourite dishes of the deceased and would either be offered at the graveyard or on a table at home placed before the altar of the family's chosen deity.

With regard to the monetary offers there were two types that would be made. The first and more traditional type was that made by folding pieces of gold and silver-coloured papers, origami-style, in the shape of nuggets resembling the ancient Chinese Yuan – apparently the main currency in use in the nether world. With each nugget made from only one piece of paper, hundreds of these nuggets were created from only a few stacks of paper - bought from the local grocery store at the cost of only a few dollars per stack - and I would often wonder how rich our ancestors must be in the other world after the receipt of all these offerings. With almost every household carrying out the same practice, there must have been plenty of rich and contented spirits with gold nuggets stacked right up to their ears.

The second type consisted of currency notes of various denominations, apparently "issued" by the authority of the God of Hades. These notes were offered to make certain that, not only would the gold and silver nugget-endowed spirits have extra cash, but also to protect them against any change in circumstances such as cash having perhaps become the main mode of exchange in place of the archaic and traditional nuggets. This was another form of insurance policy, as was also the case in the performance of two different types of wakes and funeral rites - Buddhist and Taoist.

Although food and money were the main items 'transferred' by many a filial descendant to their deceased ancestors in the other world, there were also other important chattels regularly despatched that are worthy of mention. Sedan chairs and litters made of paper and bamboo splints complete with dwarf-sized attendants and horse-drawn carriages, together with horses, were mandatory items for the well-to-do families. These were means of transport that their deceased ancestors must have at their disposal in the after-life.

Subsequent additions and modifications to these means of transport were made with the advent of modern science. While the traditional items of sedan chairs and horse-drawn carriages, together with their respective attendants and horses were still retained, there were now included cars constructed in the style and shape of the latest models of Mercedes Benz, BMW, Volvo as well as other popular and luxury makes – complete with chauffeurs, no less.

These were, as I have said, the more fortunate souls who still had devout descendants caring and providing for them, as well as the means to do so. For the less fortunate, who had either passed on to the next world without descendants to perform these deeds or the means to do it, then reliance must be placed on charitable worshippers and organizations. These less fortunate souls were the 'hungry ghosts' who, like the hungry and homeless of this world, must rely on the hand-outs, generosity and charity of benevolent bodies and individuals to feed and clothe them in the other world. There was little doubt that most of these unfortunate souls who had ended up as "hungry ghosts" were also penniless when alive, a case of being poor and destitute in life as well as in the after-life.

A similar mode of bestowment of offerings to that of the Ching Ming Festival was, therefore, necessary to ensure the successful despatch of foods, clothes, money and other material goods to these poor and hungry souls. Thus, a festival was specially allocated to them – the Festival of the Hungry Ghosts, which falls on the fifteenth day of the seventh moon of the Chinese Lunar Calendar.

On this day of the Chinese calendar groups of relatives would visit the cemeteries and graves to pray and make offerings to their ancestors. That was an obligatory filial duty, which they must first fulfil. Having carried out that duty, most of them would then turn their attention to the

Children of the Monkey God 229

poor and hungry souls of the other world. This was one of the busiest days for all the temples around town, with concerned and caring devotees arriving from very early in the morning to pray to the deities and make offerings and donations of food, plus 'hell money' to those needy ghosts. The biggest amount of food, drinks and money would be accumulated at the temple at Carpenter Street. Pork, chicken and duck, cooked in all sorts of ways, together with a great variety of cakes, cookies and buns would be laid out on low wooden stands placed before the altar. It also made it the busiest temple in town with devotees streaming in and out for the whole day and climaxing in a lantern competition later on in the night.

This was the day when we as children were warned to be extra careful where we went and what we did. This was especially the case when night fell. Games such as hide and seek were forbidden and we were told to be respectful toward the dead. This was the one time of the year when the spirits were out in great numbers and we had to take care to avoid 'bumping' into them in the things we did and to avoid offending them in the things we said. The self-appointed expert of our group on the matter, Big Testicles Soon, made the outrageous claim that sitting or squatting under a bridge with the traditional conical Chinese straw hat, very much favoured by farmers, exactly at twelve midnight on this day would give a person a second sight enabling him to see all types of ghosts. "Headless ghosts, ghosts with blood dripping from their bodies. Ghosts with their eyes gouged out, their tongues hanging out and dripping with blood. All sorts of ghosts would be seen," he said.

We never dared to test out his outrageous claim; such was the fear it generated. In actual fact, come nightfall, we were careful not to go outside the house without a companion and, weren't the dogs in the streets howling a little more than usual?

Although the night belonged to the hungry ghosts, it did not stop the humans from claiming their share of fun and enjoyment. It might be an occasion in which the needs of hungry ghosts were catered for, but there were also the poor and needy of this world to look after as well. Thus, some of the foods offered as sacrifices at the temples would, at the end of the day, be donated to charity such as the orphanages and the old people's homes, whose residents, ironically, would most probably end up as hungry ghosts - uncared for in this world and uncared for in the next.

The climax of the day came at the Carpenter Street's Siang Ti Temple. Here the food was offered to the general public at the end of the ceremony and a mad scramble would ensue at a signal from the high priest of the temple. The participants were mainly youngsters who could withstand the rough play and tactics of pushing and shoving that were employed in the mad dash for the mountains of buns, cakes and cookies made available at the end of the ceremony. Ah Kung and Ah Por said these youngsters were no different from the hungry ghosts in the way they behaved and in their desperate fight for the temple food. Perhaps they were right as it could be claimed that this fierce fight was possibly a mere re-enactment of the same scene in the after-life, a case of life imitating after-life or was it the other way round?

For my part, I was never able to understand as a young boy how it was possible for the hungry ghosts to eat the food when it didn't look as though it had been touched. It was explained to me that, while the food appeared to be intact, they had already been spiritually eaten. Apparently, denizens of the spirit world do things spiritually, including the consumption of food. There was little doubt that the elders of my generation were strong believers in offering food and other sacrifices to the spirits of the deceased ancestors and there was some concern back then that this traditional practice would be eventually abandoned by later generations of descendants. They feared that they would end up as hungry ghosts after their death – famished and uncared for by their children and their children's children. This was not an unfounded fear, especially with the seemingly successful intrusion made by Christianity into this area of the Chinese belief-system.

The Christian Orders, especially the Roman Catholic Church, forbade the practice of ancestral worship among its members on the grounds that it was against the teachings of the Bible. Ancestral worship, according to them was not only a sinful pagan practice; it also failed to acknowledge God as the one, true God. Christians, especially true Christians, should only worship God and no one else, not even their deceased parents or any other ancestors. To do so would strike at the very core of Christianity.

Chinese converts to Christianity were thus coerced into giving up ancestral worship under pain of being accused of participating in sinful and pagan practices by their local parish, although some of these converts did not require much persuasion along this line, especially when their intention of embracing Christianity was to avoid carrying on with what they considered to be an onerous duty. It was not uncommon, therefore, for some of these 'converts' to openly brag that they could avoid going to the graves of their forbears during the festivals of Ching Ming and the Hungry Ghosts without fear and with a clear conscience now they had a higher authority to answer to. Indeed, many of these converts embraced Christianity with the sole purpose of avoiding ancestral worship, feeling more than adequately protected from the wrath of the Chinese gods, for it was often said that the Christian god was far more powerful than the Chinese gods. He was far more powerful because he didn't have to share his powers with other gods, it was claimed. It was a power that came from the principle of monopolisation and from being the sole being privileged to exercise it. To the people who subscribed to this sort of thinking, it was purely a matter of mathematical logic - the Chinese gods had to share their powers, the Christian god didn't. The powers that were available were thus in the control of only one being, concentrated and, therefore, not dispersed. It was that simple.

For the worried and aging parents, no consolation or comfort could be gained in watching their children and their children's children embrace Christianity. In some families it was akin to watching the proverbial domino taking effect with one family member after another joining the Church and dropping out of the scene. To use another metaphor, the bucket got passed down the line as each son or daughter passed on the responsibility of feeding and caring for their parents after their death to the next unconverted member. Thus, it was not uncommon to hear such declarations as "If our eldest brother could become a Christian, so could I, because I don't want to be the one left to perform the onerous task of going to the graveyard every year to feed father and mother after they have passed over."

The aging parents fretted the more as to what would happen to them after their death on hearing such declarations. Various questions sprang to their mind. Would all their children become Christians after their death and, if so, who was going to feed them in the after-life? Worse still, would they become hungry ghosts in that world, condemned to an eternal after-life of hunger, poverty and begging?

One way of avoiding becoming a hungry ghost was if one's soul were to go through reincarnation and come back to this world as another being. But then reincarnation was not a process that was guaranteed to happen. There were so many variables necessary for reincarnation to occur, the foremost of which was that the deceased person must have chalked up enough good deeds in this world to have such a reward bestowed upon him by the gods, a sort of selection criterion maintained and observed by the celestial bureaucrats of heaven. Otherwise, he might end up incapable being re-incarnated, a form of death sentence as far as these believers were concerned. Or even if he was re-incarnated, he might merely re-appear in this world as a lower form of being in the shape of an animal such as a mouse or an insect such as a fly. Although this was not as bad as a death sentence, it was nevertheless an undesirable life sentence.

Lacking the confidence that they would be selected for reincarnation by the powers-that-be, many elderly people decided to do the next best thing. They became Christians themselves. To them, it was a case of "if you can't beat them, then you join them." "Look at the Christians," they said, "they don't worry about feeding their deceased ancestors in the after-life. They don't have to. They have a god who seems to have the power to feed all of them." Or "Christian ghosts or souls don't seem to require food to survive." To them this was another example of how powerful a single god could be in a mono-god religion, as opposed to the multi-god system of the Chinese. I know of at least two aunts, one from each side of the family, who'd converted to Christianity on their deathbed on this very ground.

The Christian missionaries would have liked to think that most of their converts were gained by them seeing the light in their new-found faith. They could not have been more wrong.

WITCHCRAFT AND WITCH DOCTORS

Growing up in a town like Kuching provided me with a rich store of memories and experiences, some of the most vivid being the interesting personalities who contributed to its quaint reputation.

In that respect, Omar comes to mind.

Omar was a 'bomoh', the Malay name for someone who is a shaman or witch doctor, loosely referred to these days as a 'medicine man'. They form part of the contingent of local practitioners of traditional medicine, shamans, herbalists, massage therapists, acupuncturists, temple mediums and other spiritual and traditional healers. Rightly or wrongly, 'bomohs' and 'manangs' (Malay and Iban for "shamans" respectively) were held in awe and fear by the local people, mainly from their own belief that witchcraft not only worked but was a potent force that could wreak havoc with their life. Practitioners of this craft must, therefore, be treated with respect and, unless their help was required to perform some task or other, contact with them should be avoided at all costs. At the very least, they should be kept at arm's length - without giving offence to them, of course.

Most of the traditional healers of this genre, especially the 'bomohs' and the shamans, were viewed as charlatans, quacks and con-men - collectively the practitioners existing on the fringe of society - by the more conventional and western-educated section of the population. But this view had not always been the case. There was a time before the arrival of the British and other Westerners - who brought with them Christianity, science and western medicine -

when the traditional practitioners of the healing art were, in actual fact, the mainstream practitioners. Indeed, until the arrival of these foreigners, they were the only healers available.

Every hamlet, village and longhouse would boast of at least an herbalist and or a 'bomoh' or 'manang' to take care of the sick. They were, and still are, very much a part of the community. Some would even consider the 'bomoh' in the villages and the 'manang' in the longhouses as more powerful and influential than the local chief.

They were the psychics and psychiatrists of the villages and longhouses and such were their influence and control over the residents that nearly all major undertakings must be referred to them before any decision could be made. A hunting expedition, a battle or a raid against another longhouse or a move from their present site to another could not be undertaken by the longhouse residents without reference to the shaman. He read omens in the dreams of the residents and in the cries of birds and animals. He would also be the one to ultimately make the decision to proceed with a venture. They are animists-naturalists and see life and spirits in everything. The trees and forests, the rocks and pebbles, the streams and rivers are all vehicles of these myriad spirits.

The 'bomohs' and the 'manangs' are also the resident consultants in all matters of illness, and in days gone by - before the advent of modern medical science - the one that the villagers and longhouse residents would respectively go to for all manner of sickness. Treatment of their charges would consist of traditional herbal remedies and the performance of rituals of exorcism in cases of demonic possession, as well as appeasement to the gods and the spirits of the woods, trees, rivers and land. In cases where there had been a perceived violation committed against these beings or where their charges had been the victims of black magic, a ritualistic battle to expunge the affliction would have to be carried out.

While there was wide acceptance of their practices by the local population, the Christian and Islamic authorities held a different view, taking the official position that these traditional healers were practitioners of pagan black magic and whose influence on the population was more on the negative than on the positive side.

The objections of these religious authorities notwithstanding, these practitioners were still looked upon with respect by the local population and, in some cases, were desperately sought as healers of the last resort when conventional western medicine had failed. In some cases, they were the first and preferred persons to go to when it was suspected that a person's ailments, accompanied by the appropriate symptoms, were the results of black magic, deliberately inflicted by an enemy – a jealous or jilted lover or a rival business competitor – or in some cases accidentally 'bumped' or 'crashed' into.

It was easy to 'bump' into someone's black magic in the form of evil spells and charms sent out by occult practitioners because it was everywhere. In actual fact, the town was a-washed with it, if you could believe the claims of some of its scaremongers. Night time was the 'witching' hour for these operators and that was when extreme caution should be taken, especially when going out. The advice was not to venture abroad during these hours of the night but, if you must, then you should make certain to protect yourself by wearing all sorts of protective wards and talismans.

Other means of protection against attack or, at the very least, the unintentional intrusion of witchcraft was the gathering of all items of clothing, especially those of young infants and children - who had not yet developed strong or mature 'chi' - from the clothes line just before the descent of darkness. This latter act was done to ensure that they would not be contaminated by evil spirits or the dark energies sent out by practitioners of the occult art in the night.

Further precautions to be taken included the proper disposal of one's body parts such as clipped finger and toenails, hair and saliva and to take care that these items, together with one's personal apparels and photographs, should not fall into the hands of one's enemies or some interested parties who might take them to their personal bomoh for casting spells and charms. Young girls and women were told to be extremely careful in guarding these items, lest they ended up being the willing concubine or lover of some dirty old man, their natural resistance worn down by such witchery.

Although one was more likely to come across the practices of these bomohs and manangs in the villages and longhouses of rural and native Sarawak than in the towns, there was every indication that their influences were starting to become quite prevalent in these urban areas as well, into areas largely occupied by overseas Chinese. .

The Chinese in these towns, while not entirely embracing this belief-system, had no problem absorbing parts of it as plenty of similarities existed between it and the animist-naturalist belief-system of rural China. This belief-system comprising mainly of Taoism, with elements of Buddhism thrown in, has its followers and devotees in the many temples and privately operated shrines around Kuching. These latter establishments were run by mediums from their homes, their popularity, and thus their successes, very much dependant on word of mouth spread by clients claiming to have been healed by them. Many were backyard operators who made a living by prescribing all types of talismans, wards and charms to be used against the attacks of evil spirits and black magicians.

They seldom charged a fixed fee for their services, adopting the same practice as that of the traditional herbalists and acupuncturists. The clients paid whatever they could afford, the money contained in a small red gift-wrapper.

The most common wards and charms prescribed by these operators were those scripted with Chinese brushes on yellow and red pieces of paper, roughly three inches wide and six inches long with pre-printed symbols of yin and yang and the ancient hexagrams prominently displayed on the top of the writing. While these scripts would normally be written with ordinary black ink, a more potent substance would be used if a stronger ward was deemed necessary. Instead of the normal black writing ink, the medium would, for this purpose, use his own blood for writing the warding script. Still in an apparent trance, he would run his long and ugly-looking ceremonial sword across his tongue causing a few drops to drip into a small rice bowl partially filled with water. Dipping his brush into the literally bloody ink he would, with a bold stroke here and there, complete the script with a flourish. Folded or rolled up, the warding script or paper talisman would then have a small piece of red cloth tightly sewn over it and worn next to the body with a safety pin or simply put in the pocket.

Commonly called charms, the characteristics and functions of these pieces of spiritually- treated paper were, in fact, more those of wards rather than charms or spells. This was because the mediums who dispensed them were forbidden by oaths to their patron deity from casting any charms or spells on anyone. Defensive by nature, they were used to cleanse and repel, rather than to attack or harm.

As a warding device to repel evil spirits as well as the spells and charms of black practitioners, they would be prominently pasted on the front and back doors, as well as on the doors of some of the internal rooms of the house. Their potency normally lasted a year and fresh ones had to be obtained from the temple in replacement before the passing of the expiry or "use by" date of the old ones. The used ones would then have to be destroyed by burning.

As a cleansing and healing tool they were first burned, their ashes dropped into a glass of water, stirred and drunk as one would with a couple of disprin tablets for a headache. Except that with the ashes, there was no restriction placed on what they could cure, all ailments and symptoms of a sick or unwell person, be it headaches, stomach-aches, skin rashes, fevers, etc., inevitably diagnosed by the consulting medium as mere manifestations of something that had gone spiritually askew. It was for all intents and purposes a cure-all remedy. I can't recall how many glasses of such ashes I had to force myself to drink as a boy. Plenty, although not even a fraction of the number consumed by some of my relatives, especially Ngee Koo, my second aunt from my father's side of the family.

She was, arguably, the biggest believer in spiritual healing, as well as the most devout worshipper of the Chinese gods in our extended family system. Her passion, however, had the tendency to make her a target for some of the family's good-natured jokes which, to her credit, she took extremely well. The main culprit in this area was Ah Kung, who despite his preference for my second aunt as his favourite over his other daughters, could not help but tease her over her regular annual pilgrimages to the shrines and temples.

"Off to the temple to chalk up some more credits with the gods, are you?" Ah Kung would ask with a tongue-in-cheek smile.

"How about sharing them around then?" He would continue.

His light-hearted banter was, of course, a reference to the record-keeping system claimed to be maintained by the celestial bureaucracy in heaven. Good and bad deeds are recorded in heaven, the firm believers of such a record-keeping system insisted. Whatever you do here on earth is noted by the gods in heaven and recorded for use in confronting you on your day of reckoning, they continued. To take the matter one step further, not only were a person's good deeds recorded, his offerings and sacrifices of food and "money" to the gods and hungry ghosts were similarly noted and entered in some sort of celestial ledger, to be credited to the soul of a deceased person on his day of ascension. It was often said that my second aunt would be a very wealthy woman in the after-life. Her numerous trips to the temples had guaranteed that.

As much as I could see the point of Ah Kung's rather irreverent jokes, I had also felt that my second aunt's devotion to the gods, especially Kwan Yin, her favourite, might have more to do with an accident she had in her durian farm just after her fortieth birthday. This was when a very spiky and rather large durian had fallen from a great height on her back while she was going about her work on the farm. Although she survived the accident, the aches and pains that kept on recurring had the result of forcing her to constantly look for all types of cures and elixirs.

To her and many like her, the Chinese temples with their spiritual healers were places of first resort and the clinics and hospitals with their pharmacists and doctors places of last resort. Some of them had never even seen the inside of a clinic and for a few of them it was a wholly alien place run on a completely different belief-system, claiming that illnesses were caused by tiny invisible creatures called germs and bacteria. How laughable that must have been to them. Surely, ghosts, evil spirits and someone's witchcraft were more plausible causes of illness than tiny invisible creatures that could not even be seen with the naked eye. Furthermore, the aloofness of some of the clinic staff, especially government-run clinics, put them off in wanting to go there for treatments. My mother, for instance, swore never to step inside a government clinic after an incident with a nurse who verbally abused her on her first trip to one of them. She and others like her felt more at home with the temples and their mediums.

Almost every believer had their favourite temple and medium they regularly went to for consultation, similar to the regular visits made to a family doctor or a general practitioner. While protective wards and charms were the main items "dispensed" by the medium, there were also prescriptions of traditional herbal remedies written out on plain paper for purchase later on at the local Chinese medicine shops. Sometimes the sick person would be taken to the temple for examination by the medium and the treatment that followed would include any, some or all of the following treatments - the consumption of the ashes of a healing ward, the wearing of another protective ward and the performance of various trance rituals of expurgation and exorcism.

If these treatments failed to work, the medium would then have to proceed to the next level of treatment, and that was to suggest a change of name for the chronically-sick person. This advice would normally only be made in cases of babies or very young persons whose illness just refused to go away, in spite of almost every known treatment carried out by the medium, and in spite of numerous visits made to

Children of the Monkey God

the temple by the now-distraught and desperate parents.

Something more was now required, the medium would say. It was obvious that the child's given name had attracted the attention of some evil spirit or demon and a complete change in name would help to draw away its attention from the poor child, the medium would suggest.

A new name would then be bestowed on the sick child after due consultation by the medium in his trance-like state with the gods, now the child's newly appointed spiritual guardians. If the child's health improved with this latest course of action, this new name would continue to be used until adulthood, its initial status as a mere nickname developing into an alias from whence it would begin to infiltrate into all types of official documents, such as school and college certificates, identity cards and passports. The confusion caused as a result of this new name, different from the name stated in his birth certificate, would require the child's parents to make as many trips to all the relevant government departments concerned "to sort the matter" out; indeed, perhaps more than the ones they had previously made to the temple when the child had been ill.

If this course of action in the adoption of a new name still failed to work, then a further explanation would be proffered - the medium's sight now fixing squarely on the parents – for surely they must have been the cause of the child's hitherto incurable condition, perhaps the result of some misdemeanours committed by them in incurring the ire of some unforgiving demon or spirit. The solution, then, would be to "wrest" the child from the spirit-offending parents and place him under the parenthood of another married couple, normally close relatives of the child and in most cases, an uncle and aunt. This was not an official adoption in the true sense of the word and no paperwork involving the concerned parties and the relevant government departments were required. This was, in essence, a spiritual adoption, an adoption more for the eyes of the denizens of the spirit world, designed to fool those evil demons who had been responsible for the child's poor health; a ploy indicating that the hapless victim was now no more the child of the spirit-offending parents.

The ceremony for the adoption would be conducted by the medium in his temple or place of practice and would include the "filing" of all necessary papers to make certain that the adoption of the child by his "new parents" would be recognised in the spirit world. While there was no actual passing of custody of the child from the parents to the relatives after the ceremony, he would now be told to call his adoptive parents "father" and "mother" and his own parents "uncle" and "aunt" and to treat them and behave toward them as such. This, it was said, was important not only for the purpose of finalising the adoption, but also to completely carry through with the subterfuge of fooling those evil spirits having an unhealthy interest in the sick child. Again, there would be more confusion over this latest set-up for, while those friends and relatives in the know would be quite clear on the matter, there would always be others who would be puzzled as to why a child should call his own parents "uncle" and "aunt" and vice-versa for his uncle and aunt. Although the confusion created from this mode of treatment was a different and less serious one from that involving a sick child's change of name, it was still confusing, nevertheless.

While a change involving a sick child's given name or a ploy in placing him under different "parents" were not commonplace practices, they were still not quite as drastic as a mode of treatment involving a change of sex. This mode of treatment, I may add, was more widely used on pre-puberty girls than on boys.

The whole idea of this ploy was, again, to achieve the dual purpose of not only changing the sick child's identity but to give her a disguise designed to fool the denizens of the spirit world. Like the spiritual adoption carried out by the medium in the "changing of parents' ceremony", no actual surgical procedure would be carried out on the child, merely a ceremonial or spiritual one conducted by the medium. The parents would, after the rituals, be told to treat the child like a boy. She would not be allowed to play with her dolls or permitted to wear dresses. She must wear her hair short and don only shorts, trousers and shirts and have her chest strapped and bound on reaching puberty, the bra another forbidden closet item together with high-heeled shoes and lipsticks.

It was a fairly drastic mode of treatment not only in its effect in depriving the child of her childhood and teenage years of growing up as a girl, but also because of the teasing she would receive for her male outfits and tom-boyish looks, an outcome not of her own choosing. This type of sexual "transformation" or disguise was harder for the girls than for the boys, for short of a surgical operation, they had to go through the whole motion of behaving like a boy, wearing male clothes and short-cropped hair. For the boys however, wearing an earring, normally a gold one on the left ear-lobe, would be the only act required for this treatment to work. This was all that was necessary because of the huge amount of anticipated teasing involved; for all intents and purposes a mere tokenism for their supposed sex transformation.

"Ah Lian", a girl in our neighbourhood, had to undergo such a "transformation" as a young child. Maintaining a low profile for years by cultivating a quiet behaviour and going about for most of the time in her Chinese school-boy uniform of white short-sleeved shirt and khaki shorts - her school kind enough to exempt her from wearing skirts – she was plain and ordinary in her looks until the day she stepped out as a bride. Radiant and lovely looking and in full bridal dress, she was the proverbial ugly duckling transformed into a beautiful swan.

While most mediums in the Kuching area were jacks-of-all-trades there were some who would be quite justified in their claim as specialists in certain areas. One of them was fondly called 'Chai Koh' in Hokkien, which translated into English means 'Vegetarian Auntie.' Quite plump, kind and gentle and always carrying a sweet smile, she was everyone's favourite auntie. She was also the paediatrician of spiritual healers. Many mothers in Kuching would rather go to her than the clinics for treatment of their young children's ailments such as colic, fever, diarrhoea, etc.

Her temple at Deshon Road was a busy and popular place and, although in practice the mediums and their devotees in Kuching do not make a clear-cut demarcation between Taoism and Buddhism in the classification of their privately operated shrines, Chai Koh's leanings were more toward Buddhism than Taoism. That would also account for her being a vegetarian and her practice in herbal medicine rather than as a spiritual medium - the bread and butter vocation of the local Taoist priests.

Kind though she might have been, nevertheless, I dreaded it whenever my mother took me to see her, as her concocted remedy of herbs often tasted foul and bitter, especially her recommendation of chlorophyll for colic and other stomach-related ailments. Freshly squeezed and extracted from raw green herbs (after they had been pounded into a mushy pulp by a heavy granite pounder in a big pestle) it was one of her most, if not the most difficult, concoctions to swallow. Unfortunately for us children, the chlorophyll remedy was also Chai Koh's favourite cure for almost every illness.

Children of the Monkey God 247

Sometimes though, she would recommend the use of the 'water of seven colours' to cleanse the body (a full description of which has been given in the previous chapter). This was a common home remedy used by almost every Chinese household in Kuching. However, there was another remedy that was used by some of our family members, which was shrouded in mystery and not within the province of public knowledge. From what I can make of it, it was also a remedy confined mainly within the Hakka community. It was known as writing the 'horse character'.

Writing the 'horse character' was a procedure used in emergency situations such as choking on a piece of bone or suffering from a small cut or bruise where no doctors or other forms of medical aids were immediately available.

The remedy, if it can be called that, involves the full use of all the twelve strokes required for writing the Chinese character of the horse. As it happens, the number twelve is also the number of zodiac animals appearing before the Lord Buddha in the following order starting with the mouse and then continuing on with the bull, the tiger, the rabbit, the dragon, the snake, the horse, the ram, the monkey, the rooster, the dog and finally, the pig.

The procedure that is required from the person carrying out the treatment, and it can be on himself or on someone else, is that he must write the Chinese character of the horse with his forefinger over the wounded area, in the case of a cut or bruise while silently reciting the name of the zodiac animals in the exact order in which they appeared before Buddha. Thus with the first stroke made, the name of the mouse must be silently recited, followed by the bull with the second stroke and so on and so forth until the last and final animal, the pig, has been reached. The same procedure can also be used by tracing the character over a glass of water, after which it should be drunk as one would with healing water.

Care must be taken when using this procedure and there must be absolute faith that it would work, according to its adherents. Lack of faith could undo whatever good it might have originally done. It happened thus with a cousin of mine, a son of Ngee Koo, my second aunt, who had learned the art from one of the temple mediums and who had to use it one day to stop the blood gushing from a cut caused accidentally by his own parang or machete. Alone and unaided in that part of the durian farm where he was working he decided to write the 'horse character' over it.

"The flow of blood changed from a gush to a mere trickle the moment the character was written over it," he related to us later.

"Not satisfied with the trickle that was still flowing from the wound I wrote the character a second time over it with the idea of stopping the blood flow completely. The wound opened up again and it began to gush. Lack of faith, that's what it was. Also, greed in not being satisfied with the original result. That's what it was." He said in all seriousness.

Quite unkindly, the few of us, brothers and cousins all, his small audience, couldn't stop from collapsing in a heap of guffaws.

While Chai Koh was considered a good healer whose practice was that of a 'white witch' (in western terms) who would never do harm or perform any evil deeds against anyone, there was another practitioner at the opposite end of the scale whose name was only mentioned with fear.

He was the dreaded 'Long Fingernails', arguably the most feared of all the dark practitioners in Kuching.

He was so called because of the long fingernails he wore. The oft-heard rumour circulating in the town was that he derived his powers from his fingernails; similarly to the way that Samson in the Old Testament derived his strength from his long locks. And like Samson, it was said that he would lose his powers were he to lose his long fingernails.

Mysterious and reclusive, he was rarely seen in town except in a chauffeur-driven car. Practising from his house in Tabuan Road, it was said that he had seven young and beautiful wives – women who, or whose parents or husbands, were not clever enough to realize that seeking help from 'Long Fingernails' was fraught with danger. Apparently, it was said that, not only had he an insatiable sexual appetite, he was also easily attracted to a pretty face. Not a man known for his ethical and professional conduct, 'Long Fingernails' had no qualms in using his magical charms to cast a spell on any woman he took a fancy to. Enticed by him in this manner and completely placed under his spell, they would become part of his harem and would wait on him hand and foot. It was said that they even took turns to feed him at mealtimes, 'Long Fingernails' finding himself incapable of performing this task or even the most simple manual task because of his long fingernails.

Things continued merrily in this manner in the household of 'Long Fingernails' until the day when he enticed one woman too many. This was when he took as his latest concubine the young mistress of a rich merchant. She would also prove to be his last concubine for the enraged and jealous lover wasn't going to give up easily on her. Extremely rich, he engaged the services of several local bomohs and temple mediums to gain her back. It was all for nought, for 'Long Fingernails' proved to be too powerful and strong for them. Realizing that the local experts were not strong enough against the magic of 'Long Fingernails,' the rich merchant made the decision to seek foreign help. It came in the shape of a powerful medium from Thailand who was able to do what his counterparts in Kuching could not - he destroyed 'Long Fingernails.'

"Long Fingernails" was apparently found dead in his bed by one of his seven concubines early one morning. The rumours circulating around town after the initial breaking of this news was that his corpse, barely a few hours' old, was already quite dark in appearance, apparently the result of some massive, lethal psychic attack.

Back to where we started with Omar. A good friend of my father, Omar was an Indonesian Malay, originally from Java, arguably the home of some of the most powerful 'bomohs' in the general region of the Malay Archipelago. How and why he ended up in Kuching was a mystery. Tall, with looks like Sean Connery's, Omar was nearly fifty when I met him for my first 'consultation'. The first of quite a few as it turned out. With his long well-oiled locks, almost touching his shoulders - a hair-style preceding the hippies of the late sixties by at least a decade - Omar presented a striking figure.

My "consultation" with Omar was over a skin rash that refused to go away, despite various methods of treatment attempted by my family, including one that offered appeasement to the spirits allegedly residing in the old strangler's fig tree growing next to the Henghua temple. The 'consultation' took place in Omar's house, which incidentally, was the smallest house I had ever been to. Constructed of rough-hewn timber for its walls and floor with zinc sheets for its roof, it looked more like a squatter's hut than a proper house, which was most probably what it was, together with the two or three houses next to it.

Incongruous as it might sound, it was also one of the

houses within a stone's throw from the Kuching Islamic Mosque near the old Brooke's Shipyard at the western end of the town. Islam forbids the practice of witchcraft and for Omar, who was also a Muslim, to set up shop right at its doorstep (in actual fact at the foot of the hill on which the mosque was located), was for me a most daring and peculiar thing to do. I asked my father about it later and he explained it away by saying that Omar only performed good deeds with his skills by healing victims who had been attacked by other evil 'bomohs' and, therefore, not entirely banned by the mosque authority. Omar was one of the "good guys" of witchcraft.

In actual fact, in all the time I had known Omar he never struck me as a fearsome or devious character. A witch doctor he might have been, but he had charm and charisma. With his crude smatterings of sing-song Hakka, he was able to put me at ease and made me laugh every time I saw him. He was, together with Bujang, my grand-father's close farmhand in the coconut plantation, the only other Malay I had met who was able to speak Hakka, albeit not fluently. Above all, Omar never talked down to me, despite the difference in our age. In fact, I never felt dread going to see Omar for cures with my father.

He was mostly unsuccessful in his cures, though. He seemed only to know of one spell which he would use each time I saw him and which involved the burning of an inordinate amount of frankincense. The same ritual was also used in other treatments he carried out on me.

It went like this: A small copper bowl containing hot charcoal ambers would be placed in the centre of the small living room of his wooden hovel. I would then be asked to sit on the floor with the bowl in front of me. With me in this position Omar would then recite his spells from a small, old tattered book containing Arabic characters. As he continued reciting, although it sounded more like mumblings than recital, he would, from a pouch he had in his hand, place a few lumps of frankincense into the bowl containing the hot charcoal ambers.

Long, thin white clouds of smoke would billow from the bowl as the lumps of frankincense sizzled, crackled and cracked on contact with the ambers. A pungent smell would fill the room, as my eyes began smarting from the effect of the smoke.

But worse was to come. Picking up an old sarong that had seen better days from somewhere, Omar would then ask me to bend my head over the bowl, whereupon he would proceed to cover my head with the sarong. Although it was only a partial cover, it was enough to send some more frankincense smoke into my eyes and tears would pour from them, which I suspected would have been extremely red by now. More tears would continue to pour from my eyes while Omar pressed on with his recitations from the little old book.

It seemed like an eternity by the time he finally finished. He explained afterwards that the frankincense was powerful stuff in getting rid of any evil spells that had been used against me and in the exorcism of any evil spirits that might have decided to take up residence in my body.

That was the first of a few visits to Omar that I had to make over the next few years of my life. The procedure employed by him never varied. There was the same heavy use of frankincense, the same old sarong employed as a blanket and recitations from the same little tattered book.

I remember asking my father after one of these trips why Omar had only one spell book. He explained that Omar was at one time a powerful bomoh, well known and much feared and respected not only in Kuching but in Java,

Children of the Monkey God 253

Indonesia, from whence he had originated. He had lost most of his powers in a criminal charge which he had to face years ago in Kuching, when he was accused of using the occult arts to seduce a young married woman.

Apparently, he was found guilty of the charge and one of the sentences handed down by the court was the destruction by burning of all his spell books and all other items of black magic in his possession. Somehow or other, the little tattered book managed to escape the detection of the police and was saved from destruction. That was all that remained of Omar's devices of power and it left him pretty powerless and ineffective as a bomoh.

My father further claimed that as a young practitioner in Java, Omar was able to use the power of invisibility to carry out all sorts of deeds without detection. Combining this ability with other super-human skills such as walking through walls just as easily as a person crossing the road, my father said he was able to steal huge, heavy sacks of rice right under the very noses of the owners of granary stores. My father must have seen the look of extreme scepticism on my face and must have told Omar of the lack of faith that young people have in older people, for Omar seemed to know of it when next he came to our house shortly after to perform some act of exorcism or witchery for one of the family members.

" So you want me to show you something to prove to you what a powerful bomoh I am," he said to me in his funny-accented broken Hakka.

I had no idea he had known of my scepticism and was, therefore, completely taken aback by his question. Dumbfounded, I was not able to give him a reply. Not that he seemed to expect an answer. He continued.

"Have you ever in your life known of any man who has coins imbedded in his body?" he asked.

"No," I replied, somehow finding my voice.

"Well, you're looking at one right now," he said, not without a certain amount of pride in his voice.

"Come, let me show you," he added.

With these words, he started to unbutton his shirt. Having done that, he proceeded to sit crossed-leg on the floor of our living room. He then asked me to step behind him. Staring down at his back, I was able to make out, just beneath his skin, the faint outline of a row of small round objects, the size of twenty cent coins, stretching from one end of the shoulder to the other, neatly and closely lined up next to each other. Yet the skin covering the coins was just as smooth as the rest of the body. There were no visible scars I could see on the skin to suggest that the coins were surgically implanted.

Without another word to me Omar proceeded to flex his right arm. Having satisfied himself that it was supple enough for its task he then put it behind his head. He extended it cross-wise as far as he could and rested it on top of his left shoulder. Having done that, he started to run it slowly across the top of his shoulder from left to right. The sound of coins clicking could be distinctly heard as his fingers moved slowly across his shoulder. He put his arm down by his side and said to me:

"Now do as I just did. Put your hand on my shoulder and run across it. Com' on, do it," he urged me.

I put my hand on his left shoulder.

"Come on, run across it," he said encouragingly.

Children of the Monkey God

I did – tentatively and slowly. It was one of the most eerie experiences I have ever had in my life. I could feel shivers coursing down my spine as my hand made its weird and strange journey across the top of Omar's shoulder, feeling the hardness of the coins and hearing the clicking sound they made as my fingers made contact with them.

"Now, do you believe me when I said that I am a powerful bomoh?" he asked, now with more pride than when he'd started. Omar was not without his ego.

"Yes," I managed to squeak lamely, feeling quite humbled by the experience.

Omar then explained to me that the coins were powerful wards put there by his master when he was still a young apprentice in Indonesia. Bomohs had a lot of enemies even at the best of times, he said, and the things that he and his master were doing required some form of protection. With the coins in his body, no evil spirits, ghosts or rival bomohs could hope to be successful in their attacks against him, he continued, while putting his shirt back on.

He didn't explain, though, how his master put the coins there. I didn't dare ask either. There were some places I would rather not go.

My respect for Omar grew after that incident with the coins, even though Omar was not a great success when it came to healing his clients.

Perhaps what my father said about his powers being stripped away by the court was true. But he was still a formidable seducer when it came to women. The proof of it was the few happy wives he seemed to have. Some claimed that he seduced them with his magic, especially the two younger wives, for why else would two pretty young girls who had barely come out of their teens wish to marry a man of Omar's age? Perhaps so. But with his good looks and charisma, he would not have much problem in successfully wooing them without the use of magic or witchery and there was little denying that all of them looked quite contented to share him between them.

I used to see them quite often because of the stall they ran selling banana fritters by the riverside at Main Bazaar, close to the old Chinese Chamber of Commerce, now the Chinese Museum. And there was little doubting that they served some of the most delicious banana fritters in town, crisp on the outside and succulent and moist on the inside, using the freshest fruit for frying in their huge deep wok.

This I knew, for I was a regular customer either buying them for myself or on behalf of my father or the family. At least two or three of Omar's wives would be on duty at all times with the oldest always there in charge of proceedings. Recognising me as someone who had been treated by their 'mutual husband' they always made certain to give me a more than generous portion.

The brisk trade of the stall kept them constantly busy and they all seemed to get on fine with each other, chatting and joking among themselves as they went about their work, while at the same time trying to keep a hold on their many children milling and playing around the stall, all of them off-springs of Omar's, no less. The closeness that his wives and their children had with each other, with no apparent sign of animosity towards each other, suggested that they were more than happy with each other's company.

Omar was seldom at the stall until the day he bought a huge, long Cadillac, a car which he seemed to have acquired second-hand not long after the incident with the coins. It would not have been an exaggeration to say that he was rarely seen at the stall prior to that acquisition.

However, he was now the proud owner of a luxury car, albeit a used one, and that fact seemed to have elevated his social status by a few rungs - in his own eyes at the very least. He must have felt that there was now no conceivable reason why he should not also make a public display of it as well. He now made it a point to be seen with his vehicle. Thus, Omar not only went to his banana fritter stall more often but could now be seen sitting in a deck chair placed right against his car, erasing any doubts that he actually owned the car. To make it doubly clear, he had the car prominently parked right next to his stall. It was impossible not to notice the gleaming car when it was parked thus beside his humble stall, for it was at least three times longer and twice as large as the stall itself.

Where Omar got his car and how he could have afforded it was to me a mystery. To add to the mystery was the anomaly that Omar could not drive, his previous form of mechanical transport being his bicycle. His latest and newest status symbol was for most of the time just that – a status symbol, unused and stationary. Without a driver or a driver's licence, he continued to use his bicycle to get around, while his car remained parked next to his stall, albeit well taken care of by his wives and children who delighted in giving it a daily wash and wax.

Thus, it stayed that way for quite a while until the day Omar employed a driver to ferry him around town, although it would be more correct to call him a chauffeur for he came complete with a white uniform, stiffly-starched and well-ironed, with matching white cotton driving gloves. Omar was seen around town a lot after that, always in the back of his huge car with his white-uniformed chauffeur solemnly taking the wheel in the front.

These spins around town by Omar in his American car continued for quite a while. And then they stopped. No car and no Omar. I asked my father about it, for he knew Omar and his affairs better than anyone else. Well, better than me anyway. His reply was that "the car consumes petrol like a thirsty man consumes water." Apparently, Omar had found it difficult to continue with the car's upkeeps and it had been either sold or re-possessed with the chauffeur's employment coming to a short and abrupt end.

This then was the world I grew up in, a rich multi-cultural world from which I learned to be tolerant and accepting of all creeds, faiths and belief-systems; a world full of colourful, exotic and eccentric people, endearing people whose beliefs a modern contemporary person would call quaint, weird, strange and unusual and sometimes out-of this-world. However I am a firm believer in looking at things in their social, cultural and historical context and what might seem to be outdated by today's standards would not have been the case when viewed against their relevant social and cultural time-frame. In that respect I feel that there should be no value-added judgment made on these belief-systems, something I have tried my best to avoid doing in the writing of this book. By the same token whether we agree with the adherents and devotees of these belief-systems is also beside the point. To me the pertinent point is that they not only believed in them; they, in actual fact, lived and breathed them and that's what made them so unique, colourful and endearing. And for them, that was all that mattered. Sadly though, they and the world they live in is fast disappearing (due in no small measure to the advent of modern technology) and while nothing much can be done to stop this historical and social process from relentlessly continuing its course, at least some records should be made of them and their world. I sincerely hope that I have contributed in some small way in the recording and understanding of this fast-disappearing world in the writing of this book and in the recounting of some of my experiences with them.

EPILOGUE

The first year of the new millennium saw me at Ah Kung's plantation at Sedungus. It would have been more than fifty years or so since my first trip there as a small school-boy. A large part of the eastern side of Sedungus, i.e., the beach-side, has been swept away by the sea with the rivulet on its southern border taken over by mangrove trees, creepers and vines. With its shoreline receding, the whole area is also left unfarmed and uninhabited. Untended, with not a soul in sight, the farmhouses that once belonged to Ah Kung and my uncles were nowhere to be seen. Despite our tireless efforts - a party consisting of my father, a cousin, two brothers and I - we were unable to find them, even with the use of one chainsaw and several parangs, so dense was the foliage. There were signs of macaque monkeys everywhere with some young coconuts strewn over the ground. Tracks of wild boars and monitor lizards were evidence that these wild creatures had taken up residence here. Nearly all of Ah Kung's plots had been sold; the collapse of the copra market saw to that. Yet in spite of this, the elderly residents of the nearby kampongs still spoke of Ah Kung as if he was still there owning and running the place; "a hard-working and enterprising man, strong and resilient" was one of their comments.

The demise of the copra industry also saw my paternal uncles, aunts and cousins, plus their children change from coconut farmers to pepper growers and town workers. Thus it is that the sea, the mangroves and the jungle have more or less reclaimed parts of Sedungus, on the western side of the mouth of the Sarawak River.

Children of the Monkey God

On the other hand, Telok Bandung, on the opposite side of the river mouth, where Ah Kung and my eldest aunt used to hunt wild boars is now a thriving tourist resort. With its hillside tropical rainforest and its estuarine palms and mangroves largely cleared, it is now home to a golf course, at least two international-class hotels, a "cultural" village and a horde of other infra-structure connected to the tourist industry. No more the haunt of wild animals and eerie spirits, it has been renamed "Damai" and is serviced by roads, piped water and electricity. The waters of the South China Sea flowing into this estuary can no longer proceed further into Kuching and the upper reaches of the Sarawak River, blocked as they are by a causeway constructed about twenty kilometres from the river mouth. This also means that ships and boats from Sedungus and Santubong can no longer sail into Kuching as Ah Kung was able to do in days gone by. Thankfully, the other estuaries of the river delta system remain unblocked, however, and the waters of the South China Sea continue to charge up the Sarawak River. In spite of this, the waters flowing by Kuching are now quite placid, capable of registering only a few feet in variation between high and low tide. This is in extreme contrast to those pre-causeway days where a difference of twenty feet was not an uncommon feature, either here or in other countries situated on the Equator.

Kuching itself has seen many changes over the past five decades. St Thomas' is now a government school. The Borneo Company is now defunct with its land and buildings along Thomson Road taken over by various commercial concerns, including three international-class hotel chains such as the Holiday Inn (now the Grand Margherita Hotel) and Hilton. Cinemas such as the Odeon (where I spent many a happy hour with my grandmother), Rex, Sylvia and Capital are now the sites of restaurants, cafes, shops and offices. Padungan has seen an extra road constructed on the northern side of the old one with extra shop houses built on both sides of this new road. The Henghua Temple has been demolished with the strangler's fig and durian tree next to it cut down and replaced by a multi-storey supermarket, offices and shop houses. Similarly, the Old Matriarch's traditional-style mansion on top of the hill has also been knocked down; the hill levelled and rebuilt with shop houses and offices. The playgrounds on the southern side of the street have similarly been taken over by shop and office complexes and the days when children would gather in the late afternoon to fly kites or play games of rounders, football, hide-and-seek, etc., are long gone, perhaps never to return.

These new shop houses and street offices do not have living quarters incorporated into their design and those of the old shop houses have had their upper floors converted into offices. Inner-city living has been abandoned in favour of suburban living with new housing estates springing up everywhere in newly-created areas, such as Kenyalang Park and Tabuan Jaya. Officially Kuching is, and has been for quite a number of years now, a city, in commensuration with its increased size and population. It is now much more cosmopolitan than it has ever been, with Bahasa Malaysia (the official Malay language) and Mandarin now more widely spoken than English and with the once-conservative Chinese-educated youths among the trend-setters in fashion, music and other things. Annually, numerous people of the Dayak tribes, particularly the Bidayuh, as well as migrant workers, professionals, businessmen, etc., from Peninsular Malaysia and Southern Kalimantan join the ranks of its ever-expanding population. This new demography is now quite an important instrument in the shaping of its social and cultural landscape, a far cry from the days when it was a predominantly Chinese town in the 1950s and 60s and a far, far cry from the days when it was a small humble Malay kampong that Sir James Brooke first set eyes on more than

170 years ago.

Author Biography

F. S. Choo is a retired UK-trained Barrister-at-law, born in Sarawak, Malaysia. He was a legal practitioner in Brunei from 1974 to 1987. He migrated to Perth, Western Australia in the middle of 1987 together with his wife and three daughters where they have remained since then. He never took up legal practice again, having lost the passion for it in Brunei. He then involved himself in a few small business ventures in Perth and Malaysia for a while as well as helping his wife in her homeopathic and kinesiology practice. He considers *Children of the Monkey God* to be a labor of love and is fiercely passionate in his desire to share this family story with the rest of the world.

Author's email : fasen9@gmail.com

Bibliography

Wang Tai Peng, *The Origins Of the Chinese Kongsi*

Barbara E Ward, *A Hakka Kongsi In Borneo*

Daniel Chew, *Chinese Pioneers on the Sarawak Frontier 1841 – 1941*

Robert Pringle, *Rajahs and Rebels*

Lynn Pan, *Sons of the Yellow Emperor*

Chang Pat Foh, *The Land of the Freedom Fighters*